# IRREPARABLE

A PSYCHOLOGICAL THRILLER BY

## JENNIFER TUCKER
## RUTHERFORD RANKIN

**MICHELKIN |** PUBLISHING
ROSWELL, NEW MEXICO
BOOKS.MICHELKIN.COM

Other titles from Michelkin Publishing:

*Fighting Against Gravity* by Rutherford Rankin
*The Charming Swindler* by Jeff Musillo
*Gypsies of New Rochelle* by Ivan Jenson
*The Ruined Man* by Jason DeGray
*The Knower* by Ilan Herman
*Adventures Through the Trees* by Kay Gehring
*Little Karl* by M. Earl Smith & E. A. Santoli
*Dear Sun, Dear Moon* by Deborah Paggi & Gayle Cole

ISBN: 0-9980672-8-8
ISBN-13: 978-0-9980672-8-5

## Dedication & Acknowledgements

Jennifer Tucker:
*"If you can't fly then run, if you can't run then walk, if you can't walk then crawl, but whatever you do you have to keep moving forward."*
*-Martin Luther King, Jr.*

Rutherford Rankin:
*For Grandma Joy, who, when I was a child, called me a great storyteller.*
*In memory of Papa Snuffy - Tell all the girls you seen me.*

# CHAPTER 1

Katrina Morgan was sitting on her living room sofa when she heard rain falling outside. It sounded like a soft rain, the kind that falls just slow enough and just long enough to dampen the ground, but not enough to leave behind a puddle or nourish any vegetation.

She stood up and walked over to the window to see what kind of storm was developing outside. She swallowed hard as she gazed out at the world in front of her. Just a second before, the world had been vibrant with color, but now everything appeared black and white. Kat squinted her eyes, trying to see into the distance. There, on the horizon, a tornado was beginning to form and it appeared to be coming quickly toward her.

Kat was paralyzed at the sight of the twisting whirlwind of debris as it finally touched the ground and grew in size. The distance between her and the funnel was shrinking quickly. She closed her eyes and felt her heart pounding harder. She scrunched her eyelids tight to avoid seeing her demise barreling closer. If this is how she was going to die, she just wanted it to be over without having to stare it right in the face.

Kat knew she needed to seek shelter somewhere, but she couldn't make herself move. Instead, she crossed her fingers, hoping that when she opened her eyes the tornado would be gone. But as she slowly began to open them, she found herself suddenly outside the house. She tried to make sense of the sudden changes happening around her, but rationality had rushed from her mind with the wind and anxiety had taken its place.

She was still and the roar of the approaching tornado sent chills up her spine. As she looked around for somewhere to hide, she realized the house she was standing next to was not her own, but a tiny old farmhouse falling apart from the inside out. She was in the middle of a dry field with a few rundown shacks scattered about its far edges. Dead trees, barren of leaves, surrounded a few of the shacks.

As she turned back to face the approaching tornado, Kat was surprised to see that another had developed at its side. Their winds swirled around each other and at times it was difficult to tell whether there was one or two. As they danced across the field in her direction, Kat ran toward the door of the house to seek shelter. She found it difficult to make even a small step but pushed herself forward. Each motion was like moving through quicksand and the world around her seemed to slow down.

Suddenly, she noticed a child in the field not far from the house. She realized the little girl was her at five years old—it was the little Katrina she remembered seeing in the mirror years before. As she watched her younger self, she felt what the little girl felt. What she touched, Kat felt and the emotions in her mind were reflected in Kat's. Kat watched as the little girl knelt down to touch the dirt in the field. There was no grass, no weeds, no leaves on the few trees scattered throughout the field. The area seemed deserted by everyone but the two of them and the dry, powdery dirt still felt hot from the baking summer sun.

Little Katrina picked up a handful of the soil and let it fall through her fingers. It blew away in the strengthening wind as she felt its warmth leave her hand. She suddenly felt all alone in the world. She was abandoned by everyone and everything and it terrified her, both as the little girl and the grown Kat.

As Kat turned back toward the storm, she noticed the tornadoes were no longer coming toward her. Instead, they lurked in the distance and their destructive winds spun faster and faster. The spinning made her feel dizzy and sick to her stomach and she couldn't move. She was frozen in fear of what would happen next as the entire scene went black.

Kat sat straight up in bed. She was in a cold sweat and her heart was pounding like it had many times before. She had been having this same dream or one like it since she was a little girl and it still woke her in a fright every time. She rolled over and looked at the clock. It was barely midnight and she was wide awake. Her boyfriend, Max, snorted in his sleep next to her and rolled over to face the other way. The couple had been through yet another argument earlier in the evening and she hadn't noticed when he'd finally come to bed.

She laid back down in the darkness and tried to close her eyes. Every time she did, the image of the two tornadoes spinning in the distance returned and it made her dizzy. She felt like the bed was a boat rocking back and forth on rough ocean water and it nauseated her. She listened to the ticking of the clock on her bedside table and tried to let it soothe her back to sleep. She had come to rely on the few familiar things in her life and the sound of that ticking clock had kept her grounded on many nights like this one.

Try as she might, Kat couldn't make her mind rest. She tossed from side to side trying to get comfortable enough to relax, but the tension in her body and spinning feeling in her head wouldn't subside.

After two hours of fruitless attempts to sleep, she finally decided to give up. She quietly got out of bed trying not to disturb Max and went into the living room. She got a pallet of oil paints ready and started working on her latest paint-

2

ing. Her painting hobby had been a sort of therapy to help her escape the real world and she had surprised herself with how good her work actually turned out. As the brush, wet with paint, touched the canvas, she felt herself relax. If she couldn't sleep, she would let her mind get lost in her artwork.

# CHAPTER 2

Work the following day was rough. Kat's lack of sleep the night before left her groggy and anxious. Even the short walk around the corner from the parking garage to the massive office building was exhausting. After dropping her things off in her office, she made her way to the break room in a sleepy trance where someone had already brewed the morning's coffee.

She took a mug from the cupboard above the sink and rinsed it out slowly as her mind wandered back to the night before. After drying the cup with a napkin, she turned around to the coffee pot and poured the steaming coffee until it was two-thirds full. The secretary who had brewed the coffee had made it nice and strong and Kat stared into the deep black in her mug. She liked strong coffee, but always needed to buffer it with cream and sugar to make it taste just right. She opened the refrigerator and pulled out a carton of creamer.

As she poured it into the black liquid and stirred, the two colors, black and white, spun around in a spiral. It reminded her of the dream she'd had the night before and the dizziness and nausea quickly returned. She took a sip of the coffee hoping it would be soothing, but her stomach was tied up in so many knots, the liquid couldn't make it down. She poured the still-swirling liquid into the sink, rinsed out the mug, and watched the water swirl down the drain like the tornado's twisting winds. She dragged herself back to her office knowing it would be a long day.

*****

The day wore on and though she kept busy, Kat found her exhaustion mounting hour after hour.

*If I could just rest my eyes for a minute, I'd be okay,* Kat thought to herself as she considered laying her head down for a brief moment. And yet, she knew if her boss walked by and saw her sleeping at her desk, her rising marketing career would be over. She rubbed her eyes trying to relieve the grogginess she felt, but it didn't help. She decided a splash of cold water on her face might help jolt her system to get her back on track for the day.

As she made her way to the office bathroom, her eyes were lowered to the floor. Though she could sometimes be outgoing, days like this one brought out her insecurities and anxieties. On days like this one, she avoided looking up at anyone. She would have much preferred to be at home curled up in a ball on her bed on days like this. She loved her coworkers but found it difficult to interact with anyone when her anxiety was so high and her mind so tired from a lack of rest.

Kat hunched over the bathroom sink and allowed the water to run for a moment to ensure it would be nice and cold. She cupped her hands under the faucet and threw the water up onto her face. It smeared her makeup, but she didn't care. She had to wake herself up somehow.

The frigid water took her breath away at first and she gasped and shivered. She threw another splash of water up and it was just as shocking as the first. It was just what she needed to finally refresh her body and make it through the rest of the day. She looked up and stared at herself in the mirror, the droplets of cold water still dripping from her nose and chin. Her eyes looked tired, her mouth seemed to be stuck in a frown, and her hair was out of place.

*How did my life end up this way?* she wondered as she stared at the reflection of her own eyes. The thought quickly passed as the door of the bathroom swung open and one of her coworkers, Marylyn, walked in. Kat reached for a paper towel and dried her face as Marylyn turned on the faucet next to her and began washing her hands.

"You okay, Kat?" Marylyn asked. Kat patted the water from her face and turned toward her with as much of a smile as she could muster.

"Everything's fine," she lied. "Just tired."

"Me too," Marilyn said, the quick speed of her speech contradicting the words she spoke. "It must be that late afternoon lag. That and life. The kids have been so busy with stuff for school lately. I don't know why they always pile everything at the same time every year. It'd be nice if they'd space it out a little more." Kat nodded and laughed nervously as she finished drying her face.

"That reminds me," Marylyn continued. "My daughter's school is doing a fundraiser for the children's hospital. The student who gets the most contributions wins a new bike and she's been begging for a new bike for months. I wondered if you would want to contribute?" Kat smiled as she threw the paper towels in the trash can.

"Of course!" she exclaimed, her tone becoming more pleasant and her energy rising. "I would love to contribute, especially if it's for the children's hospital. Stop by my office and I'll give you the cash."

"Okay," Marilyn replied. "You're very enthusiastic about it. Most of the people I've asked made excuses or acted like it was a chore to contribute."

"I just like helping out," Kat told her truthfully. "Can I do it anonymously, though?"

"Of course," Marilyn replied as she dried her hands. "You are just too

6

sweet!"

As Kat walked back to her office, she held her head higher and met the gaze of the others in the office. She wasn't sure if it was because the cold water had energized her or because of the rush of good feelings she got when she did something good, but she felt like it was suddenly a different kind of day.

She had sulked around her workplace all morning exhausted and anxious, but now she felt ready to face the world before her. It was like a new day had begun and she regretted having wasted the entire morning in a gloom. As she sat down at her desk, she opened the project she had been working on for the past several days and put all her effort into finishing it before the end of the day. She smiled and tapped her feet, now full of energy.

*****

Kat stayed late at work that evening to finish up her project. With her new energy, she was close to the finish line and didn't want to lose her momentum. The office quieted down as people left for the day, but a few others also stayed late to catch up on their work. Music played from one of the offices down the hall and Kat found it distracting. Her mind was racing with thoughts again. Max would probably be angry that she had stayed late at work. He would be hungry and grouchy and she didn't want to deal with him, but she also had to get this project finished and off her plate. She reached into her desk drawer and took out the clock she kept there for moments like these.

She wound the old-fashioned travel clock and placed it on top of her desk as close as possible without interfering with her work. She listened to the repetitive tick-tock to help her mental focus. It seemed everyone else used digital clocks these days and she was finding it harder and harder to find a clock that would provide the rhythmic ticking sound she needed to calm herself. Within a few minutes, the regularity of the ticking had refocused her mind and she got back to work on finishing her project. The nagging thought of going home to an angry Max was still in the back of her mind, but she was motivated by the prospect of getting this project done ahead of schedule.

It was dark when she finally finished her work and as she stepped out of the office building into the cool night air, she shuddered and felt her anxiety rising. She hated leaving work in the dark. It always seemed like something or someone was lurking around every corner. Her anxiety about going back home to Max had not only returned but also multiplied ten-fold. The extra two hours she'd spent at work would have him riled up and she didn't want another fight like they'd had the night before and so many nights before that.

*****

When Kat arrived at home, she knew she was in trouble. Outside the door of the apartment she shared with Max was an empty box from a case of beer torn to pieces. He had apparently been too lazy to walk it down to the dumpster and left it outside the door for everyone to see. She hated when he drank—he already had a horrible temper, but the alcohol only made it worse. She sighed as she turned her key in the lock and prepared for what she knew was coming.

As soon as she opened the door, Max jumped up from the sofa. The TV blared with the sound of a basketball game and he stumbled over to meet her at the door. Her eyes darted quickly around the room before the yelling began. Max had destroyed every piece of artwork she'd worked on in the past year. Pieces of torn canvas littered the living room floor, broken paintbrushes were scattered from one end of the apartment to the other, and every one of her finished paintings had been shredded to bits with a knife.

"Where the fuck have you been?" he yelled at her. She pushed the door closed as quickly as she could so the others tenants wouldn't hear his yelling. She could smell the alcohol on his breath. It wasn't just beer—he'd also had some sort of hard liquor, but she couldn't tell what it was from the smell.

"I stayed at work late to finish the project I was working on," she said softly, not wanting to upset him even more as she noticed most of her art supplies had been destroyed.

"Yeah, I bet," Max yelled. "You were probably out fucking someone else."

"No, Max," she rebuffed him in a soft, but firm voice. "I was at work. I've been working on this project for several days and I just wanted to get it done so I can move on to the next one. Let me get dinner started, you're probably hungry." She stepped over a pile of broken brushes on the floor and tried to push past him, but he blocked her way.

"You're damn right I'm hungry," he continued yelling over the TV. All the noise and the tension were starting to raise Kat's anxiety even more. She couldn't handle the violent feeling in the air and just wanted to get away. "While you were out whoring around I was sitting here starving."

"If you let me pass, I can start making you some dinner," she replied. She was finally able to push past him and dropped her purse onto the dining room table next to a spilled bottle of paint. She started to head down the hall to change out of her work clothes before preparing dinner, but Max rushed past her and blocked her way again.

"Whore!" he yelled in her face. The smell of alcohol filled the cramped space between them once again. It made her feel sick to her stomach. She'd smelled it many times before and it was always followed by something violent. She started to walk past him, but he grabbed her arm and swung her around to face him.

She felt a sharp pain in her back as her body twisted from the force. It was all happening so fast she didn't know how to react. She looked back up into Max's face as he put his arms on her chest and shoved her backward. He pinned her tightly against the wall as her back throbbed with pain from the violent twist.

*I don't believe this is happening again*, she thought to herself as Max pulled her away from the wall and then slammed her back up against it harder than the first time. Her head hit the wall and began to pound with a pain only slightly less excruciating than the one in her back. Max moved closer until his face was right in front of hers.

"I hate you!" he screamed into her face. "I fucking hate you!"

Tears began to stream down Kat's cheeks, but Max didn't care that she was crying. He held her there against the wall staring into her eyes, not an ounce of compassion or care that he was hurting her. Kat tried not to look into his piercing stare. It was humiliating to have this happening again. He had promised time and time again that it would never happen again, but here they stood face to face with Max's toxic breath filling the void as Kat's tears quietly fell to the floor.

When he finally had enough of keeping her trapped, Max let Kat go with another shove and she ran back to the bedroom. She slammed the door behind her and turned the lock hoping it would keep him out. She hobbled into the bathroom, her back now in worse pain than she'd ever felt. As she looked around the bathroom, her heart sank even more. Max had broken a beer bottle across the bathroom floor. The painting she had been working on the night before was crudely bent and shoved into the toilet. He had painted over the beautiful image of a swan, ruining it. The word "WHORE" stared back at her in thick, black paint that was still wet and dripping down into the toilet bowl. She took a bottle of aspirin out of the medicine cabinet and popped three of them to try and ease the pain.

She went over to the bed and laid down, sobbing. He always apologized the next day saying he was sorry and that he didn't mean what he'd said or done, but things like this kept happening over and over again. She had known other women who'd been in similar situations and she could never understand how they had stayed. Now she was the one making excuse after excuse to stay with a man who didn't even see her as a human being. She didn't know how much longer she could survive.

*This is it*, Kat thought. *I've got to get out of this. I've got to get away.*

# CHAPTER 3

Kat sat in her office looking out the window, lost in a daydream of better days and a better life for herself.

"Ms. Morgan!" her boss, Mr. Andrews hollered from the doorway. "Do you have the reports for the nine o'clock?" Kat jumped and turned around startled. Though it had been two weeks since Max had slammed her into the wall and twisted her back, the sudden movement still sent spasms through the muscles of her back and she winced in pain.

"Yes, Mr. Andrews," she replied, trying to hide the pain. "I emailed them to you yesterday afternoon." She forced a fake smile though she was both in pain and annoyed that Mr. Andrews would think she would forget to send her reports.

"Great, I'll see you in fifteen," he said gruffly, not waiting to finish the conversation before beginning to walk away down the hall.

*What a dick*, Kat thought to herself as she shook her head in aggravation. *I'm going to need more coffee to finish out this day.* She began gathering a notebook, pen, and copies of her reports for the meeting as she dreamed about a day when she could leave this life behind. She wanted to leave the city with its hustle and bustle. She wanted to leave her employer who was always so unappreciative of her hard work. Most importantly, she wanted to get away from Max and his repetitive cycle of abuse.

In the days after their last big fight, Kat had begun to construct an escape plan. She started hunting desperately for jobs in small towns in other parts of the country. She wanted to get as far away from Max as she could and she hoped moving to a small town would prevent him from ever being able to track her down. She needed a big change in her world and she hoped getting out of the city where she'd spent her entire life and into the seclusion of a small town might provide the contrast she needed to get her life back on track.

A few of the companies she'd applied to had seemed interested and she'd been through a couple of phone interviews, but she was starting to lose patience and hope that change would happen. She sighed as she stood up and walked down the hall to the conference room. She knew the meeting never started on time, but she always arrived five minutes early anyway. She didn't know why she did it—most of the management took no notice of anyone's punctuality or initiative. It was all about who could kiss the boss's ass the most. Still, something in her conscience forced her to be a good employee.

As she waited for the rest of the group to arrive, she thought about how pointless and predictable these meetings had become in the past few months. Everything to be discussed could have been wrapped up in a five-minute email rather than wasting everyone's time for hours on end. She knew from past experience exactly how the meeting would go and she looked around the room at the empty seats knowing exactly where each person would sit when they arrived. Rick liked to hear himself talk, so he would ramble about how great it is that sales are up and how amazing his tactics had been during the week.

*Ugh,* Kat thought to herself. *His soapbox. He's always on his soapbox bragging to anyone who will listen.*

Then there was Sarah. Kat wasn't sure what Sarah even did at the company, but she was always there at every meeting to let the others know how they needed to improve in some area while flashing her fake smile around the room to everyone, the fakest and most seductive being reserved for Mr. Andrews.

*I can see she is highly intelligent,* Kat thought. *I'd probably like her if she wasn't such a bitch to everyone.*

Mr. Elliott was one of the few people Kat actually respected at work and one of the reasons why she hadn't yet lost her shit in one of these meetings. He was such a humble man and she appreciated the fact that he didn't brag about his team's accomplishments, nor did he take credit when credit wasn't due.

Finally, there was Emily. Kat and Emily had been friends since the first grade and the two were elated when they got hired at the same company after college. Emily had the ability to make Kat laugh until she cried. She was hysterically funny, but professional when she needed to be. She was not only a coworker, she was one of her best friends. Somehow, Emily could tell what kind of mood Kat was in, even when Kat couldn't read her own feelings.

*Emily has her shit together,* Kat thought to herself. *I want my shit together.*

Kat looked down at her watch as the rest of the meeting group finally made their way in. It was already 9:12.

*That's twelve minutes of my life I'll never get back,* she thought.

Mr. Andrews took his place at the table directly across the table from Kat. She felt comfortable nestled in the corner, but she hated having to sit across from him. She focused her eyes on him as he began the meeting, but her mind was somewhere far away from the meeting, far away from the office, far away from the moment.

"Sales figures…projection…marketing plan…new services…lost a client…" she caught words here and there and scribbled a few indecipherable notes, but her mind was not in the meeting and nothing made sense. Instead, the scene of Max slamming her head against the wall that night two weeks before replayed through her head over and over getting stronger each time. It was like someone was hitting a rewind button of the same scenario over and over again and the volume increasing every time her head hit the wall. Her heart began to race and she felt herself breathing more rapidly as the scene repeated again and again. The panic rose even more as she considered the possibility that she would never be able to leave Max or the city.

A kick from under the conference table startled her back to the real world.

*What the hell?* she wondered at first before realizing it was Emily, seated right next to her, who had kicked her to snap her out of her trance. She looked over at her friend and watched Emily's lips silently mouth the words, "Pay attention." Kat clenched her jaw in frustration that she had zoned out during the meeting. Her heart was still racing from the thoughts that rushed through her mind a few minutes before.

*Focus Kat,* she thought to herself. *Get your shit together already. Be like Emily.*

"That wraps up this week's meeting," Mr. Andrews told the group as he began to gather his things. "We did a good job this week. Keep up the good work!"

*I have no clue what this meeting was about,* Kat thought. It wasn't like Mr. Andrews to be so polite to the group, but she had missed out on whatever had put him in such a good mood.

"Kat, what's up with you?" Emily asked her with sincere concern in her eyes. "Everything okay?"

"Everything is fine," Kat replied. Even Emily, her very best friend and the one who could read her like a book, didn't know about the issues she had with Max—the abuse, the way she never felt like she could get away, how she was trying desperately to get the hell out of town. Kat had hidden it from everyone and it was the one thing Emily hadn't figured out on her own. "Just a lot on my mind." She forced a smile for her friend hoping it would fool her into thinking it was the truth.

"Want to have lunch?" Emily asked. Kat just nodded in agreement, not saying anything as the images still rushed through her mind.

As everyone but Kat and Emily left the conference room, Kat felt her phone vibrate and looked down at the screen to see an email notification. She was both surprised and excited about the subject line. It read: POSITION OFFER LETTER. She smiled with excitement trying not to let Emily see her happiness.

"Actually, Emily," she said hurriedly. "Maybe lunch next week? I have to go. Something came up. Talk later!"

She rushed out of the conference room and down to her office. She closed the door behind her to open the email in privacy. As she clicked it open and began to read it over, her smile got bigger.

*Dear Katrina Morgan,*

*We at KJ & G Associates are pleased to offer you the Marketing Specialist position in our Astoria, Oregon, office. Your expected start date will be April 4.*

She skimmed through the rest of the letter looking for the salary offered. It wasn't as big as she had hoped for, but it was adequate, especially since the job was in a small town where the cost of living was significantly lower. The last line of the letter requested that she reply with her decision to accept or decline the offer as soon as possible.

*This is my break*, Kat thought. *I've been waiting for this moment and here it is. I have to take it.*

Suddenly, the excitement and hope turned to dread and misery. Her stomach churned. Now that the opportunity was right in front of her, she wondered how she could possibly pull this off without Max finding out. She stared down at her desk thinking of any way she could move halfway across the country within the next three weeks without her dick of a boyfriend finding out and finding a way to destroy her and her plans.

"Shit!" she said out loud, glad she had closed the door behind her. Her heart was racing again as she thought about what would happen if Max found out about this. The repercussions she could face would be horrible if he knew what was going on. She knew there was even the possibility he would kill her to keep her from leaving.

She took a deep breath and let it out slowly.

"I'm doing this one way or another," she said aloud trying to build up her own confidence. "I can do this. I may die trying, but either way, I'll be free." She hit the reply button on the message and typed back her response.

*It is with extreme gratitude that I gladly accept the position. I look forward to seeing you on April 4.*

She skipped lunch and for the rest of the day worked as fast as she could on her projects. It was tough to focus, but she didn't want anyone to catch the slightest hint of her plans to leave. The smallest slip-up could destroy her already fragile plan. She counted down the hours until the weekend when she would have some uninterrupted time to hash out the rest of her plan. It had to be perfect. It wasn't only about escape, it was also about survival.

# CHAPTER 4

The three weeks flew by faster than Kat expected. She scrambled to put together and execute her escape plan in such a short amount of time.

She feared Max would stop at nothing to track her down and she didn't want to leave any clues behind for him to find. It was both exhausting and thrilling to figure out the smallest details, especially since no one else knew about her plan. However, all the planning also put her anxiety-fueled irrational thoughts into overdrive.

Taking her car to Astoria was out of the question. As absurd as it seemed, an idea was stuck in her head that as soon as she changed her registration and insurance Max would surely find a way to obtain her new address. She had even pondered whether he might have placed a GPS tracker somewhere in her vehicle to track her movements back and forth to work.

She considered renting a car, but she knew he'd somehow contact the credit card company to get the details about where she ended up.

With less than a week until her move, Kat finally figured out how she would travel across the country, a way that even a determined Max wouldn't be able to figure out. During her lunch break the next day, she rushed down to the travel agency across the street from her office building.

At first, she had surprised the travel agent with her odd request.

"I need a train ticket to Astoria, Oregon, for next week," she explained to the woman. "One way only."

"Okay, can I ask why you're traveling?" the woman asked. "Is it business or pleasure?"

"Ummm…" Kat began. Despite hashing out the smallest details, she hadn't planned her answers for such simple questions. *Can't she just sell me the damn tickets?* Kat wondered to herself. "I can't really say. It's a little of both, but I don't care to share many details with anyone. No offense."

The woman behind the desk gave her a suspicious look and Kat thought her plan was going to fall through. *This woman is going to be the one who unravels all my hard work,* Kat worried as she searched for the nearest exit.

"I promise I'm not doing anything illegal," Kat told her with a pleading look on her face and scooting to the edge of the chair. She prepared to make a quick escape if the woman continued prodding. "I just need to get to Astoria and no one else can find out where I've gone. No one."

The woman turned and began typing some information into her computer as Kat fidgeted in her seat impatiently.

"This will be no problem at all," the woman finally told her. Kat's anxiety reduced a little at the woman's reassurance and she sat back in the chair. "The only issue is that no passenger trains go to Astoria. I can get you to Portland on the train and then there's a bus from Portland to Astoria."

"Oh, one other thing," Kat blurted out as she sat back up. "I can only pay cash." She put her hands on the woman's desk and noticed that they were shaking with nervousness.

The woman continued looking at the information on her computer screen before glancing back over to Kat. She reached out and placed her hand it on top of Kat's to try and calm the shaking.

"Honey, I know exactly what's going on," she said as she stared directly into Kat's eyes and got up to close the door to her office. "I've helped many women in your situation and you have nothing to worry about. No one will *ever* know where you went or when you went there."

She gave a reassuring smile, but Kat still wasn't sure the woman understood her situation.

"It's going to be okay," the woman said as she sat back down and took Kat's hand in hers once again. "He will never find out where you went."

*She does have me figured out,* Kat realized. The woman patted Kat's hand and turned back to the computer, typing in more information. Kat's eyes watered and her hands stopped trembling. This woman understood the struggle and anxiety she was feeling and something about her made Kat feel like she could trust her.

"Fill out this information card so I can book your tickets," the woman said as she handed Kat a small card to fill out. "This is how it's going to work: I'm going to set up your tickets for station pickup. You'll get them the day of your trip at the station so no one will accidentally find them in your purse or hidden away somewhere at home. Your first ticket will take you to Chicago. When you get there, you'll pick up your next ticket. At the end of the next ticket segment, you'll pick up another. You'll do this a total of five times. There's no way he or anyone else will ever be able to figure out where you finally end up. It's between you and me."

Kat nodded her head wondering if Max would really not be able to find her. The anxiety in the back of her mind told her he could be very persistent when he wanted to find something or someone and she wasn't sure even this plan was smart enough to work against him.

The woman reached over again and took Kat's hand in hers.

"I promise, sweetie," she said with certainty in her voice. "He's never going to find you unless you want him to. You just have to be smart about it. No credit cards, no mail forwarding, no taking anything with you. Have you told anyone else where you're going? A friend, a coworker, family? Anyone?"

Kat shook her head. It was true. No one else knew where she was going. She hadn't even told Emily, her best friend, about her plan or her new job. She hadn't given her current boss a two-week notice. She hadn't packed any of her things. No one else knew except her future employer in Oregon and she intended to keep it that way as long as possible.

As much as she trusted Emily, she just couldn't risk having her accidentally reveal her plan to anyone else.

"No one else knows," Kat said quietly. "It's just me, you, and my new employer."

"Good," the woman said. "Keep it that way. Even friends and family can tell the wrong person if they think they're trying to be helpful."

Kat nodded to show she understood the woman's instructions.

"I'll get everything set up for you this afternoon," the woman explained. "Come by tomorrow to pay and I'll explain how to pick up your tickets."

Kat smiled and stood up to leave. Before she reached the door, the woman hollered out to her one last time.

"One more question," she began. "You said you were paying with cash. You aren't taking it all out of the bank at once, are you?"

"No," Kat replied. "I've been taking small amounts out here and there. He thinks I've been using it to buy lunch."

The woman smiled widely as she nodded at Kat with a prideful gleam in her eyes.

"Good. You're being smart about it," she told Kat. "You're going to be just fine as soon as we get you out of here."

Kat smiled back, happy for a compliment when she was used to being ridiculed by Max and ignored by her boss.

She left the travel agency and walked back to work with a new kick in her step. Her plan was going to work. She was going to get away. Max would never find her. She might finally have a chance at the life she deserved instead of the one she'd been handed.

# CHAPTER 5

By the time the day of her departure arrived, Kat's anxiety level was higher than it had ever been before. Even with everything she'd been through in her life, those final hours before she left were full of trembling hands, pounding heartbeats, and intense, second-guessing thoughts.

She worked that day in an effort to follow the travel agent's instructions exactly. She still hadn't told anyone about her move. In the days before, she packed only a few inconspicuous things. She had purchased a small suitcase when she got the offer letter and kept it hidden in her office.

She brought a few items each day tucked in her purse and work bag to pack in her office without being noticed. She didn't want to alert Max with items and clothing missing from the house, but in the three weeks of daily packing, she had managed to accumulate several outfits, a few makeup and toiletry items, and a few things that had personal meaning to her. It wasn't much, but it would get her started on the trip until she got settled. She planned to leave her cell phone in the trash can at work when she left so Max wouldn't be able to track her phone's location. Deep down, she knew he didn't have the means or know-how to do such a thing, but with everything that had happened, she wasn't willing to take a chance.

As the morning wore on, she began to feel horrible that she was leaving her family behind without a trace. She wasn't raised to do such a thing and it broke her heart to think of her parents and brother in anguish over her disappearance to nowhere. She was also worried they might call the police and risk having her trail revealed. As much as she wanted to leave no trace behind, she couldn't leave without telling her family goodbye.

Her hands trembled as she dialed her parents' phone number. It rang once, twice, and then she heard her father's voice on the other end.

"Hello?"

"Dad, it's me," she said with a shaky voice.

"Is everything okay, Kat?" he asked. "You sound upset."

"It will be," she answered, not wanting to alarm him. "But I have some important news I need to tell you, Mom, and Jerry. Could you all meet me for lunch today?"

"Things are a little busy today, Kat," her father replied. "Could we meet for lunch tomorrow instead?"

Kat's heart sank at the thought of not being able to see her parents before heading off to her new life in Oregon.

"It really has to be today, Dad," she told him in a pleading tone. "Tomorrow will be too late. Please?"

Her father stayed silent for a moment, confused by the strange conversation.

"If it's that urgent, then, of course, we'll be there," he finally said. "What time and where?"

"Can we meet at noon?" she asked. "There's a little deli down the street from my office building that would be perfect."

\*\*\*\*\*

As Kat sat in the deli three hours later waiting for her family to arrive, she thought through the steps of her plan one more time.

Her train to Chicago left at three that afternoon. She would leave work at two without a word to her boss or coworkers, just a simple resignation letter left behind on her desk. She would walk the twelve blocks to the train station, pick up her Chicago ticket, and be on her way. She would have no baggage other than her purse and the small suitcase.

Once in Chicago, she would pick up her next ticket from the station agent. During her four-hour layover, she would find an ATM to withdraw the rest of her money from her checking account. Even if Max tracked the ATM withdrawal to Chicago, she would be making enough route changes along the way that he'd never figure out where she was really headed.

When she, at last, arrived in Astoria, she would rent a hotel room while she looked for a permanent place to live and prepared to start her new job. Though she would have only a few possessions with her, she had amassed enough of a savings through years of careful spending that she would be able to make a rental deposit, buy a cheap, but reliable car, and furnish her new place with some bargains from the thrift store and yard sales.

The plan was complicated. It was expensive. It was a little crazy. But it was also absolutely necessary, at least in her mind.

The ding of the bell on the deli's front door snapped her out of her daydream and she looked over to see her parents and brother had finally arrived. They walked quickly over to the table she had chosen and she could tell from the looks on their faces that they were all worried from her urgent call for a family meeting. She felt terrible for putting them all in this state with her vague, but pleading request for lunch.

Before they were even seated in the booth, Kat broke down in tears. Her

20

father reached across the table and took her hand. Her mother did, too, and they both looked into her eyes.

"Whatever it is, Kat, we can help," her father said.

"Everything is going to be fine," Kat said as she took a napkin from the dispenser at the table and wiped the tears from her eyes.

"What's wrong, then?" her mother asked, the look of worry not leaving her face.

"A lot has gone wrong here in the city that I can't go into right now," she attempted to explain. "So I have to leave. I have to move away."

Her family stared at her, confused by the impromptu lunch meeting and Kat's obscure explanations.

"Whatever it is, it can't be bad enough for you to need to move away," her father said.

"It's not just that," Kat continued. "That's the biggest part of it. But I also need a big change in my life. This city holds too many memories, too many emotions I can't deal with anymore. I can't even begin to tell you about them right now. Maybe one day, but not right now."

"Whatever you do, we'll support you," her mother said, tears welling up in her eyes. "We hate to see you move away, but if it's for a better life for you and Max then we certainly can't argue with that."

Kat looked down at the mention of Max's name.

"Max isn't going with me," she said, suddenly more serious than before. "And I need you all to *promise* me you won't talk to him after I leave. If he calls, don't answer. If he comes to your house, don't answer the door. Please, promise me you won't tell him you know anything about me leaving town. He can't know anything."

"But why?" her father asked, the smallest hint of anger with Max beginning to show in his voice.

Kat knew better than to tell her father about the abuse. If he knew the way Max had treated her, he'd likely kill him without a second thought. Even though she sometimes thought Max deserved to die for what he'd done to her, she didn't want to be responsible for her father going to prison for murder.

"We broke up," Kat said, hoping her cover story was believable. "He can't get over it and I want to get as far away from him as I can so he can get over me. Please, help me help him."

"Whatever you ask," her mother said. "When are you leaving?"

"This afternoon," Kat answered. "I'm leaving town at three this afternoon."

An audible gasp came from all three of her family members. Her parents held their eye contact, but her brother, Jerry, looked down at the table trying to hide how upset he was about Kat's decision. He had been unusually quiet since they'd sat down and he seemed lost in his own worries.

"That's so sudden!" her mother exclaimed, her voice breaking. "Why can't you stay a little longer?"

"I'm starting a new job in a week and I've got to get moved and settled in before then," Kat explained.

"And where are you moving to?" her brother finally asked. As he looked back up from the table, the frown on his face told Kat everything she needed to know about how he felt about her leaving town.

"I...don't want to tell anyone right now," Kat answered him. "It's really, really important for me to get away and start my new life with no one else knowing where for a while. Once I'm settled in and get comfortable, I'll let all of you know. I promise."

Her family members all nodded their heads. They were worried and a lot of what Kat said didn't make sense, but they trusted that Kat would contact them as soon as she was ready and able to do so.

# CHAPTER 6

Kat's family insisted that they meet her at the train station later that day to send her off. While she didn't want to make a big send-off scene at the station, she really did want her family to be there to wave as her train pulled out of the station, so she told them to meet her there at 2:45.

After picking up her ticket at the window, she sat down on a bench near the loading platform. The train had already pulled up to the boarding area and a few other passengers had started to step into the train's passenger cars. As she watched them, Kat wondered if any of them were taking the same type of journey. Were any of them climbing onto the train to escape to a new life, a better life?

Her thoughts were interrupted by the sound of her name being called. It was her mother's voice and as she looked over toward the entrance to the station, she saw her family rushing over to her. Her mother was already wiping her eyes. Kat hadn't even boarded the train yet, and her mother was already in tears.

Her brother carried a small bouquet of yellow daisies and he held it out to her as he walked up to her and gave her the biggest hug he'd ever given her. They held each other for a moment before her mother and father pushed their way into a family group hug. None of them said anything for several minutes. They simply stood and held each other. Their family had always been together here in the city. It was the first time one of them had left and it was difficult for them all to handle, especially on such a short notice.

Their embrace was broken by an announcement over the loudspeaker.

"Train 642 to Chicago is now completing final boarding. If you are ticketed for Train 642 to Chicago, please go to platform three immediately for boarding."

"That's me," Kat said as she wiped the tears from her face. "I better go before they leave me behind."

Her father reached back and pulled out his wallet. He opened it and pulled out a hundred-dollar bill and held it out to her.

"No, Dad," she said refusing his offer. "I've got plenty of money to get me there."

"You can never have too much when you're starting a new life," he told her as he pushed the money closer to her. "Please, Kat. It will make me feel better about you going out on your own like this."

She reluctantly took the cash from her father's hand and put it into her purse as another tear fell from her face and landed on the shiny leather of the purse handle.

"Thank you, Dad," she said through sobs. "I love you. I love you all."

"And you know we love you too," her father said. "Now, you better hurry or you're going to miss your train."

Kat rushed over to the boarding gate and handed her purse and suitcase to the security agent. The man quickly looked through both and waved her through. She handed her ticket to the man at the door of the train and made her way to her seat. As she glanced out the window to where her family stood waiting on the platform, it was difficult to see them through the tears. As she blinked, her vision cleared and she could see them waving at her. She waved back as she heard the doors of the car closing and felt the lurch as the train began moving forward.

The feelings in her heart were pulling her in two different directions. She never knew it was possible to feel so much happiness and sadness at the same time, so much hope and regret in one moment. She watched her family disappear in darkness as the train entered a tunnel and picked up speed.

 **CHAPTER 7**

Kat was exhausted. The train ride was much longer than she thought it would be, especially with the need to switch trains and routes over and over to cover her trail. She thought about how funny it was that most of her ideas ended up like this—bigger and more complicated than she originally understood.

Her mind flashed quickly to Max. Had he figured out she was gone yet? Had he gone looking for her? During her layover in Chicago, she had purchased a cheap prepaid cell phone just to keep in touch with her family. She checked it briefly to see if her parents had tried to make contact. *Surely they would let me know if Max had done anything stupid,* she thought. The uncertainty of the situation made her anxious—the unknown of the new town, her new job. The quick uproot she made in her life made her doubt whether she'd made the right decision. The fact that she was technically homeless made her doubt herself even more. She hoped the realtor she'd spoken to would be able to get her into a rental house quickly. Until then, the hotel room would have to make do.

The final segment of her trip ended as the bus screeched to an easy stop at the tiny bus station in Astoria. Kat gathered her suitcase and purse, now her only possessions. The few items she had managed to sneak away from the apartment were contained in the two small pieces of baggage. It didn't matter much to Kat whether or not she was able to keep the rest of her belongings. She had managed to collect only a few things of value over the last five years anyway, and for all she cared Max could keep every bit of it. She didn't want anything that was a reminder of her time with him. He was out of her life and she wanted him out of her thoughts and memories as well.

Max had always been too worried about materialistic things. He was always concerned about "keeping up with the Jones'". He meant it literally, too. He worked with a man with the last name Jones and he seemed to be in a constant competition with him to have biggest and best of everything. And somehow, it was always Kat's fault if they didn't have something he wanted. He rarely appreciated the things Kat did for him. It was always about what she *didn't* do for him or what he didn't have. She hoped he enjoyed it all—the furniture, the kitchenware, the cars, and the apartment. She hoped he enjoyed having it all to himself, all alone.

As she brushed thoughts of Max from her mind, Kat headed for the open bus door that welcomed her to Astoria.

It was a place she'd always dreamed of living, a place she'd always longed for, even though she'd never even visited before. She had never understood how you could miss a place you'd never been, but it happened to her. Through the tourist brochures and online image searches, she had fallen in love with the small Oregon town. Something had drawn her here, but she still didn't know why.

As she slowly descended the three steps from the bus, she took a deep breath of the damp Oregon air, enjoying the aroma of fresh rain in the early evening twilight. It was still drizzling and gray clouds filled the sky without the tiniest bit of blue sky in sight. Kat welcomed this weather. In fact, she adored it. It wasn't the type of weather she often got back home. *Home*, she thought. *That place is no longer home to me.*

Her heart was suddenly racing. Again, the unknown made her anxious. A yellow cab pulled up to the curb in front of her and the driver got out with an umbrella as he jogged over to her.

"Do you need a ride?" he asked with a smile, holding the umbrella over her.

"Sure," she responded as the man grabbed her suitcase and opened the door for her. In all the rush of planning her trip, she hadn't thought about how she would get from the bus station to the hotel. And yet, it seemed like destiny that this taxi had pulled up just as she walked out into the rain.

*Another first*, she thought as she sat down in the cab's humongous back seat. She had never ridden in a cab before. In all her years living in the city, she'd always been fortunate enough to own a car to get herself around. She felt almost like a child again for a brief moment. She was being driven around as she stared in awe of the world around her. Even as evening settled over the rain-soaked streets, she loved the way the small town of Astoria looked compared to the glaring lights of the city she'd left behind.

The cab driver moved at a much slower speed than she was used to. *The difference in traffic will take some getting used to,* she thought. Even at the slower pace, it didn't take long for them to arrive at her hotel.

Before she had time to reach over to open the car door herself, the driver had jumped out, opened his umbrella, and swung her door open awaiting her exit. It was so strange for her to be treated so politely by a gentleman that she barely knew what to say. She squeaked out a quiet "thank you" as she slid out of the car and stepped up onto the curb.

She stood at the front door as the driver retrieved her luggage from the trunk and carried it inside for her. A soft rumble of thunder sounded as they stepped through the old but well-maintained front doors.

Once inside, Kat tipped the driver generously and made her way to the front desk. She paid cash for a week in advance and hoped she would be able to find somewhere more permanent to live before it was time to pay for the next week.

"You look tired," the front desk clerk said. It caught Kat slightly off guard. She wasn't sure whether to feel offended, sad, or grateful for the woman's honesty. Truthfully, she *was* tired—exhausted, in fact. She would just have to get used to a different way of speaking. Maybe this was how people in small towns spoke to each other. She responded to the clerk's comment with a smile that simply said, "Yeah, I am."

"Welcome to Astoria," the woman said politely as she handed Kat's out-of-state driver's license back across the counter. "I hope you get some rest tonight."

"Thank you," was the only thing Kat could get out. It seemed like it was the only word she knew now that she'd arrived in Oregon. She was too exhausted to engage in any further conversation. She hoped the woman wouldn't take it personally.

Upstairs, Kat settled into her room. She knew she should unpack her suitcase so her clothes would have time to air out and unwrinkle from the trip, but instead she simply plopped down on the bed and stared at the ceiling.

Above the bed, the ceiling was painted a pale sky blue with white, puffy clouds. *It feels good to stretch out after sitting in a train seat for so long,* she thought as she got lost in the beautiful fake painted sky that lingered above her. She laughed quietly to herself as she thought about how this fake blue sky above her was like the clear sky she'd left behind in the city. It, too, had been a fake sky filled with puffy white false promises and overwhelming secrets that floated through the dry summer air and the suffocating smog of a life of anxiety. She was sure the person who painted the ceiling had meant it to be relaxing, but for Kat, it only reminded her of everything she'd left behind.

After laying still for a few minutes, she got up to splash some water on her face and change into her pajamas. Again, the urge to unpack hit her, but instead she crawled under the comfortable blankets. *I can unpack tomorrow,* she thought. *No need to do it tonight.*

Finally relaxed in the cozy bed, Kat turned on the television and grabbed her phone to let her parents know she'd made it safely to her secret destination. As she typed out the message, her eyes seemed to get heavier and heavier, drained from the days of travel. After hitting send and setting the phone on the nightstand, she closed her eyes for a moment.

She drifted in and out of a light sleep, only making out a few words coming from the news report from the TV. Street names and cities the news anchors spoke about were unfamiliar to Kat, but one line grabbed her attention.

"A thirty-seven-year-old man was arrested today on two counts of child molestation…" Kat's forehead wrinkled in frustration as she laid in bed. Those words triggered so many memories in her head.

She suddenly remembered the boy who would sneak into her bedroom at night when she was a little girl. She still remembered the smallest details—the rainbow curtains that hung above her bed, the sound of the doorknob turning when he'd try his hardest to be silent. He *was* silent to the rest of the house, but Kat's heart would jump every time she heard that doorknob turn.

Laying in the hotel bed, she tried not to think about it, but she swore she heard the doorknob across the room turning slowly around and around in circles as memories flooded her worn-out mind.

The boy would walk quietly to her and ease onto her bed. He would never speak. He'd only touch her. Afraid and unsure of what to do, she had never said anything, as if her throat were closed shut. Her little body would simply lay frozen, hoping it would be over soon.

A single tear rolled down her cheek just then and she tried to snap herself out of the moment and back to the present. Kat wiped the tear, trying to brush it off. The news was just finishing up and she wondered where the time had gone. Lost in her memories, the world around her had continued ticking on minute by minute. Not aware of how much time had passed, she turned off the TV and fought her hardest to go to sleep.

As hard as she tried to relax, memories of her childhood kept playing through her head as if someone was once again hitting the rewind button over and over. Kat couldn't get the reel of tape to stop playing in her head and it made her angry. She sat up in bed, frustrated. All she wanted was sleep. Her body needed rest after the long trip and she couldn't understand how she could be so tired, but so unable to fall asleep.

She massaged her temples over and over. *Why was I such a coward? Why didn't I fight? Why didn't I scream? Why didn't I tell him to stop?* The questions kept racing through her mind as her heart raced.

Jumping off the bed, she paced around the room. Her body started to tense and more tears trickled down her face. Her memories were poisoning her and all she wanted was the antidote. All she wanted was a way to make them stop, but she didn't know how. She reached into her suitcase and grabbed the clock she always kept close to her for times like this.

She crawled back into the bed and placed the clock on the pillow beside her. *Tick, tick, tick, tick...* Kat focused on the only noise she knew would eventually ease her. She pushed everything else out of her mind, only allowing the sound of the clock to fill her thoughts.

*Tick, tick, tick...*

The tears slowly stopped.

*Tick, tick, tick...*

She felt her heartbeat slow down.

*Tick, tick, tick...*

In time, Kat finally drifted off into a night's slumber.
*Tick, tick, tick...*

*****

The next morning Kat woke early. The anxiety and memories of her past hindered her ability to get a good night's rest, but she had an appointment to meet with the realtor at ten and she wanted to be sure she had time to get ready and find her way there in time.

She was glad to find a coffee maker tucked away inside a cupboard in the hotel room. It hadn't been used in some time, but she was glad she could have a strong cup without having to leave her room. She took a quick shower as the coffee brewed and sipped from a chipped coffee mug as she finished getting ready for the day.

Kat was excited to meet the realtor and had high hopes that she would be able to find a place quickly so she could settle into her new home before her new job started. Still, she knew better than to be too optimistic—her optimism had gotten her into trouble before.

As she finished putting on her makeup, she ran through the list of items on her to-do list. Find a place to live, find a new bank, call utility companies, furniture, groceries...the long list went on and on and Kat let out a long sigh. She was overwhelming herself again. *Let's just focus on a house right now*, she thought. *One step at a time, one day at a time.* She stared into the mirror and her cold blue eyes stared back. *Did I do the right thing?* she wondered as she dabbed pink blush onto her pale cheeks. She checked her watch, took one more glance at herself to adjust her hair, and left for her appointment. Ten o'clock rolled around sooner than she expected.

*****

"Ah, rain boots," Kat whispered to herself, adding another item to her list. She enjoyed the walk to the coffee shop the realtor had suggested as their meeting place. She loved how so many things were within walking distance to her hotel. In fact, everything in Astoria seemed to be within walking distance of everything else, but the rainy climate made getting around on foot all the time questionable. *Car*, she thought, adding another item to the mounting list of to-dos or things needed. *Maybe I didn't plan this out as well as I thought I did,* she questioned, second-guessing herself. Her forehead began to wrinkle with the disappointment of her quick and foolish decision to move so many states away from home.

The smell of rain overtook her senses and the cleansing scent washed away her self-doubt. She loved the rain. Most people hoped for blue skies, but Kat had always admired gray skies and drizzly weather. She preferred to be outside when overcast skies were in the forecast as if the dark clouds understood her and protected her.

"Katrina Morgan?! I'm Mr. Lawrence," an older white-haired man shouted with enthusiasm outside the coffee shop. Kat nodded as the man walked over and began shaking her hand. "So pleased to finally meet you! How was the ride to Astoria?" Kat responded with a smile. The get-up-and-go in the man's voice was a breath of fresh air. He was full of energy and that pleased Kat. As much as she loved her solitude, she needed good company occasionally and now was one of those times. She needed someone to reassure her that she'd made the right decision.

Mr. Lawrence motioned Kat toward his SUV and she climbed into the passenger side as he closed the door for her and walked around to the driver's side.

"So Miss Morgan, it's just you, correct?" he asked as he slid in behind the wheel and put the vehicle in gear.

"Yes, sir," Kat replied joyfully. *Just me*, she thought. "Nothing too big, sir, but something comfortable."

"I have a few in mind, but we'll look at all of them," he said, speaking as if he was out to defeat the world that very day. Kat smiled in appreciation of his ambitious and outgoing attitude.

\*\*\*\*\*

After a couple of hours touring different apartments and houses for rent, Kat began to feel disappointed. She knew exactly what she wanted, even if she couldn't put it into words, but none of the places she'd seen so far had fit her idea of home. Her stomach growled with hunger adding to her frustration and disappointment.

"Do you have anything without so many neighbors?" Kat asked with hope in her voice.

"Actually, I do, but it's a bit larger than you asked for," Mr. Lawrence replied.

"Ah, what the heck, let's see it anyway," Kat giggled with a soft smile. "I haven't found the one yet, and I'm enjoying the company so we might as well give it a try." It was the first time she had laughed in weeks and it felt good.

Mr. Lawrence drove to the end of town. He turned onto a short winding road. Tall trees fenced the road on both sides and their branches, filled with leaves, arched over the roadway. Kat had never seen so many trees together at one time. Other than a few scraggly parks, the city she'd come from didn't have many trees at all. The trees in Astoria were vibrant with the first green of early spring, another thing she wasn't used to seeing in the smoggy city where trees choked on air pollution and their roots searched for water under asphalt and concrete.

30

The SUV slowed and Mr. Lawrence turned right into a long gravel driveway. The trees arched even more over the driveway. Kat gasped in wonder. The house was beautiful. She adored the wooden deck that wrapped around the two-story house. You couldn't find this type of house in the city.

As soon as the vehicle stopped, Kat jumped out and leaped up the four steps onto the deck. The view from the deck had already won her heart. Even if the house was falling apart inside, it wouldn't have mattered. Her mind was made up.

"I love it!" Kat announced in excitement. The white-haired gentleman laughed.

"Well, let's see inside the house first," he suggested. Kat already knew this house what exactly what she wanted, but she followed Mr. Lawrence inside the front door as he requested.

The wooden floors creaked slightly as they walked through and the house smelled older, perhaps even a bit musty. *Character*, she thought and fell more in love with it. The living room was to the left of the front door and directly across from the living area stood a room with white French doors. The doors opened into an office. *That would make a perfect art studio*, Kat thought.

She followed the realtor down a small hallway that led into a kitchen and small dining area.

"This is perfect," Kat exclaimed in growing excitement. As they wrapped up the tour, she fell even more in love with the house.

"If this is what you want, let's go do the paperwork," Mr. Lawrence said humbly as they walked down the front steps.

"Let's do it!" Kat replied hoping she could move in soon. She was relieved that even after a mostly fruitless search, they had found the perfect place on the first day of house hunting. Things seemed to be falling into place. *Maybe this was the right thing to do*, she pondered.

 **CHAPTER 8**

Kat slowly eased her eyes open and scanned around the room. Outside the bedroom window, birds were chirping and in the distance, she could hear the waves crashing gently against the rocks. She laid in the bed for a moment enjoying the soothing sounds. They were so different from the sounds of the city. Sirens were replaced by the constant chant of seagulls. The only morning traffic noise was the soft rumble of the freight train and the occasional bellow of a boat in the harbor on the other side of town.

A different thought suddenly filled Kat's mind and she sprung from the bed in a panic to make breakfast. She made it across the room and halfway down the hallway toward the kitchen before she stopped to think.

*I don't have to do shit,* she realized. For the first time in five years, Kat took a deep breath and felt the reassurance that she no longer had to wait on anyone hand and foot. Max was nowhere near Oregon and there was no way he could possibly find her. The distance between them engulfed her like a comforting hug and made her feel warm and safe. She took another deep breath and let out a relieving sigh.

With her panic now under control, Kat walked slowly and calmly to the kitchen and brewed her morning coffee as she stared out the kitchen window at the beautiful view she had been waking up to for the past three days.

Walking out onto her deck, she took a sip of the hot coffee and sat down on the Adirondack chair that had come with the house.

The sights and smells now mixed with the sounds she heard earlier and the blend was invigorating, almost overwhelming her. Salty sea air mingled with the freshness of the trees and the softness of damp earth. She was happy she still had a few more days of relaxation and peace before starting her new job. The move had taken a lot out of her and she still had more to do to spruce up the place to her satisfaction. *Well worth it,* she told her anxious mind. But thoughts weren't enough to convince herself.

"Well worth it!" she said out loud, finally getting through to the inner layers of her mind.

She loved her new house. She hadn't lived in a house since she'd moved out of her parents' home, and even then, the houses in the city were crammed together with barely a backyard to separate them.

In this part of Astoria, there was plenty of space for each house and Kat loved the privacy her new home offered. It was something she never got while sharing the old apartment with Max.

It was an older home, but she loved everything about it, including the owner. Mr. Lawrence had helped her get a great deal and the owner had allowed her to sign the lease and move in without having started her new job. The owner had left all the furnishings for her to use at no additional cost. Kat could tell he was a good man, not like the slumlords that so often owned the rentals in the city.

Escaping from that cramped hotel room helped ease some of her anxiety about the decision she made to move to Astoria. When she walked through the house the first time with the realtor, she knew right away it was meant to be. Everything, down to the furniture that came with it, was like Kat—well worn, but with plenty more life inside.

Even the things other people might see as annoyances didn't bother Kat. The screen door slammed a bit. When she walked through the house, the old wood floors would creak just like they did the first time she'd seen it. It didn't matter much to her—instead, she still maintained that it added character to the place.

The living room was painted in a light blue, while her kitchen had a soft yellow touch to it. The pastel colors and the sunshine pouring in through the windows brought peace and hope into her life. The house was perfectly tucked away off the main road. In a few short days, it had become her nest, her escape. The one thing she had desperately dreamed of, she now had—her own place away from the world...away from Max.

Kat enjoyed unpacking and decorating the house to her own liking. Even though a few days had passed since she'd moved in, she took her time to make sure everything was just how she wanted it.

After spending a few hours organizing her clothes in the bedroom closet, her stomach started to grumble for lunch. The bologna sandwiches, the only food she had in the house, were getting old, so she decided it was time to check out the diner that had caught her eye several times in town.

She slid into a clean pair of light-colored blue jeans and a gray t-shirt that fit well against her body. On her way out of the house, she grabbed her favorite blue sweater with the extra-large hood and walked outside.

She was in the process of buying a cheap, but reliable car from a woman in town that Mr. Lawrence had suggested, but the sale hadn't yet been finalized, so Kat made her way into town on foot. It wasn't a long walk and she enjoyed being outdoors in such a gorgeous setting with plenty of clean air to breathe.

Astoria was a small town with just over 10,000 people. Everybody seemed to know everybody which was both a blessing and a curse. Still, the lack of seven million people buzzing about was a welcome change, Kat realized as she rounded

34

the corner and walked toward the front door of the diner. An old bell clanged as the door closed behind her.

The inside had the same character as her new home. It was an older structure, but it was clean and had been well taken care of. She loved it the moment she walked in the way she'd loved the old house the week before.

She scooted into a booth near the back and opened the menu. Looking over the different options, she finally settled on the classic burger.

*You can never go wrong with a burger,* Kat thought after the waitress took down her order and shuffled back to the kitchen.

As she waited for her food to arrive, Kat glanced shyly around the room. She heard joyful laughter from the other side of the diner and turned to see a group of police officers on their lunch break enjoying themselves.

Kat didn't realize she was staring at the men until one of the officers looked her way. For a brief moment, he turned his attention away from his buddies and focused on her. As he gazed at Kat, he smiled warmly. Their eyes met and Kat blushed and quickly turned away. After a few seconds, she peeked back over at the man across the room and saw that his eyes were still locked on her. She finally got up the courage to smile back.

"One classic burger with fries?" the server said, interrupting Kat's silent conversation with the man across the room.

She turned to the man standing next to her with her order in his hand as she nodded.

*Yum,* she thought to herself as she looked up to the server and smiled. *Astoria sure has some handsome men.*

She looked back over to the police officer and their eyes locked again.

"Are you visiting or new in town?" the server asked cheerfully as he sat the plate down in front of her.

Kat was a bit annoyed and turned her eyes away from the officer apologetically to give the server the attention he was still seeking.

"New in town," she answered him as she forced a smile. "Just moved here a few days ago."

The man slid into the booth on the side across from Kat and held out his hand for her to shake. It was a big hand, a strong hand, and she stared at it for a moment before shaking it.

"I'm Kyle," he said, introducing himself. "I own the place. I'm usually around so let me know if you need anything. I'll be glad to assist with anything you need." He smiled with excitement and Kat had to look away. That smile was almost too much for her to handle.

"Thanks, Kyle, that's very nice of you," she replied as she continued shaking his hand. "I will keep that in mind if anything comes up."

Kyle stood up and walked back toward the kitchen. Kat glanced over to take another look at the police officer, but the group had already left in the few minutes she'd been speaking to Kyle.

"Fuck," she whispered to herself as she picked up the burger and took a big bite that was just as satisfying as she expected it would be. She chewed slowly, savoring the burst of flavors against her taste buds as she turned around to see if Kyle was still within view. She sighed when she saw that he was already back in the kitchen and out of sight.

When she finished her lunch, Kat left some cash on the table to cover the meal and a generous tip and walked out into the afternoon sunshine peeking through the low clouds.

The road was still damp from the morning's rain. She made the ten-minute walk home take a little longer as she enjoyed the world around her. As she turned off the main road and walked toward the house, she appreciated the giant trees all around her. They gave her a sense of adventure. She climbed the few stairs up to her deck and turned to take another look at the place she now called home.

There were no interstates nearby, no tall buildings to block the view of the horizon. No loud traffic or millions of people crowded her like they had in the city. The crisp air and the smell of the coast flooded her nostrils. She knew moving to Astoria had something special to offer. She could feel it, but she didn't know yet what it was. She knew it would be life-changing. The move there started a new chapter in her life and she was excited to embrace it and live it to the fullest.

# CHAPTER 9

"Bananas, I can't forget the bananas," Kat whispered to herself as she rushed around the supermarket.

*Just a few more items and grocery shopping will be done,* she thought with a feeling of accomplishment. But her excitement was short-lived. She walked and walked for what seemed like hours before turning the corner where she thought the produce aisle would be.

*How much farther do I need to go before I find the bananas?* she wondered silently, still pushing the shopping cart past other fruits and vegetables and skimming the area for the familiar yellow color.

Looking up from the displays of fruit, Kat stopped dead in her tracks. The aisle before her now seemed to stretch on like it was half a mile long.

She swallowed a big gulp. "Did it just get darker in here?" she asked herself quietly.

She began pushing the basket slowly down the aisle again, but every step only seemed to make the end of the aisle further away. She stopped for a moment trying to shake off the eerie feeling pulsing through her veins, but it didn't work. She simply wanted to get out of the store and be done with the entire experience. It felt as if something bad was imminent and she didn't want to be around to see what it was.

Disappointed and anxious, she continued pushing the cart. As she finally reached the end of the aisle, Kat smiled when she saw that past the aisle the rest of the store was fully lit and everything seemed to be normal. At the corner, she eyed the supermarket carefully and rejoiced that she'd finally found the bananas.

"Weird," she said aloud softly as she pushed her cart next to the bin of bananas and began selecting the bunch that was to her liking—not too green, not too yellow, just ripe enough. She turned to grab a plastic bag for the bunch she chose, but when she looked at the roll of bags, she realized she was too short to reach for one. Even standing on the tips of her toes, she couldn't seem to reach far enough to get a bag in her grasp.

A glimpse of her hand caused her to jerk back, drop the bananas, and hold both of her hands in front of her face. She examined them closely.

"Oh God, these are not my hands," she said in a panic. "These are too little to be my hands." She pulled the tiny hands up to touch her face and examine the rest of her body. She gulped again nervously, unsure of what was happening to her.

"Oh little Katrina, where are you?" The familiar voice in the distance made her shiver. Trapped in little Katrina's body, Kat began to sweat. She wanted to scream out in fear, but something seemed to trap the scream inside. Instead, she paced quickly around a bin of apples.

*That voice*, little Katrina thought. *I know that voice. I hate that voice.* The little blue-eyed girl searched desperately for the store's exit, but she couldn't seem to find the doors she'd come through only a little while earlier.

*Thump...thump...thump...* Little Katrina heard the noise coming closer. She could feel the vibrations of the approaching thuds under her feet. As her eyes rose from the floor, little Katrina saw an enormous elephant charging toward her. The pale-skinned, black-haired little girl tried to scream again, but once again her mouth remained silent.

Finally able to move her legs and run, little Katrina took off as fast as her little legs allowed her to.

"Oh Katrina, come back here. I won't hurt you." She heard the familiar voice call out for her again. She turned back out of curiosity and saw that Daniel, the neighborhood boy who'd traumatized her, was the one calling out her name. Atop the elephant, he used the enormous creature to taunt Katrina. Turning back to run once again, she tripped and fell, distracted by the boy she'd discovered riding the elephant. She rolled over and, laying on her back, Katrina looked up at Daniel and the elephant quickly approaching her. She knew the gigantic animal would crush her little body. Bracing for the bone-crunching impact, she was finally able to shout an intense and agonizing scream.

Kat bolted up in her bed, still shrieking at the top of her lungs. Her heart was pounding and beads of sweat dripped from her temples. She threw off the blankets and switched on the lamp beside her bed.

Still frightened from her nightmare, Kat squinted in the dim light to read the clock across the room. It was 11:09 p.m.

"At least I have time to get some more sleep before my big day tomorrow," she whispered to herself in the darkness. She wanted to go back to bed, but Daniel's face was still stuck in her mind. Even in the dim light of the room, she felt his eyes staring her down from atop the elephant. Her stomach growled and she rubbed her belly as she got up and headed downstairs to the kitchen.

She poured a late-night bowl of cereal hoping a full stomach would settle her enough to be able to fall back to sleep. She carried the bowl into the living room and plopped down on the sofa as she crunched a spoonful of the sugary sweetness.

It was too quiet, so she reached over to grab the TV remote and waited for the screen to buzz to life. She began to flip through channel after channel trying to find something that would distract her from the nightmare.

"Fuck, Kat, you're a grown-ass adult," she said out loud to herself angrily. "It's a fucking elephant for crying out loud!" She was irritated that once again a simple dream had her so on edge and upset. But it wasn't a simple dream. It was a dream she'd been having since childhood, just like the ones with the tornadoes. But even after all these years, the dreams still left her just as terrified. If nothing else was a constant in her life, those recurring nightmares certainly were.

Channel after channel flipped in front of her eyes until she stopped on an old rerun of *I Dream of Genie*. The main character's magical laughter had a way of easing her mind and calming her down. She slurped the last bit of milk from the edge of the bowl as the genie nodded and disappeared from the screen. As the show went to a commercial break, Kat's phone made a beeping sound to notify her of an incoming text message. She sat her empty bowl on the table and grabbed her phone, wondering who was messaging her so late at night. As she read the message, she froze, afraid to move. She held her breath as she read the message a second time.

*Late night snack, Kat?*

The message came from Max's number and as she read it a third time, her heart pounded through her shirt. *How did he find me? How?*

A million thoughts and questions flooded Kat's exhausted mind. As she struggled to process what was happening, she heard a rustling in the trees outside the window. It was more than just two branches rubbing against each other—she knew there was someone out there looking in.

"Oh God, he's outside my house," Kat whispered to herself as she squinted and tried to see through the glass into the darkness outside. A glimmer of something in the trees made her jump off the sofa to run for the stairs.

As she scrambled across the room, she tripped on the leg of the coffee table and the cereal bowl she had put down just minutes earlier hurled into the air. Her body tumbled over as she lost her balance. Just as she was about to land on the floor, she woke up and jolted off the sofa in a panic looking at the living room around her.

"Damn it!" she yelled as she realized it had only been another nightmare. Not trusting the world around her, she picked up her phone to help reassure herself of reality. She sighed with relief as she saw there was no message from Max on her phone.

Kat glanced at the time hoping for a few more hours of sleep. The time glowed back at her in the dim light—5:14 a.m. She sighed again. *Might as well make coffee and get ready for my first day,* she thought as she stood up and headed to the kitchen.

She sipped the cup of coffee slowly as she watched the first light of dawn breaking in the east through the kitchen window and thought about the dawn of a new era in her life. With her mug empty and the caffeine beginning to wake her up, she headed upstairs to begin getting ready for the day.

Kat took a cool, refreshing shower hoping to wash the events of the night from her mind. The nightmares always made her feel unclean and out of place.

Standing in front of the bathroom mirror a while later, she admired the outfit she'd selected for her first day of work in Astoria. The royal blue blouse fit well and made her eyes stand out from the rest of her face.

She styled her long, shiny black hair into loose curls and carefully darkened the edges of her eyes with a thin, black eyeliner pencil. As she looked at herself in the mirror, she thought she looked too pale, so she dabbed her cheeks with a little blush to give them some color.

As she finished brushing mascara onto her long eyelashes, she took one more confident glance at herself.

"You got this, Kat," she told herself confidently and courageously. "Today is a new day."

# CHAPTER 10

Kat turned onto Commercial Street where most of the businesses in Astoria were located. The car sale had finally gone through before her first day of work and she was glad to have the freedom to go anywhere on her own again. No more walking or waiting for cab rides—besides, people in Astoria often gave her strange looks when she pulled up to places around town in a taxi. They weren't used to anyone using the taxi service unless they were headed to or from the bus station or the airport in Portland.

The car certainly wasn't anything special, but it ran well, had been maintained with care, and fit her budget for the time being. She drove slowly down the street admiring the old buildings in the downtown district with their vintage-style signage. It still had that classic small-town appearance that had disappeared from so many other downtowns decades earlier, and yet it was still modern enough to keep up with the times.

Kat smiled, cautiously pleased with her decision to move. This very short drive from her house to the downtown area was her new "rush hour" and it was quite the change from the bumper-to-bumper traffic jam she'd crept through when she lived in the city.

As she neared the end of the street, the sign for her new employer's office came into view: *KJ&G Associates*. It was the last building on the street and Kat was pleased to see that it was on a corner that appeared to have excellent views of both the town and the Columbia River. Her heart began to race out of both excitement and nervousness.

"You got this, Kat. You got this," she told herself out loud.

She pulled the car into the tiny parking lot behind the building that held, at most, ten cars.

"Wow, such a difference," she exclaimed as she remembered the ten-story parking garage outside her city office. She took a deep breath and looked in the rearview mirror for one final check. She grabbed her lip balm from her purse and coated her lips one more time with the waxy, tingling substance before stepping out of the car.

With her bag in hand, Kat took in the view of her new workplace. She was in awe once again of the beauty of Astoria. Standing next to her car, she was able to see the river draining into the Pacific Ocean to the west and the state of Washington just across the famous Astoria-Megler Bridge.

The downtown was so quiet in the morning that she could hear waves colliding gently against rocks in the distance and the sounds of seagulls flying overhead helped to ease her nervousness. The lack of honking and thousands of people hurrying to work made her happy she'd chosen a change to the small-town life.

She opened the glass door at the front of the building and was immediately greeted by a polite and outgoing gentleman who had clearly been awaiting her arrival.

"You must be Katrina Morgan," he said with a genuine expression of excitement on his face. "We are all so pleased to have you!" Kat felt her nerves calming as the man's kindness made her feel welcomed and comfortable with her new job. He reminded her of her brother—the expression on his face always seemed to say that he had another joke waiting in his back pocket. She could tell from the small wrinkles at the corners of his eyes that this man was always smiling.

"I'm Luke Stevenson, office manager, but you can just call me Luke," he explained with amusement. "Did you find the place okay?"

"Oh yes, no troubles at all," Kat replied shyly.

"Good to hear! Let me take you to meet the rest of the herd," he said with a burst of laughter. "But please, don't tell them I just called them a bunch of animals."

"Your secret is safe with me," Kat said with a warm smile as Luke guided her down the hallway.

There was a much larger room in the back of the office where the other employees were already settling in for the work day.

"We all work in an open area. We feel it's better to see faces while we work," Luke said with more laughter and smiles. Kat enjoyed watching him and seeing his happiness. It lifted her mood.

"We're here forty hours a week, we don't want to feel as if we're in a cage all day," a woman across the room added.

"Plus, this way we all get to share the amazing view," Luke chimed in again. Kat walked to the opposite end of the room where a big window in the office covered an entire wall.

"It's gorgeous," she exclaimed. As she turned around, a red-haired woman walked over to introduce herself.

"Good morning, Katrina. My name is Aubrey," she said as she shook Kat's hand. It was humbling that everyone was so kind and welcoming to her. No workplace in the city had ever been this warm and hospitable.

"This is Jane and Lisa," Aubrey said as she continued the introductions.

Both women smiled genuinely and greeted Kat with a friendly wave.

"Okay, Aubrey," Luke interrupted as he headed back to his desk in the corner. "I'm gonna sneak away to respond to some emails I have lingering. Please help Katrina get settled in."

Kat followed Aubrey across the room as Luke chimed in one more time from his desk. "Glad you're here Kat!"

"Well, alright then, Katrina, let's get you to your desk and get you all set up on email," Aubrey said getting down to business. "Then I'll go over the client list and we can talk about some of your previous work." She seemed sincerely interested to hear about Kat's work experience and it made Kat feel even more welcome among the group of professionals. Aubrey took her by the arm and directed her to her new desk.

The training on office standards and procedures went by quickly without Kat realizing the morning was nearly over. It wasn't until Luke walked over rubbing his belly that she even thought about lunch.

"Who's hungry?!" he asked loud enough for the entire office to hear. "Let's take Katrina to the Silver Salmon Grille for a welcome lunch." The three other ladies in the office nodded in agreement with his suggestion.

"Hope you like seafood!" Jane exclaimed as she grabbed her purse and switched off her desk lamp. Kat didn't respond to the question but instead stood with her head tilted with a questioning look on her face as she pondered whether or not she did like seafood. "Oh shit. You don't like seafood, do you?" Kat shook her head slowly, not sure whether to be embarrassed or amused.

"You do know where you moved, right?" Lisa asked with a chuckle as they all headed down the hallway toward the front door.

"Um…I guess I didn't think this whole move out thoroughly, did I?" Kat replied jokingly.

"It's okay, they also have some pretty amazing burgers," Aubrey said, coming to Kat's rescue. "Besides, just because you live here doesn't mean you have to like seafood. It's a misconception about coastal life."

"Let's roll, ladies. I'm starving," Luke said impatiently with another smile as he held the door for the group and locked it behind them.

Kat couldn't get enough of the scenery in front of her eyes as they walked through the downtown district. The sidewalk was still damp from the early morning rain and a slight fog still hung in the air. The group of five came to a small, fancy-looking building with a brick facade and a maroon overhang that read *Silver Salmon Grille*. At first, Kat felt uncomfortable. She never liked going to fancy places. She always felt out of place.

Her new coworkers quickly settled her nerves as they walked in and took their seats at a large table covered in white paper.

"Here, take a few crayons," Aubrey said as she handed Kat a few different colors. "You'll need them in a minute."

When the group had placed its order, Luke stood and made an announcement.

"In honor of Katrina and her first day at a new job, I would first like to raise a toast of this amazing Coca-Cola," Luke raised his glass and the others followed with their glasses. Kat blushed from the extra attention. "And second, you all have to draw something on the table to describe your first day with us. Katrina, I know you haven't been with us long, so we won't make you draw for us just yet."

"Please, everyone, call me Kat," she said, looking around the table at her new coworkers who already seemed so much more appreciative of her presence than her fellow employees in the city had been.

The group began sketching on the table with their crayons as Kat scribbled and waited patiently for the others to finish. Everyone was quietly concentrating on their drawings, but Luke chuckled every few seconds as he reminisced about his first day and did his best to capture the story.

Just before the meal arrived at the table, Luke announced that it was time to share everyone's artwork. Lisa stood and shared her story first. Her drawing was a car battery and she explained that on her first day, she was more than two hours late because she had left her headlights on the night before, running her car battery down.

"But Mr. Stevenson, I mean Luke, was so understanding," Lisa shared with a smile. "He didn't care that I was late and he even drove me to get a new battery after work."

Jane told her story next. She had drawn a stick figure with a head full of frizzy, curly hair.

"I thought it would be a great idea to get my hair done before my first day," Jane said. "You know, new job, new me. It turned into a bad idea when I tried to perm my own hair with one of those at-home perm kits." She paused and put her hand over her mouth to cover a giggle as she recalled the results.

"Well, I did it wrong and ended up ruining my hair. My hair was so puffy my first day of work that I couldn't get it under control. But the worst part was that all day my hair kept breaking off. I felt like I was shedding all over the office." The group burst out in laughter as Jane finally let out the giggles she had tried so hard to hold in.

"But Kat, I want to be sure you know that on that first day, not one person at KJ&G made a rude remark or made me feel insecure about my hair. I knew then that it would be a wonderful place to work and I can't see myself anywhere else."

As Jane sat down, Aubrey stood up to share her story. Her drawing was simply five telephones lined up side-by-side.

"When I started at KJ&G I had just left a place I'd worked for ten years. In fact, I had worked there since the age of sixteen and it had been my only job until that point. When I was first hired, I was the receptionist for KJ&G and Luke had me answering calls on the very first day," Aubrey explained. "On my first call, I answered with my old employer's name." The group chuckled.

"Oh wait! It gets better," Aubrey continued. "You would think at that point I would have learned my lesson and caught on. But truth is that I didn't do this just once that day. I didn't do it twice, either. I didn't do it three times. And I didn't do it four times. I did it, ladies and gentlemen, a total of five times." The group was now roaring with laughter, but Aubrey was only halfway through her story.

"I'm not done, yet," Aubrey said, shaking her head with a smile. "The best part of this story is that one of KJ&G's clients at the time was my former employer. They just happened to be the fifth call that came through and let me tell you, they were confused when I answered with the name of their company."

Aubrey sat down as Luke reached over and gave her a pat on the back.

"I might have you all beat," he said as he stood up. The group looked over at his drawing and tried to make sense of the strange image. "My first day was way before any of you ever started at KJ&G and I don't think I've ever shared this story with any of you. On my first day, I thought I was something special. I thought I had it made. I know you wouldn't think it now with as humble as I am, but I used to have quite an ego."

Jane, Lisa, and Audrey rolled their eyes and Audrey let out an audibly sarcastic, "Ha!"

"I know, hard to believe!" Luke joked. "Well, that first day I decided to kick my feet up on my desk about halfway through the day. I was in the middle of a phone conversation with a very important client when I heard a crack. The main bolt holding my office chair together snapped and I crashed to the floor like a knocked-out boxer."

The four ladies, including Kat, were bent over with uncontrollable laughter as Luke continued his story.

"The phone flew off the desk directly into my left eye, my full coffee cup spilled all over my white shirt, and my pants ripped in the crotch. The entire office got very quiet and no one moved. I think they were afraid I was dead. I spent the rest of the day with my jacket tied around my waist, coffee stains drying by the minute, and nursing a black eye. But I will tell you, we kept that client."

The server showed up to the table with their lunch order and Luke sat down as he finished his lesson.

"Kat, as you've heard everyone here had something embarrassing or unlucky happen on their first day with us," he said as the server placed plates down in front of each of them. "Considering that you've made it halfway through the day without an incident, I'd say you've outdone us all already. Welcome to KJ&G and we hope you have an embarrassing story to share with us someday!"

During lunch, Kat and her new coworkers enjoyed each other's company and bonded quickly. As they laughed about jokes and stories, the staff from

KJ&G Associates learned about Kat and her old life. She left out the parts about running away from her abusive ex-boyfriend and the terrifying nightmares that had always filled her nights. But by the time they walked back to the office, they were acting like old friends.

*****

Kat finished off the rest of the afternoon completing stacks and stacks of new hire paperwork. She had forgotten how much paperwork was involved in a new job, but her new office had such a positive change in the environment that she barely noticed time passing by.

"Alright, Katrina. Time to kick you out of here," Luke called out to Kat as he stood up and put on his jacket.

"Oh wow! I didn't even notice it was five o'clock," she replied as she began gathering her belongings. "It snuck up on me." The group headed for the door and parted ways cheerfully in the parking lot.

"Well, you made it the entire day without anything embarrassing happening," Luke joked as the other co-workers chuckled in the background. "I think you might be eligible for some kind of award or something."

"Haha! Very funny!" Kat replied as she waved goodbye to everyone with a smile.

As Kat drove home from work, a soft rain began to fall on her windshield. She cracked the window on the car just enough to smell the rain as she made her way leisurely across town to her comforting new home.

Still full from her big welcome lunch, she made herself a cup of hot chocolate and grabbed a few graham crackers from the cupboard. She walked out onto her deck to enjoy the rain with her marshmallow-filled mug of liquid heaven. She felt at peace, even after the vivid nightmares the night before.

Most people felt lonely when found themselves without company, but Kat desired her alone time, even though she had enjoyed her first day of work. She longed for isolation. She couldn't even imagine another relationship after the one she'd finally escaped from. As she watched the water dripping from the edge of the porch roof, she wondered if she was even capable of loving anyone else. She wondered if she even loved herself.

She leaned back in the chair. With her cozy pajamas already on, she pulled her knees up to her chest and continued to sip her hot chocolate to the sound of the falling rain.

"Crap, I forgot to check the mail today," she said out loud to herself as she stood up quickly and sat the mug down. She looked down at her bare feet and pajamas and shrugged her shoulders. *The hell with it*, she thought. *A little rain never hurt anybody.* She took off down her long driveway barefoot as the precipitation increased from a slight drizzle to a pouring rain.

She felt free as if she were a child playing in the rain. Her senses were almost overwhelmed. The wet earth beneath her feet, the cold raindrops pouring down onto her hair and face, and the greenery that surrounded her on all sides gave her a sense of joy that she couldn't shake. In the midst of her run to the mailbox, Kat carelessly spun around in her driveway with her arms wide open. She laughed at herself as she made the last few steps to her mailbox.

"I don't think I've ever seen someone look as graceful as you dancing in the rain before," an unfamiliar approaching voice called out. Kat jumped a bit, startled that someone else was nearby. As the dark-haired man drew closer in the rain, she noticed it was the police officer she had exchanged smiles with in the diner. He was dressed for a jog and the winded way he spoke told her he had been running for some time.

"Oh God," Kat whispered to herself low enough that he didn't hear. She knew she looked terrible drenched in rainwater. Her long hair was now a stringy mess laying on her shoulders.

"Um...I didn't think anyone was watching," Kat said, her embarrassment adding an attractive blush color to her pale cheeks.

"Haha, don't mind me. I promise not to tell anyone...well, except all my friends," the man joked with Kat.

"Oh, well aren't you just a gentleman now?" Kat teased back at him.

"Oh, I have my moments," the man said with a smile.

*Oh goodness, there's that smile again,* Kat told to herself as she remembered the man's irresistible smile that day in the diner. It was a smile that reached up to his dark eyes, a smile that revealed deep dimples on his cheeks.

"I can see that," Kat said returning a smile of her own. She started to shiver, forgetting for a moment that she was soaked from the rain. She pulled open the mailbox and grabbed her mail, returning to her original task as she continued her conversation by introducing herself. "It was nice meeting you. I'm Kat, by the way."

"Well, Kat, the pleasure is all mine. I'm Nicholas," he said with a big grin on his face. "I'll see you around, yeah?"

"Yeah, maybe," Kat laughed, though her eyes said no.

"I can handle that, I guess. Okay, nice meeting you, Kat. I must continue on my run," Nicholas said as he started to take off on a sprint again.

He was already at the end of the road when Kat shouted back at him. "You know it's raining, right?"

Nicholas turned around to face Kat and began jogging backward. "It's one of my favorite things to do! Running in the rain!" He smiled and turned around to continue his jog along the narrow wooded road that led away from Kat's house.

She paused a moment before she headed back to take shelter from the downpour. She watched Nicholas in the distance until she could no longer see him through the rain. Once he was out of sight, she ran up the driveway and inside the house away from the cold and rain. She was drenched by the time she got back in.

"Hmmm, Nicholas," she said out loud. *One more time,* "Nicholas." Kat liked how his name rolled off her tongue. She shivered in her damp clothes as she climbed the stairs to take a long, warm bath to finish off her day.

*This has been one of the best days I've had in a long time,* she thought as she warmed her body in the cozy bath water minutes later. The thought made her smile as she realized she would have plenty more days like this. Safe. Quiet. Fun. Alone—just the way she liked it.

# CHAPTER 11

Kat slowly opened her eyes and looked at her surroundings trying to make sure she wasn't dreaming. She laid in bed and listened to the quiet house—it was calm like her emotions had been lately. She welcomed the quiet. The thought that Max didn't dominate her life anymore put a smile on her face. She couldn't remember the last time her life was so at ease. Everything had always been so chaotic in her life, but she put on a brave front. She kept most of the chaos to herself, locked in her mind where no one else would find out about it.

She rolled over and noticed it was 5:34 a.m. and dawn was already breaking outside the bedroom window. The sun was rising earlier as the days got longer. It was still early, but Kat finally felt rested for the first time since her move to Astoria. For weeks she had been running on a few measly hours of sleep each night, buffering her exhaustion with coffee. Now it had been almost a week without a nightmare and she had at last been able to sleep through the night without waking multiple times.

Laying in her warm bed, Kat hugged her blanket tighter. She loved the fact that she was alone in her nest, but she also felt guilty that she was enjoying a new life in Astoria away from her problems while her family was so far away and missing her presence. She wished she had her family closer to her new home because there was no way she could ever move back to that city again.

She knew her father would never entertain the idea for more than a few seconds. Her brother would never move to Astoria either—he loved his hometown too much. He always talked about building his journalism career in the city. Jerry was highly intelligent and very driven, but he was stubborn. *I don't know what he sees in that city,* Kat thought to herself. There were too many painful memories she could never shake to be able to move back to that place.

Kat scolded herself for being so selfish. This was her adventure, her time for personal growth, development, and healing. She had no right to expect her family to uproot their lives to join her in her new life.

It was painful, but she hoped her family would forgive her for moving so far away. She was grateful for them and it had been difficult to leave on such short notice and with such little explanation. But she couldn't risk having them involved too much with her plan. She frowned at the mere idea of Max finding out that they even knew about her move. He only knew destruction and Kat could never forgive herself if something happened to her family because she had brought Max into their lives.

Though they were thousands of miles apart and she missed them like crazy, Kat looked forward to a day when they would come and see her new life, her better life, even if it was only for a few days at a time. Her parents had promised to visit a few times a year and Jerry promised to visit in the fall when his work slowed down. The thought of what kind of mischief they'd get into made Kat chuckle out loud. Jerry and Kat either loved each other or hated each other, but one thing they both shared was an ability to make trouble together.

"I think it's coffee time," Kat said out loud breaking the silence of the house. She pushed off her blanket and made her way downstairs to the kitchen. She listened to the gurgling of the coffee maker as she stared out the window and tried to remember whether she had anything to do that morning.

With the strong brew in her cup, she walked out to her deck and sat down. This deck was her new favorite place, a place she could call her own. The sun was still rising, and the soft purple glow that came with it cast a calmness over the entire area. Kat smiled, pondering what to do with her Saturday. She sipped on her coffee as she watched the glow in the sky getting brighter by the second. She smiled even though no one was there to see her smile. The stillness of the morning was her favorite part of the day. That moment between night and day, the transfer between dark and light brought her hope. Dawn was when she was at peace the most, likely because it meant a fresh day and a fresh opportunity for things to go right instead of wrong.

Kat enjoyed days like this when there wasn't much movement in life and no duty for her to interact with other people. Some people called these types of days boring, but Kat looked forward to the freedom and isolation they provided her.

She would never understand why so many people she knew back home thrived around people. They looked forward to parties and events, but Kat wanted the opposite. She felt anxious just getting invited to something that involved a lot of people and noise. *Maybe it's just my personality,* she thought to herself. *Maybe it's a defect in my mind.*

As the light changed from purple to yellow over the horizon in the east, the faint sound of waves in the west reminded her that she hadn't yet spent any time at the beach since moving to the coast. "Ah, perfect!" she exclaimed with joy as she began planning a relaxing day on the beaches of the Pacific Ocean. A day near the edge of the salty water was just what she needed.

An hour later, as she stood in her towel rummaging through her closet, she realized she didn't have much to wear to a beach. In fact, she didn't have many revealing clothes at all. Max always seemed to think she was dressing up for someone else.

"No Kat," she stopped herself. "Today, you will not think of Max. Today is *your* day." She grabbed a pair of jean shorts and a white and gray striped tank top. *This will do,* she reassured herself. She blow-dried her hair and gave the long strands a few loose curls. She thought it was probably silly to get so done up for a day at the beach, but it was her day and she wanted to feel beautiful. She lined her eyes in black and put on her mascara as she hummed a song to herself. With her work done, she stared at herself in the mirror. No matter how much makeup or hair styling she did, she was never happy with the way she looked.

"This will have to do," she told herself in a disappointed tone accompanied by a frown.

The drive down the narrow road from her house felt good. Kat had her favorite music playing on the radio and the weather was perfect enough to keep the windows down. She drove at a steady speed, winding around the curvy, wooded roads. The feeling of freedom grew as the wind blew through her hair. *This is a good day,* she reminded herself. *I'm in control of my day.*

Trees became sparse and she could smell the saltiness in the air increasing as she got closer to the coast. As the road made one last curve, she could see the blue water span across the horizon broken by a craggy rock and foamy waves here and there. They were sights she'd never seen in person before, but she welcomed them easily.

With her car parked at the edge of a small hill, Kat walked down the easy slope and gazed out at the expansive ocean before her. This was the view she'd been homesick for, though she'd never even seen it before now. Even after arriving in Astoria and being in awe of the sights and sounds of her new home, she still didn't understand how one could be homesick for a place they'd never been before.

She walked down to the sandy beach where only a few other people were enjoying the day. Seeing the emptiness of the beach made her even happier.

"No crowds," she said out loud, though she knew it likely wouldn't last long on such a beautiful day.

Nestled against a boulder at the edge of the beach, Kat dug her feet into the cool sand. She was in wonder of what surrounded her. The sounds of the water crashing against the rocks reminded her of the chaos that had once been in her life, the times she'd been thrown against rocks of her own. And yet, the seagulls gliding in the air above her reminded her of the peace she felt today, her own ability to glide over everything that had been done to her. She grabbed a book out of her bag and indulged in the first few chapters as the warm sun rose higher in the sky.

*****

51

Kat was lost in the fairy tale love story she'd been reading when a dog crashed into her legs. She looked up, startled, and saw the golden retriever running to his ball. A man ran over to her and apologized several times.

"I'm so sorry, ma'am, I overthrew Murphey's tennis ball," he explained sincerely. Kat looked up and quickly recognized the handsome man—he was the owner of the diner she'd met during her first week in Astoria. Kat thought it was strange that she kept running into the two men she'd noticed that day, but brushed it off as one of those coincidences of living in a small town.

"Oh goodness, he's so cute. Come here, Murphey," Kat called to the man's dog. "No worries. He's too adorable to be upset with." As the dog scrambled over to her, she scratched behind his ears. The man gave her a curious look.

"Hey, you're the new girl in town, right? I'm Kyle, I own the diner on Eighth Street," he said in excitement as he recognized Kat from their initial meeting.

"Oh yes, I remember. How are things?" Kat responded politely as she also remembered the man's unintentional interruption of her moment with the handsome cop that had been sitting across the diner. *Well, if you want to call it a moment,* she thought to herself. A bit annoyed with the memory, Kat picked up Murphey's ball and threw it far across the beach for him to fetch.

"You could probably use some friends here in town. Can I take you out for coffee sometime?" Kyle nervously asked her. *How does he know what I need?* Kat asked herself with frustration. He was obviously hitting on her, and she was both annoyed and flattered at the same time.

Caught off guard, she responded politely to his request. "Uh…sure, that would be nice, Kyle."

"Great, I can meet you tomorrow at nine. There's a coffee shop just down the street from the diner," he offered, patiently waiting for Kat's approval. She smiled and agreed to meet him for the impromptu casual date.

"Come on, Murphey, let's let the lady get back to her book," Kyle said with a grin.

"Thank you," Kat laughed as the man ran away with his dog close behind. Kyle was certainly interested in her, but she didn't know exactly what to think of him. *Are people always this eager?* There was something about him Kat just didn't trust. Maybe it was his motives. *What does he want with me?* she wondered. *Why does he want coffee and why tomorrow? Why so sudden?*

"Why didn't you just say no, Kat?" she asked herself out loud. Her mind began to race with dozens of different scenarios. *Maybe Max sent him.* The irrational thought jumped into her head. Right away, she jumped up from her cozy place in the sand and looked around the beach nervously, expecting wholeheartedly to see Max standing at the top of the hill laughing at her before storming down to drag her back to the city by her hair. A few of the other people on the beach looked her way wondering why she seemed panicked.

52

"Okay, Kat. Let's not be crazy," she said softly, trying to calm herself down. "It's just coffee and this is what people do. Normal people. They socialize. Calm the fuck down. It's just coffee." She sat back down and tried to look as casual as possible. *Get yourself together, Kat,* she reassured herself.

She let out a heavy sigh as she realized she was letting Max get to her once again. She didn't understand her irrational thoughts and why they persisted even when Max was out of the picture. It was frustrating. She wasn't with him anymore, so why did he still consume so much of her life, her thoughts, and her dreams? It was always about him or the neighborhood boy who had taken advantage of her childhood innocence. Her decision-making, her whole perspective of people and their motives were skewed by her experiences with those two horrible people. They had ruined her.

Kat grabbed her book and tried to get back into the exciting story, but she had trouble focusing again. *Maybe a walk would do some good,* she decided. She gathered her things and headed back to her car.

"Find walking trail near me," Kat said into the GPS app on her phone. It responded with a beep and a list of twelve trails near her location. Conveniently, the first one had a trailhead right at the edge of the beach below.

The walk was beautiful, with views of not only the Oregon coast but also the forestry at its edge. She wished her father was there with her. He was an avid hiker and he would have loved the awe-inspiring combination of geographies. She planned to bring him here to this very trail the first time her parents came to visit. Her mother could come too, and together they would enjoy a picnic somewhere along the beauty of the trail.

As the trail rounded a small hill and moved closer to the coast, Kat saw what looked like the remains of a shipwreck on the beach. As she walked closer, she read the information signs explaining the origin of the ship, named the Peter Iredale. It had been on the beach for more than one hundred years wasting away in the salty air. She'd never seen such a thing in her life and as she walked about the decaying ship's skeleton, she felt like a character in a book discovering a wonder of the world.

The continued story of the ship was explained on other trail markers surrounding the wreck. After losing control of the ship's course in 1906, the captain was unable to direct it into the mouth of the Columbia River nearby. Instead, it crashed onto the sandy beach where it had been ever since. The soft sand had provided a perfectly safe surface on which the ship could come ashore without the loss or injury of any of the crew.

As Kat leaned on one of the information markers, she gazed at the unusual view in front of her. The waves reminded her of her own emotions threatening to sink her ship and drown her in an ocean of anxiety. *But now,* she thought to herself, *I've found a soft, sandy beach to land on.* Like the Peter Iredale, she'd gotten off course in a storm called life and it had pushed her ashore, luckily with a landing on a soft section of the Oregon coast that would result in her safe rescue.

Kat continued her walk, leaving the shipwreck she'd stumbled upon. She would certainly be back some day, how could she not? She identified personally with the story of that ship and it was inspiring to stand among its remains and ponder the future.

It was quiet as she walked along the path before her. She heard only the ocean's pulse of waves in the distance as she ascended up the hills that separated the coast and the forest. Birds chirped around her in the stillness and she was lost in thought as she took in the natural wonders on every side. Suddenly, a few steps behind her, she heard the sound of leaves crunching. On edge already, she couldn't ignore the sound.

Out of curiosity, she turned around to see what made the sound behind her. Further back on the trail, an older gentleman was kneeling down and staring directly at Kat. She gulped hard. *Breathe, Kat,* she told herself silently. The man stood up quickly and started at Kat with a pace that made her uncomfortable.

She turned back around and started to walk as fast as she could, trying not to draw any attention to herself.

"Hey! Hey! Come back here!" the man shouted with a thunderous voice at her back. Kat's heart began to pound and she tried to quicken her pace without breaking into a run. *Who is following me? Why? Oh God, Max really did send someone for me.* She couldn't ignore the thoughts racing in her head.

She started to run as fast as her sandals would allow until the trail split into a fork. She took a left at the fork and leaped over the brush that had grown out onto the trail's path. She looked back as she ran and saw that the man was still following her, now at a steady jog and with something in his hand that she couldn't quite make out in the chaos.

Kat continued to dodge branches that got in her way as the trail began to cut through a thicker area of the forest. *This is too familiar,* she thought. *Being chased, like in my dreams.* The night terrors she'd experienced since childhood were now becoming a reality. *Maybe this, too, is just a dream,* she wondered. *But it feels too real to be a dream.*

As she began to leap over a large branch that had fallen across the trail, her sandal caught a rough piece of the tree bark and she didn't quite make it over. She felt herself quickly going down hard and smacked her face on the dense ground underneath her. With soreness taking over her body, Kat slowly turned over to her back and saw the man approaching her. She panicked and screamed at the top of her lungs.

"No! No! Get away!" she yelled, hoping someone nearby would hear her cries for help. She burst into tears and tried to get back up. She immediately fell back down again, unable to put much weight on her foot.

"Ma'am, ma'am! I'm not going to hurt you. I won't hurt you," the man was talking quickly as he tried to catch his breath and relieve Kat of her fears.

He seemed unsure of the situation that had just unfolded before his eyes. "You dropped your phone. I tried to get your attention to give it to you."

The man reached his arm out with the phone in hand, trying to make a truce with a terrified Kat. She took her phone without saying a word, still trying to process her overreaction. Defeated, she laid down on the ground, not wanting to face the situation she had caused. Her foot was throbbing and her face stung, but her pride was bruised more than anything else.

"Ma'am, you're bleeding. Can I help you?" the man said with concern in his voice. Kat was dazed, not sure how to answer him. As she laid motionless on the ground, she heard sirens in the distance growing closer. She leaned up slowly on her elbows, looking at her surroundings with a confused look on her bruising face.

# CHAPTER 12

"Over there! Over there! Here, this way!" Kat could hear a woman's voice yelling at someone. Within seconds, paramedics surrounded her.

"Ma'am, can you tell me your name? Are you in any pain?" the first paramedic asked quickly.

"Um, Katrina Morgan. I'm Katrina Morgan. I'm okay. I just fell." Kat wasn't sure why there was so much commotion over a fall on the trail. The paramedic began to put pressure on a wound near Kat's left eyebrow.

"Someone heard lots of screaming," the paramedic explained. "They called 911." Kat started to feel overwhelmed and embarrassed.

"Her pulse is rising," a paramedic who had been measuring Kat's heartbeat announced.

"I'm just overwhelmed. I'm fine, really," Kat pleaded with the paramedics taking care of her injuries. They helped Kat up and walked her to the ambulance with a slight limp. *This is a bit much,* Kat thought. *Who called an ambulance over a trip and fall?* She sat in the back of the ambulance while the paramedics finished examining her. She was able to move her foot and luckily, it wasn't broken.

"Are you sure you don't want a transport to the hospital, Miss Morgan?" one of the paramedics asked as they packed up their instruments.

"No, thank you. Really. I'm okay," she answered pleadingly. The paramedics seemed reluctant to release her, but she wanted nothing more than to go home and be alone with her damaged ego.

"Hey Phil, do you mind if I ask Miss Morgan a few questions?" a police officer politely interrupted.

"Hey, no problem. She's all yours. See if she'll let you get her some first aid for those scrapes," the paramedic said as he patted the officer on the back while stepping away.

"Miss Morgan, you had a pretty hard fall. Witnesses said they heard a pretty vicious scream. Did someone hurt you?" the officer asked as he looked at Kat with a sympathetic expression on his face. Kat stared into the officer's eyes—it was Nicholas, the officer from the diner and the evening when she'd been dancing in the rain. Embarrassed, Kat tried to relay exactly what happened.

"It's really just a misunderstanding on my part, officer. I thought the gentleman over there was following me, so I ran away. I ended up tripping and then I turned over and saw him running towards me. I got scared and I screamed. But I dropped my phone earlier on the trail and didn't realize it. He saw it, I guess, and all he was doing was trying to give it back to me," she explained at a fast pace. Every word she spoke sounded more ridiculous as it left her mouth.

"So, he didn't hurt you?" the officer asked, trying to reassure himself.

"No, he was only trying to help. I'm so sorry for causing such a panic. I don't know why I thought he was following me," Kat continued. "I mean, he was...but..." She had no other words to make the situation sound any better.

"Don't be sorry. You thought you were in danger. Don't beat yourself up, Miss Morgan," the officer said, trying to ease Kat. She looked down at his name tag and noticed it read *Officer Mendoza*. She had finally learned his last name, but she wished it had been under different circumstances. "One thing, though. Do you have a reason to believe that you were being followed?" Officer Mendoza's eyes were firm on Kat, full of concern. *Oh God,* she thought. *How can I explain all of this without sounding like a total whack job?*

"No, I don't. It's a new place and...and I just moved here a couple of weeks ago. I must have just spooked myself." *I'm telling the truth,* she reasoned with herself in her head. *I'm just not telling the whole truth.*

"Okay, Miss Morgan. Just making sure. I'll follow you home to make sure you get there safely. Is that okay with you?" He waited patiently for Kat's approval and as she nodded her head, Nicholas and one of the paramedics helped her limp back to the parking lot where her car was parked. She didn't have the energy to argue by that point.

"Alright, boys. All clear. I'll make sure she gets home safely."

She pulled away from the parking lot with her pride aching more than anything else. She checked her rearview mirror and, just as he promised, Officer Mendoza was right behind her. She drove into town and turned onto the road that led to her house. She made the winding path slowly until she reached her driveway. Officer Mendoza pulled in right beside her.

Kat grunted as she got out of the car. "Ouch!" she said out loud. The officer was getting out at the same time. Kat caught a glimpse of herself in the reflection on her car window as she closed the door.

"Oh shit," she said loud enough for Officer Mendoza to hear her. She ran her fingers along her face examining her wounds for the first time.

"You're pretty banged up, Miss Morgan. Do you need help cleaning the wounds?" the officer offered kindly.

"You can call me Kat, by the way. And it's really okay. I'm sure you're busy and I can do this myself," she replied gratefully, but with a hint of annoyance in her voice.

Office Mendoza laughed. "Stop being so stubborn. You look like hell.

58

Come on. I'll help you," he said, refusing to take no for an answer.

Kat proceeded to her deck and hobbled up the few steps. "Thanks for your honesty, officer," Kat said while returning the laughter.

"Where's your first aid kit?" the officer asked as Kat eased herself down on the sofa.

"It's upstairs in the bathroom cabinet," she answered.

"Got it, I'll go get it," Nicholas said as he ran up the stairs.

*Oh God, I hope I didn't leave any dirty clothes laying around,* Kat worried to herself. Even though she enjoyed the company at the moment, she hated unexpected visitors.

"Found it," the officer shouted with excitement as he bounded back down the stairs and sat at Kat's side.

"I really appreciate all this, officer," she said as he opened the first aid kit and took out a cotton ball and a small brown bottle.

"Ah, just doing what I do. Plus, please call me Nicholas. Stop being so formal." He smiled as he opened the bottle of peroxide and poured a little onto the cotton. Kat gulped hard. His eyes were beautiful and as she looked over his face, she focused on his smile, a dimple appearing next to his mouth.

"Ah," she gasped as Nicholas cleaned the scrape on her eyebrow. He was gentle with his touch and Kat thanked him silently for that. He moved the cotton down to her face, cleaning the cut on the bottom of her lip.

"How you doing?" Nicholas asked sincerely as Kat chuckled.

"I'm fine, really. I'm just a sissy for pain," she said, grinning, then wincing from the pain as the smile hurt the cut below her lip.

"I'm sure it will heal soon," he predicted while dabbing antibiotic cream on Kat's scrapes. "That should do it, Miss Morgan." He stared softly into Kat's soft blue eyes.

"I thought we were done being formal, officer?" she said with a smirk. As much as she enjoyed the moment with Nicholas, she quickly put a stop to it.

"Oh yes, I apologize," he said, breaking from his trance and gathering up the first aid kit contents. "Also, have a hiking buddy with you next time you decide to venture off. It's the smart thing to do—the safe thing." He spoke in a firm voice. Kat saw that he wasn't joking and appreciated his concern.

"Yes, sir. With the dozens of friends I have made in the last few weeks, I'm sure I can find one so easily," she said sarcastically.

"Feisty now, are you?" Nicholas chuckled.

"It comes and goes," Kat laughed back. "Thanks, Nicholas." She gave the clue that it was time for him to leave. He picked up on it well and respectfully headed toward the door.

"Good night, Miss Morgan," he said as he stood in the doorway. "One more thing, can I get your number? I want to call and check on you in the morning." He pulled out his phone and prepared to enter her number, but Kat hesitated.

"That's really not necessary," she replied. "I told you, I'm fine." She didn't know why she was so against him having her phone number, but she was firm in her answer.

"No big deal," Nicholas said as he started to put the phone back in his pocket. "I can just stop by instead." He gave one more look to Kat, smiled, and continued out the door.

"Wait!" she shouted after him as she followed him onto the porch. "I don't want you coming all the way over here to check on me. I'll give you my number so you're not going out of your way." He pulled out his phone and handed it to Kat to enter her number. She handed it back with a shy smile.

"Talk to you tomorrow, Kat," he said with a wink and stepped off the porch to his patrol car as Kat walked back inside the house.

*Well, there went my day of rest,* Kat realized. Not only was she in physical pain, but she also couldn't figure out why she had freaked out the way she did. It was irrational to think that Max had not only tracked her down but also that he had hired people to follow her on his behalf. Kat let out a heavy sigh. *Tomorrow I can figure that out,* she told herself. *Tonight, I need sleep.*

She took a painkiller and headed up to her room to turn in early for the night.

# CHAPTER 13

When night fell, Kat wondered if sleep would treat her well after what happened on the trail. She was confused by her overreactions and anxieties. She had been away from Max for several weeks by then. She finally had her quiet—she had her peace. She could never understand why the nightmares still haunted her and left her restless. Here and there she would have a good night's sleep, but then the dreams would slowly creep back, stealing her nights.

There were days when even the slightest noise would make her want to crawl out of her skin. There were other days where she would leave work feeling like she'd been holding her breath all day long, only able to breathe once she got into her car alone. There were also days when she could feel the rage boiling in her blood and everyone and everything irritated her.

*I'm not a mean person,* she thought. But sometimes her anger made her feel as if she was. She didn't know why she felt tense at work. It was a great office and the people were amazing. She couldn't imagine herself working for any other company in the near or distant future.

*If only I could talk to someone who would understand, someone who wouldn't pass judgment on me,* she wished silently. But she didn't know anyone she could trust that much. For now, she would do what she'd done as long as she could remember: smile to the world, laugh, and put on a happy face because that's what the world wanted and expected.

It was something she'd learned long ago—the world wants to know when things are going well for you. People love to hear when success lies in your path. Society does not welcome your conversation about the nightmare you had the night before. Instead, people want to drink their coffee and discuss the date they have scheduled for Friday night. They would rather talk about the new movie that's coming out over the weekend than the struggles of life.

*The world hides their problems as much as I do mine,* Kat realized. *How does the world begin to fix its problems if they're never spoken about? Maybe it's just human nature— it's easy to see the good and it's too much of a challenge to fix the bad like the crisis in Syria or hunger in third-world countries.*

Her eyes began to droop as she thought about the world and she finally fell into a deep sleep.

The ringing of her phone the next morning startled her. It took her a moment to realize it was Officer Mendoza calling to check on her. She had forgotten she'd given him her number the day before.

"Hello," she answered groggily and with a hint of nerves in her voice.

"Hey, how you feeling?" Nicholas' charming voice asked on the other end.

"Okay, I guess," Kat replied with a yawn. "I slept pretty well, but I'm still a little sore."

"You hungry?" he asked mischievously.

"Starving, actually," Kat answered even though she wasn't remotely hungry. She rarely ate breakfast and started her day with little more than a cup of coffee. Still, she was open to seeing Nicholas again.

"Would you like to accompany me to breakfast?" Nicholas asked, the handsome grin on his face carrying in the sound of his voice.

"Umm…I look like hell right now and I'm still in my jammies," Kat giggled.

"Well, to be fair, you looked like hell yesterday on the trail and I didn't mind," Nicholas said as he burst into laughter.

"You have a way with compliments, now don't you?" Kat laughed back.

"It truly is a crafted skill," Nicholas continued in laughter.

"Ugh, come get me in ten, I'll do my best to look decent," Kat replied with a giggle.

She hung up the phone and jumped out of bed to quickly freshen up. Thankfully, the pain in her foot had been short lived and it no longer hurt to put pressure on it. She brushed her teeth and washed her face, careful to be gentle around the scrapes on her brow and chin. Her long, black hair actually looked good for second-day hair, especially after the day it had been through the day before. She lined her eyes and applied a bit of mascara and blush.

Kat rushed to her closet and grabbed the first thing she found, black leggings and her favorite rock band t-shirt. She ran down the stairs knowing the ten minutes had already passed and grabbed her pair of black boots. Before heading for the door, she slipped on her favorite dark blue sweater with the oversized hood.

She felt a bit of anxiety. She didn't want Nicholas to be upset if he had been waiting for her. She grabbed her phone and wallet and checked out the front window. *Crap! He's already in the driveway!* Kat rushed out of the house, quickly locked the door, and hurried to the car where Nicholas was patiently waiting.

"I'm so sorry I made you wait," Kat said apologetically. Nicholas blinked a few times with a grin on his face.

"Yes, the whole two minutes you made me wait. You *should* be sorry," Nicholas laughed and eased Kat's worry. Her face relaxed as he continued. "But seriously, don't be sorry. You haven't done anything wrong."

He gave her a confident smile. His eyes spoke truth and sincerity. He was genuine and he made Kat feel safe and comfortable. But his eyes also spoke heartache. They hid his vulnerabilities deep within him. Kat sensed that he hid his pain with humor so the world couldn't see. Though Kat could see through the mask he wore, she wondered if he could see through the one she hid behind as well.

She smiled and thanked him silently. She didn't have to explain herself to Nicholas and she appreciated that.

"I'm taking you to my favorite café down by the bay. Their breakfast is amazing," Nicholas changed the tone in his voice.

"I'm trusting you on this," Kat giggled. "Don't disappoint me on this." She grinned at him.

"Oh, I'm full of disappointments, Kat, but my food choices are not one of them," Nicholas chuckled. Kat loved that she and Nicholas could have both genuine and serious moments, then playful banter. She laughed quietly to herself thinking how much she enjoyed the way she felt when Nicholas was around, even if she'd only been around him a few times.

*****

The view of the bay from the café really was delightful and she knew she would never get tired of the coast, no matter how many times she saw it. Nicholas had his favorite spot on the café deck and they were seated there immediately upon arrival. The staff knew him well and already knew his order by heart. Kat wondered how many other women he'd brought to this same place.

The air was crisp outside, but comfortable. The wooden deck laid right next to the bay. Sunshine snuck through the clouds from time to time keeping them just warm enough to be comfortable in the damp morning air.

Kat thought Nicholas looked beautiful when the sunlight would shine for a moment each time the clouds broke. She couldn't keep herself from admiring him. It wasn't only his physical attributes, but also the way he listened and showed he cared. He didn't get bored and carried on intellectual conversations. That was something Kat desired in other people—the ability to have an intelligent discussion. His character was something she'd never seen before in a man. The knowledge he held was quite extensive.

An hour and a half flew by without either one realizing it. Their conversations during the tasty breakfast ranged from world history to current events and they made time feel as if it didn't exist. It was conversation with substance and Kat appreciated the fact that Nicholas treated her like an intelligent person, not someone to be looked down upon. It was something she needed, something Max never even tried to give her.

"What do you have planned for this afternoon?" Nicholas interrupted the end of their conversation.

"Um, nothing specific. Maybe work on a painting?" Kat responded, immediately regretting revealing her hobby. She had just finished replacing her art supplies and she hadn't had a chance to create anything she felt was really good.

"You're an artist?" Nicholas' eyes widened. "Can I see your work?" He had an excited expression on his face that Kat couldn't turn down, even if she was shy about sharing her paintings with other people.

"Yeah, for twenty bucks. No free art show," Kat said sarcastically.

"Deal," Nicholas laughed as he signed the credit card receipt for their meal and they headed for the door.

The drive back to Kat's house was filled with more conversation and laughter. Kat forgot her troubles while she with Nicholas, especially this day, and that made her smile. She unlocked the door and directed Nicholas a few steps until he was standing in front of the French doors. She had finally turned what was supposed to be an office into her art studio as she had planned during that first walk-through of the house.

The wood floors creaked as they walked toward the room. Kat placed her hand on the doorknob, but instead of walking right in, she stopped suddenly to prepare herself for Nicholas' reaction. Nicholas bumped into her lightly, unaware of her abrupt stop. He didn't readjust his body, he just stood there with his chest leaned against her back gently. She gulped as she felt the warmth of his body behind hers.

Nicholas breathed softly behind her, silently waiting for Kat to speak. She turned her head slowly and whispered. "Don't lie to me if they're not good." Nicholas reached for Kat's cheek and cupped her face in his hands. He directed her body to turn more toward him until her eyes met his. Her heart began to race as she gazed into his dark brown eyes. Again, she thought she could see his vulnerabilities deep inside his gaze. He stood still with his hand still placed on her cheek and spoke softly.

"Kat, I will never lie to you. Know that." Her breathing shook a bit as she nodded in silence, then turned around to lead Nicholas into her studio.

Canvasses, some bigger than others, lined the walls around the room. Kat stood by the open door as Nicholas walked slowly around the room observing each one. Kat hadn't realized until that moment how many pieces she'd done in the few weeks since she'd arrived in Astoria. Nicholas moved to each painting giving each one its fair amount of examination and time.

"You don't paint with much color, why?" Nicholas asked curiously with his back toward her. Kat walked across the room and stood by his side as they both observed the same painting.

"I'm not sure why. I paint to express how I feel. Maybe there's not much color in my emotions," Kat theorized as she kept her eyes on the painting. This time, she wouldn't allow Nicholas to see the vulnerabilities in her eyes. It didn't matter anyway—he'd already seen it, regardless of whether he could see her eyes or not.

"They're beautiful," Nicholas said genuinely, keeping his eyes on the paintings. He reached for her hand dangling next to his and held it in his tight grip. Slowly, he maneuvered his body toward Kat's. She turned to mirror his position and they looked into each other's eyes. Kat could tell he wanted to say something, but he was being careful with every word that was spoken. She gulped again as she noticed his eyes were glued to hers.

Nicholas lifted his hand and gently caressed Kat's cheek. He slowly leaned into her, stopping as his lips touched hers softly. He was waiting for permission to kiss her. Hundreds of thoughts raced through her mind at that very moment and she knew thoughts were probably racing through Nicholas' head at the same time. She placed her hand on the back of his head giving him the permission he desired.

As he kissed her, she welcomed every bit of it. He kissed her firmly, but at the same time, it was a gentle kiss. Kat embraced the warmth he offered. The feeling of his body pressed against hers felt good. A kiss like this was indeed a first for her. A kiss like this had seemed to only exist in books and in movies, but never in real life. It was truly a fantasy that had, for a brief moment in time, walked into her reality.

Nicholas pulled away slowly, clearly not wanting the kiss to end, but needing to get on with his responsibilities for the day.

"I shall let you continue your day in your art," he whispered. Kat smiled and blushed as she nodded in approval. "Can I see you again soon?" he asked politely.

"Of course you can," Kat responded softly. She gulped and, at a loss for words, thanked him for breakfast and walked him to the front door. She watched from the doorway as he walked to his car and drove away. She didn't turn to go back inside until she could no longer see his car in the distance. Her mind felt foggy. She caressed her lips where Nicholas had just laid his. Whatever she was feeling was a new feeling and she hoped it would last.

As she turned to walk back to her studio, a horrible feeling that she had forgotten to do something that morning hit her like a truck. She ran through her to-do list in her head, but she was at a loss for anything on her schedule. Kat ran through the past few days in her head when she remembered her encounter with Kyle on the beach. She had made plans to meet him for coffee, but her mishap on the trail had wiped it from her mind.

"Can I meet you for coffee tomorrow at nine?" Kyle's invitation popped into her head as a feeling of guilt hit her. It wasn't like Kat to flake out on a meetup, even if it was one she didn't particularly want to show up for. She had always been a woman of her word and she felt terrible that she had accidentally stood Kyle up.

*I don't even have his number to apologize,* she realized. She started to search the house for an old phone book, but she thought an apology by phone would be too impersonal. She sighed in frustration as she reached for her car keys and headed for the front door.

She drove slowly to the diner in town hoping Kyle was working that afternoon so she could just get this over with. As she pulled up outside the diner's front door, her heart began to race. What excuse could she possibly use? She didn't think he would appreciate the truth—that she'd skipped out on her date with him to go to breakfast with another guy. As much as she hated dishonesty, she felt it was better in this case to lie.

As she entered the diner, the bell on the door dinged the same way it had that first day in the diner when she'd seen both Nicholas and Kyle for the first time. She quickly glanced around the room looking for Kyle's face. It was nowhere to be found.

"Can I help you, honey?" an older waitress asked as she walked by. "Are you here to meet someone? Maybe I can help?"

"I'm actually looking for Kyle. Is he in today?" Kat asked the woman, hoping for a moment that he was off so she had more time to prepare herself for her apology.

"He's in the back, hon," the woman answered. "In the kitchen. But he's not himself today, so I'd make it quick. Just peek your head in the swinging door and watch out for the servers coming through."

Kat made her way to the back of the diner and her hands shook as she approached the swinging doors. A server swung through and barely missed Kat on his way to deliver a tray of food to a table. She pushed one of the doors open just a bit and peeked her head through trying to see if Kyle was in sight. She glanced around the cramped kitchen space but didn't see him anywhere.

"Excuse me!" another server hollered behind her as he carried a tray of dirty dishes to the back. "Can I help you?"

"I'm looking for Kyle," Kat answered. "Is he in?"

"He's back in his office," the server said impatiently. "Follow me and I'll take you back. I just need to drop these off first."

Kat moved out of the man's way and followed him through the swinging doors. He stopped by a large industrial-size sink and put the tray down before heading further back in the kitchen.

"Right back there," the man said as he pointed to an open door on the back wall. "Just knock before you walk in."

Kat approached the office slowly as she prepared her explanation. She peeked her head around the doorway and saw Kyle sitting at a small desk with papers neatly stacked on top. He was looking over a form with a look of disappointment on his face. Kat knocked on the door lightly.

"Excuse me," she said softly. "Kyle, it's me, Kat." Kyle didn't look up from the form he was reading.

"I missed you this morning for coffee," he said in a nonchalant tone pretending he didn't care. "I waited for a while, but when you didn't show up, I figured you stood me up."

"I'm so sorry, Kyle," she said quickly, interrupting him. "Something happened yesterday afternoon after I talked to you and…and…"

"It's okay, Kat," he said, still not looking up at her face. "You're not interested in me and that's fine. I just wish you would have said that yesterday. It wouldn't have gotten my hopes up. No need for excuses now."

"Please, Kyle," she begged. "I just want to be clear that I didn't intentionally stand you up. Something happened and I slept late. That's all."

Kyle finally looked up from his papers and glanced at Kat. His eyes grew in size when he saw the scrapes on her face. He jumped up from his office chair and rushed over to her.

"What the hell happened to your face?" he asked with sudden concern in his voice.

"That's what I was trying to tell you," she explained. "After I saw you at the beach yesterday I went hiking and…it's a long story. To make a long story short, I tripped and fell. I'm fine, but I was so tired that I forgot about our plans and slept right through. I'm so sorry."

"No, I'm sorry," Kyle said sympathetically. "Here I was thinking you stood me up and the whole time you were hurt. I'm such an asshole."

"No, don't say that," Kat said, the feeling of guilt growing as Kyle began putting the blame back on himself. "It was just a mistake on my part. You didn't know what was going on. I would have been upset too if I were you."

"Well, in that case, maybe we can try for tomorrow or another day?" Kyle offered. Kat stood in silence for a moment trying to think of a reason not to accept this new invitation. She clearly had an interest for Nicholas, but she felt nothing for Kyle. Sure, she thought he was handsome, but she didn't see herself having anything serious with him.

"Look, Kyle," she began. "I didn't want you to think that I intentionally missed our meeting this morning, so I came to explain about that, but I also don't think we should plan anything in the future either. I just don't see us together."

"Hey, whoa, Kat, I just wanted to get coffee," Kyle interrupted. "That was it. Just a cup of coffee between friends. I'm sorry if you took it as anything more." Kat's face blushed in embarrassment. *Well, now I feel like an idiot*, she thought to herself.

"That's a relief to hear," she said. "I appreciate your offer of friendship. I really do. I could definitely use some friends in Astoria, believe me. I just have trouble with social situations. It's something I'm working on, but right now I don't know if I'm up for meetups with anyone, friend or otherwise."

"Tell you what, let's not set anything up right now," Kyle said. "When you feel like you're ready for some friend time, let me know. You know where to find me." He smiled at Kat and while his smile was handsome, it wasn't nearly as attractive or genuine as Nicholas' smile was.

"That would be nice," Kat replied. "I'll let you know when I'm ready. And again, I'm sorry."

"Apologies aren't necessary," Kyle responded as he walked Kat out through the swinging doors and to the front door of the diner. "I'm just glad you're okay. It looks like it was a pretty bad fall. It's a wonder you weren't hurt worse."

"Thanks, Kyle," she said as the bell rang on the diner's door and she stepped outside. Kyle gave her a small wave and she walked to her car as he watched from the diner's doorway.

*That wasn't so bad,* Kat thought as she drove back home. She was glad Kyle said he didn't expect more than friendship, but she also didn't know whether he was telling the truth. She couldn't read the honesty in his eyes the way she could Nicholas'.

# CHAPTER 14

"No, no, no! Stop, Max…please!" Kat cried to Max, begging him not to start another fight. The stench of alcohol on his breath suffocated her and she knew any fight would quickly escalate with him in an intoxicated state.

"You're nothing but a whore, Katrina!" Max shouted back to her, drops of his 80-proof spit landing on her face. She couldn't hold back the tears, but it didn't matter. Max didn't care if she cried. Tears were invisible to him.

"I'm sorry, Max, I'm sorry," Kat continued to cry out. Max paced into another room giving her the chance she needed to get away from him. She ran to the bedroom and locked the door. Her heart was racing and she was breathing heavily, unsure of what to do next. *Hopefully, he won't come back,* she thought. *Hopefully, he'll get distracted by another drink.* She stood at the door with her ear placed on it, listening for him coming back.

*Bam…bam…bam!* Max pounded on the other side of the door angrily.

"Open the fucking door, Kat!" Max shouted.

"Just leave me alone, Max. I don't want to fight with you," Kat nervously shouted back to him through the door.

"Don't lock me out of my own fucking room, Kat!" he shouted as his pounding on the door became more violent and the door began to move slightly with each strike. Kat trembled as she wondered whether he could actually break down the door.

"I…said…let…me…the…fuck…in," Max screamed slamming his body against the door with each word until he was successful at knocking it loose from the frame. Kat's heart sank as she rushed to the other side of the room desperately searching for a place to hide.

Max grabbed her and swung her around slamming her into the wall. She cried out in pain as her neck whipped from the force. He was now just inches from her face and as he continued to shout, Kat's eyes burned from the heavy liquor-filled air pouring from his mouth. She struggled to catch a breath of fresh air in the cramped space between them. Max slid his arm to her throat, slowly cutting off her air supply.

"Max, please…stop," Kat choked on the few words she was able to get out. He pushed harder on her throat and Kat helplessly struggled for air. She stared into the eyes that tortured her. Bloodshot and full of rage, their centers were black and empty like there was no soul inside. *I don't want to die,* Kat thought as she tapped one more time on Max's arm pleading him to let her go as she began to slip into darkness.

"No!" Kat awoke with a chilling scream. "Stop, Max, stop!" She yelled out as she grabbed at her throat and gasped for air. She scanned around the bedroom in a panic trying to place where she was. She sat up in her bed breathing heavily and desperately tried to ground herself in reality.

"I'm okay, I'm okay…" she said aloud until she started to sob. She continued to rub her throat where she swore she'd really felt Max's hand squeezing the life out of her. It had felt so real. Tears fell from her face onto the bed and her heart continued to pound. She felt scared and alone. The feeling was overwhelming and paralyzing to her body.

She continued to catch her breath as she moved to the side of her bed and sat up on the edge to calm herself. *Just a nightmare, Kat,* she thought. *Just a nightmare.* She laid back down and wiped the tears with a plush blanket her mom had made her years ago. She tried to focus on the harmonic sound of the drizzly rain hitting her bedroom windows. She took in a deep breath as another tear streamed down her cheek.

Suddenly, she remembered that though it was Monday, she didn't have to go work. She was thankful for the three-day weekend. It meant an extra day to whatever she wanted without work or life to worry about.

The house was quiet and isolated, just the way she liked it. But at the moment it was too quiet, too isolated and she felt more alone than ever. The nightmare replayed through her head. What had she done in life to deserve to be treated the way Max had treated her? She glanced over to check the time—her clock read 8:36 a.m. The rain had hidden the sunrise and it had thrown off her normal internal clock. She didn't like sleeping so late into the morning.

Kat tried to make her mind wander somewhere else. Sometimes it was the only thing that saved her from her own sanity. "Nicholas," she whispered to herself. There was something enticing about him. Something about him was able to occupy Kat's thoughts when she needed it the most. She caressed her lips where Nicholas had kissed her the day before. *He tasted good,* she thought. She wasn't sure what to think about the kiss between them. She knew she was attracted to him, that was certain. But what was to come from it? Nothing. Even if there was the possibility of romance between them, Kat was in no shape to even think about dating.

She didn't know how long it would take for the nightmares to stop completely. Perhaps they would never stop, and that wasn't something a future boyfriend would likely find appealing. Her paranoia about Max and the way it influenced so much of her life wouldn't help either. She would be no good for

Nicholas or any other guy who was interested in her. It would be impossible to explain the anxieties that stopped her from embracing people. *Who would want a fragile girl anyway? A coward? I would be no good*, Kat thought, discouraging herself.

Even with the doubt that flooded her mind, curiosity overtook for a moment.

*Hi, Nicholas. Going to see the sea lions today. Wanna join?*

She stared at the text message after typing it out wondering if she should hit the send button. She finally built up the courage to press send and waited for a message back. Several minutes passed with no response. Kat frowned, disappointed. *He's probably busy,* she thought. *He can't just sit around waiting for a message from me.* She hopped out of bed and hobbled down to the kitchen to start her coffee.

While she waited for a response and for her coffee to finish brewing, she hopped in the shower. The hot water streamed over her body and provided the relaxation she needed. She took longer than usual in the shower letting the heat melt away some of her anxiety and frustration. She enjoyed the newfound freedom of doing things at her own pace and at her own will. She was able to make her own schedule and she could come and go when she wanted without having to answer to Max or anyone else.

The hot water continued to fall on and around her as she covered her eyes with her hands allowing herself to feel every drop of water. It was difficult for her to feel reality, to feel the moment she was actually in. She really had to stop and put effort into feeling what was around her. Unintentionally, she often stepped out of reality and into another world. The numbness had always helped to make her days pass less painful.

It was almost as if she was stepping out of her body and watching her life in a blur below. Pain or numbness were her only two choices and she preferred the numbness to the pain. She was tired of hurting and being hurt and stepping out of reality helped save her mind from remembering all of the past abuse she had experienced. Her mind wandered as she enjoyed the comfort and warmth of the shower and she wavered between the past and present. Her mind finally settled on a memory from the past.

"What the fuck Kat! You didn't do shit while I was gone!" Max shouted as he busted through the bathroom door. Kat stood naked in the shower, frightened and helpless. Through the steam, she could see a group of Max's friends in the living just outside the doorway.

"Max! Close the door! You have your friends out there!" Kat screamed back.

"I don't have to do shit, Kat. I told you they were coming over. The apartment hasn't been cleaned. What the fuck, Kat?!" Max shouted again.

71

"I told you I was sick, Max. I'm still running a fever. I can hardly breathe." Kat started to cry as she tried to hide her naked body from Max's friends.

"You're nothing but white trash, Kat. You and your family, both," Max shouted as he slammed the door hard behind him.

Kat opened her eyes and panic filled her blood. Memories like that left her feeling as if they had just happened and she would never forget the way they made her feel. She gasped at the confusion and turned off the water in a panic. She reached out of the shower door for her towel and wrapped herself as tightly as she could, shielding her body from the view of people who weren't there.

*What was that?* she wondered frantically. *Am I sleeping? Am I dreaming?* She cupped her face in her hands to be sure. She knew she was awake, there was no doubt about that. "But it felt so real," she whispered to herself. She couldn't make sense of what was happening. The day of that memory was so many years ago, but it was still so fresh in her mind.

She quickly scampered to her closet to dress. She felt violated and had the desperate urge to cover herself as quickly as possible. She tried to shake off the memory as best she could, but rage started to sneak into its place. Anger and hate steamed from Kat.

"I was so fucking sick that day, Max! I fucking hate you! I hate you!" she screamed as she grabbed a handful of hangers off the rack in the closet and threw them angrily across the room. She fell to the floor, sobbing. Her breathing was heavy as she pushed that day from her mind.

Max had humiliated her in front of his friends and those men just stood there watching him belittle her as she stood naked in the shower. She wasn't sure which was worse, the one who tortures or the one who knows the torture is happening and does nothing and allows the torture to continue uninterrupted. Perhaps it was worse when the one who could have helped turned their back on the helpless.

Kat let out her last cry, wiped her tears, and finished getting ready so she could fetch her coffee and get her day off to a better ending. She thought perhaps she was simply confused and emotional because she hadn't yet had her coffee.

She took a deep breath and enjoyed the first sip from her mug. An alert sounded from her phone as she sipped, letting her know she'd received a new message. It was finally Nicholas' response.

*Hey, can't today.*

The message seemed short and impersonal and it made her uncomfortable. The lack of further explanation disappointed her. *Did I do something wrong?* she wondered. Doubt and confusion once again filled her thoughts.

"No!" Kat yelled out to herself. *He's busy. I get busy too,* she thought to herself. *It doesn't matter anyway. I'm not able to give myself fully to someone, so why even start something I can't finish?* Instead, she decided a day to herself, a day that was all her own in the fresh air, would do her good.

After she sipped on her coffee, Kat brushed and braided her long black hair to one side. She wished she had the confidence to leave the house without makeup, but it gave her the boost she needed to not totally hate herself. The puffy redness around her eyes from her tearful morning made it difficult to apply the makeup she desired, but she did her best to cover it up and make herself look "presentable" to the world.

She stopped by her studio on the way out the door and grabbed her black messenger bag with her sketchpad and pencils hoping she would find time to sketch later in the day.

The curvy road into town was always a joy for Kat. The greenery always gave her a sense of peace. *It would be a good time to call my dad,* Kat thought as she grabbed her phone. He would certainly want to hear about her plans for a mini-adventure to the East Mooring Basin Boat Ramp on the other side of town. She and her father had always taken mini-vacations, day hikes, or just short road trips to unexplored territory. Whatever it was, they always had fun and Kat wished he was with her now as she made the short drive to see wild sea lions for the first time.

Her father was pleased to hear from her and shared Kat's wish that he was there to join her. The conversation lasted longer than her short drive across Astoria, so she parked her car in a small parking lot next to the entrance to the boat ramp and turned off the engine as she finished her conversation with her father.

"Okay, sweetie. Have fun and be safe. Take lots of pictures!" Mr. Morgan said as they ended their call. It had been refreshing to hear her father's voice and it felt like a new day. She grabbed her bag from the passenger seat and walked down to the boat ramp where she could already hear the barking of the sea lions.

She never imagined there would be so many of them gathered in one place and she loved seeing the way they played with each other, teased one another, and seemed to pose for the photos people were snapping. She felt as if she was seeing the world through a new pair of glasses. She found a bench and sat down to observe the view that laid in front of her.

She pulled out her art supplies and began to sketch out the hundreds of sea lions lying on the dock basking in the sunshine that had broken through the clouds. The boats that lined the harbor took up another couple sketches. As she lost herself in her drawing, time was nowhere to be found. Kat took herself to new places when she drew, places that were not of her world. They were places where she could escape and they allowed the thoughts that constantly haunted her to be shoved away somewhere else for the time being.

A smile filled her face. It was times like this that she loved. It was peaceful. There was a quiet in her mind and a quiet mind was what she desired the most. As she looked around her, Kat wondered if she had ever really experienced true joy in her life before moving to Astoria.

Her growling stomach interrupted her intense drawing session. She knew she needed to eat soon. The coffee she'd enjoyed as her breakfast was wearing off and she knew it was time for something with more substance. As she packed her sketching tools back up, she remembered seeing a pizza place just a block away. *Pizza sounds amazing,* she thought as her mouth watered.

The pizza was satisfying, but the homemade chocolate pie she ordered for dessert really hit the spot. Nicholas came into thought as she waited for her food to settle and her bill to arrive.

*I hope your day is going well.*

She typed out the message to him and debated herself on whether to send it or not. Surprisingly, once she did decide to hit the send button, a quick message was returned.

*Going good. Just tied up all weekend.*

Kat let out a small sigh. She was disappointed again. She was sure he was trying to tell her subtly that he was no longer interested in her. *Why did he even kiss me? Why did he help bandage my wounds? Why did he take me out for breakfast? Why do I even give a fuck?* Kat pondered the questions piling up in her mind. The confusion exhausted her. *I can be cold too. Fuck him.* She decided she was done thinking about Nicholas for the day.

Instead, she plopped down some cash to pay for her lunch and headed out the door to spend the rest of the weekend shopping for her new home. Even though it came furnished, she wanted to continue adding her own touches to it. Besides, she needed a new toaster. She had left behind the one she'd shared with Max. *Fuck him, too,* she thought as she climbed into her car, rage boiling in her veins. *I hope he electrocutes himself trying to figure out how to use it without my help.*

 **CHAPTER 15**

The ambiance of coastal life was starting to fill Kat's new home. She adored the new lamp she'd bought over the long weekend. She flipped the switch to turn it on as she got ready for work on Tuesday morning and basked in its soft glow.

It was shaped like a miniature lighthouse and soothing yellow light glowed through the opaque glass. She needed a lighthouse to rescue her at night. She hoped it would serve as a refuge when the night terrors attacked her again, an object she could focus on to help distinguish dreams from reality.

Now she could seek that comforting lighthouse when she was drowning in an ocean of terrifying memories. If she could only find an anchor to keep from being blown over in the midst of her storm, she felt she might be able to survive among the gigantic waves constantly crashing her against the rocks. She needed something concrete and stable in her life. Her thoughts created havoc and she hoped adding comforting elements like the lighthouse to her home would offer the peace she sought.

As much as Kat hated shopping, she was pleased with the unique décor she had found at the small shops downtown. Overall, she felt the entire weekend had been decent. It was certainly the most relaxing time she'd had since moving to the Oregon coast. Even the fact that Nicholas had distanced himself from her hadn't ruined her rest.

She checked her phone as she sipped her coffee knowing there would still be no message from him. Every time she checked it over the weekend it had been blank, nothing from Nicholas or anyone else.

"I need to stop setting myself up for disappointment," Kat said out loud to herself. She tipped her mug and finished off the coffee as she dropped her phone into her work bag and promised herself she wouldn't check it during the entire work day.

Waiting for a message was beginning to become an obsession and she didn't have time for it at work. She had been assigned her first big project and she was excited to get started on it. There would be plenty of work to keep her busy at *KJ&G Associates* and she was excited that she could always stay as late as she wanted to continue working without repercussions from Max. The thought made her smile as she headed out the door to head to work.

*****

Luke arrived at the front door of the office at the same time Kat did and he seemed to be in a good mood as he unlocked the door to let her in.

"Hi, Miss Morgan! How was your long weekend?" he asked with politeness and genuine excitement. He was always dressed well and he was always clean and freshly shaven. He was much older than Kat, and she certainly wasn't interested in him, but she could tell he was still in good shape.

She watched his arms as he turned the key in the lock. One of his arms was probably two of Kat's put together. He looked intimidating although he really wasn't. *I'm sure he could be if he needed to, though,* Kat thought.

Unlike some bosses, Mr. Stevenson was approachable and easy to talk to. Kat knew if she ever needed help, he would be there in an instant without being annoyed or impatient. He was fiercely driven in everything he did, but he never boasted about his accomplishments.

"Good morning Mr. Stev—I mean, Luke," Kat chuckled as she remembered to call him by his first name. "My weekend was good. Relaxing, actually. Oh, and I saw the sea lions at the boat ramp for the first time." Mr. Stevenson pulled the door open and held it as Kat walked through. They headed down the hallway to their workspace in the back of the building.

"I'm glad you had a good week—" Mr. Stevenson suddenly stopped his sentence and grabbed Kat by the arm frantically pulling her back into the hallway from the main office.

"Luke, what the hell—" Kat started to complain, but she stopped as she turned toward the back of the office and realized why Mr. Stevenson had pulled her away. Her heart began to pound and she could it feel it rising in her throat.

Shattered glass covered the floor near the big window that looked out over the town and the river. The damp breeze blew through the opening where the window used to be, gently tossing papers around the room.

"Be careful and don't touch anything. I'm going to call the police," Mr. Stevenson said as he walked back to the front of the building. Kat barely heard what her boss had to say. All she could focus on was the pounding against her chest. She wondered if this would be the time her panic finally caused a heart attack.

She scanned the room again. Desks were trashed and keyboards were thrown to the floor and smashed to pieces. Kat saw her projects had been thrown to the floor as well.

"Max…" was the only thing she could get out. Even the whisper of his name made her shiver. The thought that he was nearby made her heart race even faster.

"Oh my goodness!" Aubrey said as she snuck up behind Kat and peeked into the office. It made Kat jump.

"Fuck! Aubrey, shhh," Kat snapped at Aubrey without giving it a second thought. She didn't like the way she'd been startled. Aubrey's eyebrows raised with concern. This wasn't a side of Kat anyone in the office had seen yet. It wasn't like her to snap at anyone.

"I'm so sorry, Aubrey. I was startled and you made me jump a little bit. I'm just on edge. Forgive me?" Kat pleaded. Her mind was racing. Not only was she in a panic, now she was creating unwanted drama with a coworker.

"It's all good, Kat. I didn't mean to scare you. Just don't let it happen again," Aubrey joked as she saw the panic on Kat's face. "Luke just told me what happened. Sorry if I scared you."

"I don't think anything was taken," Kat said as her voice shook. It was hard for her to think straight, let alone talk. Her words were shaky as she spoke and her mind continued to race with hundreds of thoughts.

"Are you okay, Kat?" Aubrey asked, concern growing in her voice. "Hey girlie, it was probably just some punks here in town. Don't let it get to you. That's what they want. Aren't you from the city where this kind of stuff happens all the time?" Kat smiled as best she could to please Aubrey.

"I think I just need some fresh air," Kat said as softly as she could, forcing her voice to settle. Dazed, Kat hurried as fast as she could down the hallway to the front door. *How did he find me? I have to move again. But where? Wait, but I like it here.* The speed of the thoughts and questions in her mind matched the quick pounding of her heartbeat still thumping against her chest.

Kat wasn't paying attention as she rounded the corner and she slammed into a police officer arriving to check out the scene.

"I'm so sorry," Kat said in a panic. As she looked up at the officer, she was dismayed to see that Nicholas was the one she'd slammed into. Her panic transformed into frustration. In the height of the situation, the possibility of Nicholas being the responding officer hadn't crossed her mind.

"Hey, it's okay Kat. Are you okay?" Nicholas asked, seeing that Kat was clearly upset.

"Yeah, I'm fine. I just need fresh air," Kat continued to walk around Nicholas without a second look at him.

As she was walking out, another two officers greeted her as they stepped inside. Mr. Stevenson was hanging up a phone call and proceeded to follow the officers inside. Kat rushed to the parking lot and tossed her bag on top of her trunk. Breathing heavily, she leaned herself against the car with her arms extended out in front of her trying to calm herself.

*I just need to calm down,* Kat reassured herself as her thoughts continued to race. She looked up and tried to focus on the view in front of her. She tried to allow only the calling of seagulls to occupy her mind, but she was too distracted by everything else.

*I want to stay here, I don't want to leave. What if he's watching me right now? What does he want? Is he taunting me?* No matter how far she ran from Max, she couldn't seem to escape the demons that lurked inside her head, left there by his abusive behavior.

"Kat," a familiar voice called. "You don't seem alright." Nicholas had come outside to check on her. Kat kept her back to him not wanting him to see her in her current state. She couldn't allow him to see the fear that laid deep in her blue eyes and she knew he would if given the chance. She was a mess and she didn't want her co-workers to see her this way either.

A tear trickled down her cheek, a tear that Nicholas noticed from the side. She knew she couldn't mask the pain that killed her any longer. The panic, the extremes she went to in order to protect herself couldn't be bottled up anymore. The endless nightmares, the memories playing continuously, she knew she had to share them with someone, but she didn't want it to be Nicholas. Another tear rolled down her cheek.

"I'm not…I'm not alright, Nicholas. But I don't care to share with you. Please…leave me alone…you've been pretty good at that the past few days," Kat said with defeat. She didn't care what spewed from her mouth.

"I'm sorry, Kat," Nicholas' forehead wrinkled with worry. He hadn't expected Kat to call him out on his behavior over the weekend. He stepped even closer to her and reached out to pat her back. Kat shrugged his hand away.

"Don't touch me, please," she snapped at him.

"I'm sorry, I shouldn't have…" he replied apologetically.

"It's not you, Nicholas, it's me. I just don't want to be touched right now," Kat continued with a snippy tone in her voice. She could feel the tension in her body and wiped the tears from her face as she slowly turned to face Nicholas. "I'm just having a bad day. I just need to go home." She softened her tone and tried to ease the panic from her voice. She wanted Nicholas to believe she was okay.

"What's going on, Kat? Talk to me, please. I can help," Nicholas said with concern. His face was stern, though Kat could see the gentleness in his eyes. He really did want to help her and his expression said he would refuse to accept her false excuses.

"I don't know how to tell you without sounding crazy," Kat admitted, finally looking up at Nicholas.

"You're scared. I can see you're scared, Kat. Did the break-in frighten you?" Nicholas continued pleading for answers. She was starting to get irritated. He had ignored her after *he* kissed her and now all of a sudden he cared about her well-being. No, that wasn't good enough. Her mind started racing again, this time filled with anger toward Nicholas.

"Now you care?! Now you fucking care, Nicholas?" Kat's voice rose as she let him know exactly how she felt. Nicholas started to say something, but she cut him off. "No. No. I don't care for your fucking excuses, Nicholas. I don't fucking care. If you didn't want to see me, that's fine. If you regret kissing me, that's fine too! But open your fucking mouth and just tell me, 'Kat, I'm not interested'. Would that have been so hard?"

Kat began rubbing her temples to try and calm herself, to try and calm the frustration growing inside her. It was odd to Kat that Nicholas had just stood there taking what she had to say. He didn't yell at her, he didn't argue. Half of her was more upset that he wasn't fighting her, that he was just letting her make her point whether it was valid or not. Instead, he waited until she was finished and spoke calmly back.

"I know. I know, Kat. I was a jerk…I am a jerk. I knew exactly what I was doing. I didn't *not* want to see you, but I didn't know if I could keep seeing you. But I didn't want you to go away. I'm sorry. That's all I got, Kat. It's a crappy answer, but it's the truth. I'm sorry I kept you in limbo. It wasn't fair to you. It was selfish and maybe I'll explain in a better way later," Nicholas said as he begged Kat for forgiveness. Kat could tell he was being genuine, and as more confusion filled her mind, tears started to fall more heavily from her eyes.

"I have to leave, Nick…like, leave town. I only moved here to get away from my ex. He's…umm…he's mean. He's really mean. I think he found me. Nothing was stolen from the office, Nicholas. Nothing! He's just taunting me! Can't you see, Nicholas?" Kat cried out, revealing her story as more tears fell from her cheeks. "It's Max. And I'm scared, Nicholas. I'm so fucking scared right now. I'm scared he's going to hurt me and I'm scared my boss is going to find out about it and it's going to be the end of this great job…" Kat trailed off as she wiped her tears with the sleeve of her jacket. "I don't know what I'll do if he finds me. I feel like I'm losing my mind, Nicholas." Kat couldn't bear to look at him. She couldn't handle his judgment right now.

"Oh, Kat. Fuck. I won't let him hurt you. I won't. I understand the fear you're talking about…more than you know, Kat," Nicholas explained, trying to comfort her as best he could. He knew it wasn't the right time to give an optimist speech, he knew it was best just to listen and offer help however he could. "We can do close patrol if you would like?"

He waited patiently for Kat's response. He could tell from her expression that it was something she had to think about deeply. Finally, she gulped loudly and opened her mouth to respond.

"I would like that, thank you," she said as she felt the tension in her body start to ease. "Nicholas, I don't even know if it really was him. I thought he was following me on the trail that day. It wasn't him then, and maybe it's not him now. I…I just feel like I'm crazy, Nicholas." Kat paused, wondering why she had even told Nicholas any of it. If she had had any chance with him, she'd just blown it.

*I just told him I think I'm crazy,* she thought. *Wait until he finds out about the nightmares.* She took a deep breath and wiped her face of the few tears that still trickled.

"I really don't think it was him, Kat," Nicholas said, trying to reassure her. "It just doesn't seem likely that he could have done all of this. Besides, we've had a few of these types of incidents in Astoria in the past few months and this fits the same characteristics. But if it will make you feel better, we can definitely keep an eye on your place tonight and for the next couple of days."

Kat nodded, looking down at the ground as his words sunk in.

"Thank you for the extra patrol tonight. I better go help clean up the damage and then I'm going home for the day," Kat told him as she grabbed her bag and began to walk back to the office.

"I'll walk with you," Nicholas said uneasily, not sure if she would allow him to. He was reassured when Kat gave him a small smile. It wasn't her usual happy smile, but it was an attempt at acceptance. He returned it with a smile of his own and they walked in silence through the parking lot and back to the front door.

Kat didn't understand his intentions or his motives. *What does he want with me? What could he possibly see in me, the crazy girl?* He did make her feel safe and she liked that feeling. Still, she thought she was in no place to be anything more than a friend to Nicholas. She wondered if she should give him the same speech she'd given Kyle that day at the diner. Maybe she just needed to explain her intentions with Nicholas.

Before stepping back into the main office area, Kat looked into Nicholas' eyes one last time.

"Thanks again," Kat spoke softly and walked away without giving Nicholas a chance to say anything else.

"Okay, your report will be ready in a couple of days. You can pick it up then," one of the officers explained to Mr. Stevenson in the corner.

"Thank you, officers," Mr. Stevenson replied back. As the policemen walked out of the office, Nicholas couldn't keep his eyes off Kat. Each of them gazed back at the other until Kat could no longer see him down the hallway.

Immediately, she felt her cheeks blush with embarrassment. She knew her coworkers had noticed Nicholas smiling and staring at her as he left.

"Ooh, Katrina! Officer Mendoza was totally checking you out," Aubrey shouted from across the room over the noise of a vacuum cleaner sweeping up bits of glass.

"Stop it...no he wasn't," Kat managed to get a slight giggle out.

"Then why are you blushing, Kat?" Jane chimed in playfully.

"It doesn't matter anyway. I'm not interested," Kat said, halfway telling the truth. She really was interested, very interested, but she knew it couldn't go far. She just couldn't handle it.

"Hey, can I go home for the day? I'm not feeling well. I'm a bit shaken up by everything," Kat asked Mr. Stevenson after she cleaned up her work area.

"Yeah, go ahead. I'll be sending everyone else home as well. I called someone to come board up the window until it can be replaced tomorrow," Mr. Stevenson replied. *God, he's always so calm and cool about everything,* Kat thought. *His business has just been vandalized and he hasn't lost his composure. He's truly a good boss and a great leader.*

Kat grabbed her work bag and headed home. All she could think about was taking a nap, a very long nap. She was happy she didn't have a long commute home. Today would not have been a good day to deal with a traffic jam. *What if Max is waiting for me at home?* Her thoughts turned back to Max. *Was it even him that broke in?* Kat continued to ponder the hundreds of questions as she pulled into the driveway.

She put her car in park and debated whether or not to go inside. Surely, she was crazy and she was blowing this whole thing out of proportion. She reached into her bag and grabbed her phone, gripping it tightly in case she needed to call for help.

"Oh!" she exclaimed aloud as she looked down at the screen and noticed two unread messages from Nicholas. A small smile erupted on her face as she read the first one.

*Hey, I checked out your house for you. Everything is intact. And no signs anyone has been there but you. :)*

Kat felt an instant relief and continued to read the second message.

*I promise to message you later. :)*

A bigger smile appeared on her face. She was happy Nicholas had thought of her, but all she wanted for the moment was rest. It had already been a long day and it was only ten o'clock in the morning. Kat crept quietly into her house and shut the front door behind her. She made sure both locks and the deadbolt were turned before moving on.

Even though Nicholas had checked it out, Kat had to do a quick run-through of the house just to be certain, just to reassure herself. Nothing was out of place, just like Nicholas had told her. *Maybe I should start trusting him a bit more,* she told herself.

She dragged herself up the stairs and threw herself onto the bed still dressed in her work clothes. Sleep was a must and she hoped sleep is what she would get. She reached over and switched on the lighthouse lamp. She smiled in its warm light as her eyelids became heavy and her breathing slowed.

# CHAPTER 16

Kat knew she should have dressed warmer for the cooler weather at the higher elevation, but she hadn't expected to be out so late. It was supposed to be a fun drive up into the mountains to get away for a few hours. Now the fog was heavy and even with the heater running in the car, she was still able to see her breath in the cold air. She had ventured further into the mountains than intended, but the mini-adventure was exactly what she needed.

For some reason, it seemed as if it had gotten dark a lot sooner than normal, but she chalked it up to nothing more than the fog and the mountains blocking the last rays of sunlight. *I should turn around,* she thought to herself. *I've gone far enough and I need to head back.* Kat drove a little further until she spotted a small pullout area to the right of the road that would allow her enough space to get turned around. *Perfect,* she thought as she signaled with her blinker on the deserted road and pulled over.

There was just a bit of moonlight shining through the fog here and there, but otherwise, the road was nestled deep in the woods and was pitch black. Only the tiny slivers of moonlight and the headlights of her car lit the path in front of her as she turned around and started her way home. She took her time on the winding road in the darkness, afraid to take a curve too sharply and fearing that some type of mountain wildlife could jump onto the road any second.

Suddenly, she didn't feel so good about her spontaneous adventure and panic and irrational thoughts started to set in. It was dark—too dark. She knew she hadn't been gone that long and even with the fog, there should have still been a bit of daylight to guide her home.

The fog was still thick and its fingers crept slowly across the road in front of her. The tall trees that lined each side of the road seemed larger than they had been before and they seemed to take on a menacing character. *Something isn't right,* Kat thought. *Or am I just being paranoid again?* At this point in her life, it was difficult to distinguish between rational fear and paranoia. She couldn't tell whether she should fear something or not—it was impossible for her to recognize whether there was a valid reason to be scared. Everything seemed to put her on edge these days.

*Clank…clank…clank…* Her car made an awful noise and she felt it slowing to a crawl on the road.

"No! Don't you dare!" Kat yelled at the car. *This would be the worst time for my car to break down,* she thought as she looked around at the darkness and tried to remember the last time she'd seen another car on the road. Her cell phone was dead and it was freezing. In her light clothing, she would get hypothermia trying to walk to find help.

She hit the dashboard of the car a few times, hoping her nonsensical approach to auto repair would fix the problem. Strangely, the noise went away for a moment and she smiled, happy with her success. Her happiness ended less than a mile down the road, however, as the noise returned stronger than before.

"No, no, no!" Kat cried aloud as the car came to a complete stop in the middle of the roadway. The headlights dimmed and flickered out and the heater sputtered to a halt. Her heart began to pound. It was so cold outside and she could already feel even more frigid air sneaking in with the heater off.

Kat breathed hard as she tried to make a plan. She wondered for a moment whether she could coast the car down the steep mountain road safely. *At least that would get me into the valley where it's warmer,* she reasoned with herself. *That's not safe, you dummy. You have no headlights and who knows whether your brakes are even working now.* The image of her car careening off the side of a mountain popped into her head and she shuddered at the thought. Her thoughts were racing and she was panicking. The fog continued to creep along the damp pavement in front of her.

She gulped loudly and tried to calm herself. She squinted in the dim light and as the fog opened a bit she spotted a payphone about thirty feet ahead of her on the side of the road.

"Perfect," she whispered to herself. Without hesitation, Kat opened the driver's side door and placed her black boots on the pavement below her as the fog swirled around her feet.

The sound of her car door slamming echoed through the dark woods. The loud bang startled her and Kat hoped it had startled away anything or anyone else that was out there as well. She wrinkled her forehead in worry as she looked at the forest around her. She hated drawing any unwanted attention from whatever might be lurking in the trees.

She crossed her arms as she headed for the pay phone. As much as she wanted to run, she couldn't. The fast-paced walk would have to do. *Almost there,* she thought. She did her best to keep her eyes on the payphone in front of her to avoid spooking herself any more than she already had.

Confusion struck her as she approached a road sign. She wasn't able to make out the words that towered above her on the tall sign. *Is that German?* she wondered to herself trying to sound out the language that seemed so foreign. *Surely not, there's no way.* She stopped in front of the sign and tried to whisper its

84

words out loud to herself.

She rubbed her eyes trying to reread the unusual words on the sign when a crackle came from the darkened woods. It sounded like a branch breaking nearby. Kat gulped as she tried to determine where it had come from. She began to take steps backward toward the car not knowing what or who was beyond the side of the road in the woods.

Another crackle, louder this time, popped and echoed through the woods. Another one sounded right after, even closer. A panicked Kat tried to let out a scream, but nothing sounded besides the crackles in the woods. Her scream was silent. More unwelcome noises slowly emerged from the woods and onto the pavement.

Kat didn't want to see what was behind her. She didn't even know if it was right behind her or back where she'd heard the sound. She ran as fast as she could back to the car. The thirty feet she'd walked before now seemed so much further away.

She continued to run, confused as to why a walk that had been so easy before was now such a challenging run back. The air was even colder and it hurt her lungs as she gasped to try and catch her breath in the fog. Finally, her car came into view. *Just keep going,* she encouraged herself. *You're almost there.* She could feel her heart pounding up into her throat.

Her fast spring slowed into a jog as she approached the car. She finally felt close enough to the car to look back. Curiosity got the best of her and she had to see what was chasing her in the darkness, if it even was chasing her. As she braced herself for the terror that was about to come, Kat turned around quickly. She gasped, ready for an impact, but to her surprise, there was nothing. Only the fog lurked and the dark road in front of her looked to be empty.

She quickly scanned the entire area, panicked, but she still found nothing. Her heart continued to race. *I know what I heard,* she thought. *I'm not crazy. There was something out there.* She examined her surroundings one more time.

There, behind her car, about fifty yards away, a shadow stood still. She couldn't make out what it was, but there was definitely something there. A shrieking scream bellowed from Kat's lungs as the shadow started to approach her quickly. Kat flung herself against her car, desperately trying to open the door handle slick from the fog. It wouldn't open no matter how hard she pulled, and Kat was left alone and unsheltered to fight whatever demon was gaining ground behind her.

She was too frightened to watch the shadow get closer and avoided looking back.

"Please, please open," she screamed, begging the locked car door to give her the shelter she needed from the beast behind her. She refused to look at the monster, but she could hear every movement getting closer.

As she pulled the door handle with all her might, she could see the dark shadow leap to attack her. Kat closed her eyes tightly and braced herself for what was about to come.

Shrieking screams sounded from Kat's mouth as she sat up in bed. Breathing heavily, she was still terrified from the nightmare she had just woken from.

"Fuck! Fuck! I hate this!" Kat screamed as she rushed to turn on her bedroom light and lock her door. She rubbed her temples frantically, desperate to calm herself down. "It was just a dream, Kat. Just a dream."

The clock on the nightstand read 1:14 a.m. Kat wasn't sure how she would make it until dawn broke. Even the lighthouse lamp didn't seem to provide any comfort in the loneliness of nights like this one. She felt like a child all over again. All she wanted was her mother.

"Mama," she whispered softly in a child-like voice. "I need you."

It wasn't the first time Kat had dreamt that dream, it was one of the several that haunted her since childhood. It was one of the many she had prayed to God to rid her of, but now, many years later, they still appeared on a regular basis and Kat couldn't understand why her prayers had never worked.

She sat up on the bed with her knees pulled up to her chest and stared at the cross that hung on the other side of the room. Kat had grown up in church and she had always trusted God. At one point in her life, she felt she was a good Christian. She had been obedient as best she could, her faith was strong, and she tried to seek God in times of trouble. Still, the nightmares of her childhood continued on into her adult life with no relief.

Kat had prayed hundreds of times before. She had asked for the abuse to stop, begged for the nightmares to calm, but deliverance never occurred. She questioned why God would allow such pain in the world in the first place and why He allowed her to continue to be tormented.

She felt guilty even doubting God, for questioning Him and not trusting Him. Exhausted, Kat pondered the confusion of religion. She needed sleep. It had been a long two weeks at work as she toiled to finalize her first big project and please her bosses and clients.

Kat's eyes began to get heavy, though she was still too spooked to sleep. She allowed herself to get more comfortable and forced herself to focus her thoughts on other things, more positive things. *Nicholas*, she thought with a smile. It was a name that never got old, a name that comforted her.

Nicholas had taken Kat out on his boat days a few days earlier. He had messaged her just as he promised. Although Kat welcomed his attention, she was still unsure of his motives or whether anything could come of the two of them. She could tell he was interested in her, but she couldn't see why. Still, when he said he wanted to take her out on *his* boat, she was impressed. She couldn't think of a single person she'd personally known who owned their own boat.

He had offered to take her whale watching along the coast as an apology for flaking out on her sea lion day at the boat ramp. Even though it sounded like a lot of fun, she still had to force herself to go with him. Lately, staying home sounded much more enjoyable than going out and facing the world. Her sudden unmotivated personality was starting to take precedence over her willingness to see Nicholas.

The thought confused her—she very much liked her mini-adventures to see the new world around her, but lately, her weekends were spent in bed with several naps throughout the day. Some days she couldn't get out of bed at all unless she was motivated by work. Even then, it was usually only the anxiety about the consequences of missing work that served as her motivation for facing life outside her front door.

As Kat laid in her bed thinking about that day on the boat, the noises that popped and creaked as the house settled through the night spooked her, reminding her of the noises from her dream. She tried her best to ignore them and enjoy the memories of the day with Nicholas.

They had sat on the boat waiting to spot a whale or two making small talk. As they became more comfortable with each other, Nicholas began to tell Kat a little about his own demons he tried to hide from the world. Some of the things he mentioned about his time serving as a police officer and the things he had seen made Kat feel guilty for the difficulties she had in her own life. It was as if her problems, her past, were petty in comparison to the things Nicholas had experienced.

"If I would have made a different decision that day, my partner would still be alive," Nicholas said with a stern facial expression that Kat found difficult to read.

"You can't blame yourself, Nicholas," Kat responded. She was at a loss for anything else to say.

"It's hard not to, Kat. I was in charge that day. I was responsible for him. I failed him and his family," Nicholas said softly, his face riddled with guilt and regret. "It will be something that always haunts me. But some days are better than others."

The conversation they had that day was much different than the other conversations they'd had. It was serious conversation. As the gentle waves lapped against the side of the boat, Nicholas and Kat's conversation made its own waves. Those waves were unsettling, and they hit harder than the ones that gently rocked the boat. These were waves that pulled both of them under to drown them in an ocean of memories.

"You do it too, Kat." Nicholas' face was unchanged. He was still serious.

"What is that?" Kat asked. She already knew the answer, but she wasn't ready to admit it out loud.

"You blame yourself for things you had no control over. I can see it," Nicholas answered, unafraid of Kat's response. Kat smiled slightly and put her head down for a quick second. She thought for a moment before lifting her head back up to face the truth.

"Is it that obvious?" she asked.

"It's not, actually. Well, to the rest of the world, anyway. But to someone who goes through the same thing, yes. I saw it that day I picked you up for breakfast," Nicholas explained, his face still carrying that stern look that said he would stand his ground against any of Kat's denials. She was taken aback, but she remained silent to avoid revealing that what Nicholas said was true.

"Also, I'm a cop, so…I can read people pretty well," Nicholas said as he burst into laughter to break the serious tone. Just as his laughter echoed off the deck of the boat, a whale broke through the surface of the water several yards away, but close enough for them to get a good look.

Kat was in awe of the creature's size. She knew whales were large, but this animal seemed to be more massive than she had ever imagined. Its skin glistened as water poured off its back and it began to submerge itself once again in the ocean. The whale's movement in the water created a wave that rocked the boat even more and though she tried to hold her balance, Kat tipped over and fell into Nicholas' arms.

"I'm sorry," Kat said. "Didn't mean to fall over."

"It's okay," Nicholas said with a smile as he helped Kat back to her feet. When she was standing, Nicholas' face became stern once again. "You know, the amount of times you apologize for wrongdoings you didn't do or had no control over was my first clue that we're alike. But you also hold something darker, something deeper. I'm just not sure what that something is." Nicholas smiled, reassuring Kat that her secrets were safe with him, but only when and if she was ready to share them.

She hadn't asked any more questions about Nicholas' traumatic events. She figured he'd tell her if he wanted. Of course, her morbid curiosity wanted to know every detail, but she wanted to give him the same respect he showed her: no questions, no details, just an ear to listen when needed.

Whatever he'd been through couldn't have been good, whatever he'd seen could never be unseen. Whatever he'd done could never be undone.

As she stared at the lighthouse lamp next to her bed, Kat let out a heavy sigh. She could feel her body becoming less tense and more tired. *We underappreciate our police,* she thought. *They do things, they see things so that the rest of us don't have to.*

Kat's eyes were heavy and she began to drift in and out of light sleep. She was grateful for Nicholas, more than he would ever know.

# CHAPTER 17

Kat was tired of the nightmares that haunted her. She was tired of thinking that Max was following her, lurking around every dark corner. She tried her best not to allow the dark things in her life affect her quality of life, but it was difficult.

She actually had an optimistic outlook on life. She loved setting and achieving her goals. Most importantly, though, despite everything that had happened in her life, despite the way a few people had betrayed her and damaged her, she genuinely loved people, all types of people.

Kat had a special place in her heart for the helpless. She hoped that someday, somehow she would be able to offer some sort of humanitarian aid where it was needed. It broke her heart more and more every time she watched the news. Children were dying of starvation in Yemen, innocent civilians were being bombed and killed in Syria, and the homelessness in the United States alone was heartbreaking.

To make matters worse, it seemed that even those trying to do good in the world were being targeted. Just the week before, several police officers had been ambushed and killed in the Southwest. The thought made her heart even heavier than it already was.

With the amount of shit going on in the world, Kat wondered how some people could get so upset if they didn't have the right kind of house or a nice enough car to make a social statement. She would never understand how someone could get so excited to stand in a massive line waiting for the newest phone to go on sale when there were thousands upon thousands of people in the world waiting in line for their only meal of the day.

Kat let out a heavy sigh. She wished she could do more to help the world even if she couldn't even help herself. She remembered something her father had told her once before when she'd been depressed about the evil in the world. "If you can't help the world, help one person," he had told her. He was right—it was impossible to help the world, so instead, she would have to help one person at a time. *If we all just helped each other a little more, the world would become a better place*, Kat thought to herself. *Less hate, more love.*

An alert sounded from her phone breaking her thoughts. A message from Nicholas popped up on her phone's screen.

*So there are some amateur fights tonight in Portland. Wanna go?*

Kat had never been to an organized fighting event, but she thought it sounded like it could be fun, especially if Nicholas was there.

*Sounds like a good time. When should I be ready?*

She started to walk upstairs to look through her closet as she waited for Nicholas' reply.

*It'll take a while to get there, so around 3…we can catch dinner there too.*

His reply made her smile. As much as she wanted to stay home and finish cleaning her house, she thought an evening out of Astoria would be good for her. She hadn't ventured far from her new town since the move and she wanted to become more familiar with the rest of Oregon.

*What does one wear to a fight?* Kat wondered. *Hmm…this will have to do.* She grabbed a tight-fitting black v-neck t-shirt and a pair of blue jeans. *I should really go shopping for some new clothes,* she thought. *But I hate shopping and these clothes are really fine.* Her mind returned to the problems of the world once again and she felt guilty for wanting new clothes when so many people went without. She had plenty more than the homeless people she often saw living under a bridge back home in the city. *Really, I'm fine with what I have,* she reassured herself.

She heard a faint knock on the front door and made her way to the staircase trying to see who was on the other side. *Who's here?* she wondered as a slight panic took over her mind. It was barely 1:30, so she knew it wasn't Nicholas. She had never liked unexpected visitors, but especially not now when little things put her so on edge. She preferred to be left alone as much as possible. *A courtesy call would have been nice,* she told herself silently as she walked down the stairs and toward the door. She thought it was rude for people to just invite themselves over.

The knocks came again and Kat rushed to the door.

"I'm coming," she shouted as she approached the door. She took a deep breath and put on her fake friendly face before opening it.

"Good afternoon! I just wanted to introduce myself," an older lady said with a smile. "My name is Mrs. June McKay and I live next door with my husband. I'm sorry it took almost six months to introduce myself. My husband has been in and out of the hospital for some time now."

Kat smiled warmly, the annoyance melting from her face and heart, kindness taking its place.

"Nice to meet you, Mrs. McKay. I'm Kat Morgan," Kat said while eyeing the plate of cookies the woman held in her hands.

"Oh, these are for you. Please enjoy them. If you ever need anything, please let me know," the woman said as she turned and walked away to her own house next door. Kat had just met her, but already knew she would like her. She could be the grandmother she never really had.

Kat daydreamed for a quick second. The warm and genuine smile the woman gave her really did make her feel welcome, even if it had taken her a while to do. Kat had actually seen her and her husband a few times while getting in and out of her car. She could see their porch in the distance from her driveway. On occasion, she had seen the older couple outside feeding the birds that came to visit them. She thought it was adorable and knew the relationship they shared was the way a relationship was supposed to be.

Kat finished getting herself ready for the evening out with Nicholas. As she styled her hair with loose curls and lined her blue eyes in black, she took the time to appreciate the way Nicholas treated her. He hadn't tried to sleep with her, which a new experience for Kat when dealing with men.

In the past, before she'd met Max, Kat gave in to sleeping with every man who took her out. It wasn't like she'd said no—she didn't even consider that she had the option to say no. She had never set any boundaries with her body before and she wasn't even sure she knew how. If it went past kissing and a shirt came off, Kat had felt obligated to finish what had started whether it felt right or not. Even when she hadn't wanted it to happen, it had never dawned on her that she could actually say no.

*Does it really matter, though?* she wondered. *It was just sex.* Sex meant nothing special to her, though she wasn't sure why. She knew sex was supposed to be a personal thing with someone you love. She allowed her mind to continue wandering as she finished getting ready.

Sex was more like an out-of-body experience where her mind had taken her elsewhere. When it was over, she'd had no problems getting dressed, leaving, and continuing her day without another thought.

Kat didn't feel emotion during or after sex like some of her friends would talk about. It made her doubt her ability to ever be in another relationship.

Another knock came from the front door, but this time she expected it.

"Hey Kat," Nicholas greeted as she opened the door to let him in. Kat caught him scanning her from head to toe taking in the view. It made her blush, but it didn't keep her from calling him out on it.

"Hey! My face is up here," she laughed.

"Oh…yes, yes. I forgot for just a second," Nicholas joined her in laughter.

*****

The drive to Portland wasn't as bad as Kat thought it would be. It was a two-hour drive, but she and Nicholas conversed well and the time flew by quickly. Along the way, they had seen a road sign with Nicholas' last name on it. He had pulled the car over and Kat snapped a picture as he stood in front of the highway sign that read, "Mendoza Drive, Next Exit." Nicholas was proud of his last name and he even told Kat about a town he'd once found named Mendoza. As he told her the story, Kat thought about how much she loved the way she felt when she was with Nicholas and she wondered if he felt the same way about her.

Kat and Nicholas walked into the convention center and Kat quickly observed the other women in the crowd. *I'm definitely not dressed for the occasion,* she thought as she looked around at the crowd. There were so many people and it was beginning to make her uneasy.

"Hey, I don't like the crowd either, but we'll ignore it together for one night," Nicholas smiled as he sensed Kat's uneasiness.

"I guess I didn't get the memo about wearing miniskirts and stilettos to fight night," Kat joked to him.

"Well, that's unfortunate," Nicholas teased back with his charming grin. "Would you like a beer?" Kat hesitated.

"No thanks. A soda would be good, though," she responded casually trying to hide her discomfort. Nicholas picked up on her hesitation and decided to join her in drinking a soda instead of a beer.

As the event began, Kat realized she was having more fun than she had expected.

"I can't wait until the heavyweights come out. I wanna see someone get knocked out," Kat exclaimed with excitement.

"You know, that's really hot—a girl getting excited over a fight," Nicholas replied, his charm making Kat blush once again. She took the compliment the best she could.

"Thank you, I think," she laughed. She had never handled compliments very well. With all the commotion going on around them with the crowd rooting and shouting and the overhead announcements, Nicholas had been staring at Kat without her even realizing it.

He examined every hair on her head, every wrinkle that appeared when Kat smiled. Nicholas couldn't keep his eyes off of her. He studied her every movement.

"What?" Kat asked softly after catching him staring at her.

"You really are beautiful, Kat. In so many different ways," Nicholas said with confidence in his voice. Kat's pale cheeks blushed and she couldn't keep her smile hidden, even in the dim light of the audience.

"Thank you," she responded shyly. "You're not so bad yourself." She giggled to keep the moment from becoming too awkward.

When the last fight was over, the two headed out for the parking lot. A heavy rain had started to fall during the event, so Kat and Nicholas ran for his car. They were sopping wet by the time they made it into the car.

On the way home, Nicholas began to share more of his insecurities with Kat.

"That was a big thing for me, Kat. To be around all those people and all the noise," he explained. "I'm actually quite proud of myself."

"You should be," Kat responded with a smile. Inspired by her warmth and understanding, Nicholas continued.

"I feel like I always have to watch my back. Like there's always someone wanting to kill me. It's very difficult to actually enjoy something like tonight, but I did. So thank you." Nicholas spoke softly as he continued to focus his gaze on the dark highway in front of them.

"I thought I was the only one who had an issue with crowds," Kat said, matching Nicholas' serious tone of voice. "I feel like I have to hold my breath in a large crowd. I feel tense and nervous. I feel like everyone around is judging me. It's like they know about everything I keep hidden from the world." She felt like she could trust Nicholas in her moment of vulnerability.

"What is it that you hide from the world, Kat?" Nicholas' curiosity sprung from his mouth before he could stop it. Kat's heart began to race. She had never said out loud any of the things that haunted her the most. The most she had ever told anyone else was the day of the break-in at the office when she'd finally admitted to Nicholas some of the truth about Max. But that didn't even put a dent into the heap of things that drove her crazy every day. She wasn't even sure if she could put into words what had happened in her past.

"Um…some things happened to me as a child. And…um…my relationship with my ex wasn't very good," Kat explained the best she could at the moment. She trusted Nicholas not to judge her on her past, but she still found it difficult to talk about it. *Maybe one day I'll be able to tell my story,* she thought. *Tonight, though, is not the night.*

"Fuck, Kat. I'm so sorry. Really, I am." Nicholas didn't have much to offer, but Kat knew there wasn't much one could offer after hearing something like that. *What's done, is done,* she thought. "I'll never judge you, Kat. I won't. And no pressure to tell me. Seriously. Just know I'm here if you ever need an ear." Nicholas did his best to reassure Kat he was there for her without delving too much into her business.

"I tried to kill myself before," Nicholas announced. His sudden confession quickly changed the mood in the car. Kat's eyes grew with concern. She had never considered that whatever demons he fought could resort to him trying to take his own life. It hurt her to think that he could be in so much pain. She wanted to take his pain, too, if she could. He masked his pain with laughter just like she thought when she'd first met him.

93

The rest of the world couldn't tell, but Kat had been able to. She saw it in his eyes every time she looked into them the same way he had seen her vulnerabilities in her eyes.

"The round didn't go off. It must have jammed. I was ready for it. I had come to peace with the thought that my family would be better off without me," Nicholas said, still speaking in a soft voice.

"Why did you think they'd be better off without you?" Kat asked.

"I felt like if they didn't have to deal with my outbursts of anger, my depression, and the craziness I brought, that they'd be better without me causing problems. I didn't want to be a burden any longer," Nicholas explained in his soft-spoken manner.

"And now?" Kat asked with gentleness in her voice.

"Now? I'm better sometimes. I still have my days with crazy thoughts. I still have flashbacks from the day my partner died. I still think people want me dead. I still see my partner lying there dead. It's just something I'll have to deal with and learn ways to cope better. Some days will just be better than others," he answered.

"I'll never think you're a burden," Kat smiled as she offered the only thing she could—emotional support.

For the rest of the way home, the mood became lighter as the two discussed current events, the insane election season that had everyone at each other's throats, and playful banter back and forth. When Nicholas turned into Kat's driveway, it was just after midnight.

"I'll walk you to the door," Nicholas offered as he got out and quickly ran over to open Kat's door.

"Well, thank you, good sir," Kat giggled.

"Pleasure is all mine, madam," Nicholas mirrored Kat's playfulness.

"I had a good time with you. Thanks, Nicholas," Kat smiled as she unlocked the door.

"Eh, you were okay too," Nicholas laughed. "No, but I really did have a good time with you, Kat." He unexpectedly leaned in and kissed Kat on the cheek. He didn't give her time to respond as he whirled around and walked back to his car.

Kat watched as he drove away and gave one more wave before he disappeared. She was both grateful and offended that he didn't try to make his way into her bed. *Is something wrong with me? Am I not good enough for him? No Kat! He's just being a gentleman*, she argued with herself inside her head. She was too tired to entertain the thought any longer. She locked the front door behind her and made her way upstairs to bed. She hoped it would be a dream-free night, just like she hoped for every night.

# CHAPTER 18

Kat woke one morning a few weeks later well-rested, but in a panic. She had been able to get a good night's sleep the night before, but her heart was pounding when her eyes opened, though she couldn't figure out why.

She decided coffee was not the best thing to consume with a heart that was already racing so early in the day. She threw the blankets off and headed for the bathroom. She splashed warm water on her face trying to calm herself down from whatever placed her so on edge. She hadn't had a nightmare in a few nights and her friendship with Nicholas was growing stronger. She was confused why her heart raced and she found it difficult to think clearly.

It was Friday morning. *Only one more day before the weekend,* Kat thought. *If I can just make it through the day I'll be fine.* Since she was skipping her usual morning coffee, she hurried as quickly as she could to get out the door to work. The walls felt like they were closing in on her and she needed out of the house and into some fresh air. She gathered her things frantically and rushed out the front door.

*Clank...clank...clank...* Terrible noises came from her car as she tried to start it. *No, I have a meeting with a top client today. This can't happen,* she thought to herself. With high hopes that it was simply a fluke, Kat turned the key a second time. *Clank...clank...clank...*then nothing. Her breathing became more rapid and she rubbed her temples trying to convince herself to calm down. *I can't call my boss,* she thought. *This is a huge day. What will I tell them? I have to get to work in twenty minutes,* she told herself.

She tried to take a deep breath and think rationally. *Maybe Aubrey will come and pick me up.* Kat dialed the number from her contacts list, but the other end didn't even ring—it went straight to voicemail. *I can't handle this. Not today.* Kat panicked and her anxiety rose with every second. She jumped out of her car and stormed inside slamming the door behind her. Pacing back and forth up and down the hallway, Kat tried to develop a plan to get to work. She felt her mind racing. The sleepless, nightmare-filled nights were still wearing on her. The paranoia grew more intense and it was exhausting her. She felt alone with no one to turn to. *Nicholas,* she thought. *No. I don't want to bug him,* she told herself as she pushed the thought aside.

Kat ran upstairs to her room and continued her frantic pace back and forth. She had moved hundreds of miles away to start a new life, but the life she left still haunted her daily. She felt stuck like she couldn't outrun her past no matter how far away she went. She didn't know how to stop the playback in her head. She didn't know how to get rid of the nightmares that haunted her. She wanted to feel at ease and she wanted the pain from the constant tension in her neck to go away.

She was tired of being on high alert all the time—it wore her out. Her energy was being drained by the havoc in her head and she was losing her grip on life. She was tired, so tired of fighting every day. The prayers, the good vibes, the dream catchers, nothing seemed to be able to rid her of her troubles.

Kat leaned against her bedroom wall and slid down to sit on the floor. Tears started to fall from her eyes as she burst into a sob. She felt like she was crazy, like she was losing her mind. *What if it's already gone,* she wondered. Her thoughts went dark, darker than they had ever been before.

*There are pills in the kitchen, lots of pills,* Kat thought as she pondered an easy way out.

"No!" she quickly yelled out to herself as she tried to redirect her thoughts. She closed her eyes trying to regroup. All she could see was memory after memory, nightmare after nightmare replaying in her head. Her breath was heavy and she was beginning to scare herself.

She had never before thought about taking her own life, but it seemed like it was the only thing that would rid her of the suffering of her own mind. She could finally stop the images that looped over and over in her head. Her mind was flooded with memories, ones she was tired of seeing over and over. There were memories of that door opening, the creaking sound when Daniel would close it behind him. Memories of him touching her and the way it made her feel: ashamed and disgusted with herself.

There were also memories of Max slamming her against the wall, pushing her off the bed, and humiliating her in front of his friends. There was the constant name-calling and belittling from him. There were the alcohol-filled nights with Max so drunk he didn't even know how badly he was hurting her.

*Why didn't you fight? Why didn't you scream? Why did you take it?* She asked herself why over and over as the thoughts played over and over again. She hated herself for the coward she had been and the coward she still was.

The pills were sounding better with each passing moment and every critical thought. She would finally be able to shut the door on her mind. She didn't want to burden anyone with what played in her head. She wanted her parents more than ever, but she had hidden her heartbreak for too many years. It was heartbreak that she indulged and held onto so that her parents wouldn't have to. *This isn't me,* she thought. *I can't think like this.* She continued trying to talk herself out of ending her life on that early Friday morning. *Nicholas. I can call Nicholas.*

Kat's heart pounded even more. She didn't know what sort of consequences might be in store for her if she called him. Nicholas was a cop and she wasn't sure if he would be obligated to take her to a mental health facility. *I can't go to a psych ward*, she reasoned with herself. The truth was, she didn't want to die—she just didn't want to live with the memories and nightmares that tortured her. She took out her phone and dialed nervously.

"Nicholas," Kat strengthened her voice as best she could.

"Yes? Kat, are you alright?" Nicholas could hear the weep in Kat's voice.

"Can I talk to you as a friend, not a cop?" Kat asked, unsure if Nicholas knew what she meant.

"Yes, Kat. I am your friend. What's going on?" His voice reassured her that he could be trusted.

"Nicholas, I don't know what's going on with me. I'm scaring myself," she explained without giving too much away over the phone.

"Hey, I'll be right there. Don't do anything stupid, Kat. I'll be right there." Nicholas' voice was stern and made it clear that he was concerned for his friend.

A few minutes later, Nicholas put his hand up to knock on the door, but instead grabbed the doorknob and let himself in.

"Kat! Where are you?!" he shouted. Kat was embarrassed. *Why did I call Nicholas?* She could have just figured everything out without him. Regret ran thickly through her blood. "Kat!" His shouts were getting louder and more concerned as he ran upstairs and found Kat defeated on the floor of her bedroom. Tears drenched her face.

Nicholas approached with caution remembering the day in the parking lot when she had been so apprehensive to him. He was careful with every move and made sure not to touch her.

"Nicholas, I can't get the memories to stop. I can't get the nightmares to stop. I try, Nicholas. I try so hard. I've prayed. I've prayed so many times. They just keep replaying in my head. I'm always scared to sleep at night because I don't know what's going to haunt me. I'm so fucking exhausted, Nicholas. I just can't keep going. And to top it off, my car wouldn't start," Kat cried as she spewed her troubles out for Nicholas.

"Kat, look at me," Nicholas commanded gently. "Breathe. You have to breathe. Breathe in deep through your nose and out through your mouth." He tried to calm her down. She followed his instructions, breathing in and out slowly to calm her heart rate.

"Nicholas, I wanted to die. But I don't want to die. I just want a quiet mind," Kat sobbed as she continued taking deep breaths in and out.

"Kat, I know what you're going through right now. I understand. But it will pass. You have to allow it to pass right now. And your car...we'll get that fixed. Don't let that stress you out. I'm here to help," Nicholas continued. "I promise you, you're not the only one going through this."

He leaned down to sit next to Kat. "May I sit next to you?" he asked, still being cautious in his movements. Kat nodded her head in approval. After a few minutes, she finally got the courage to look up at Nicholas. She had been holding her head down in shame, but she could feel her emotions calming.

Nicholas continued to talk, but Kat didn't catch everything he was saying. She had lost herself in his eyes. They helped to ground her back to where she needed to be. Kat could see the sincerity in those eyes. He truly cared about her and her well-being. She knew he was still talking, but only because his lips were moving. She tried to focus in on what he was saying.

His voice was soothing as well. It was difficult to focus on what he was saying when his voice was so therapeutic. She shook her head trying to come back to the reality. She felt like she'd been somewhere else. She knew she was breathing deeply in and out and that Nicholas was there to calm her. It felt like she'd been millions of miles away, but she was slowly coming back. She was calm now but worn out. Her emotions had been out in full force and now she was exhausted and emotionless.

Nicholas watched her with curious eyes. He hated seeing Kat this way. *This is what she hides from the world*, he thought. "Here, take this," Nicholas told her as he reached for his wallet and pulled out a business card. Kat read the card and immediately felt embarrassed: *Dr. Melvin Sampson - Psychologist*. "Don't freak. It's the guy I see. Kat, therapy can really help. I promise. Please, call him. Make an appointment. Do it for me," he pleaded.

"Okay," is all Kat could get out.

"I'm going to come back over tonight. Okay? I'll bring a movie and pizza. Will you be okay until then?" Nicholas didn't want to leave Kat alone, but as he read her face, he felt like she was safe to leave for the day. "You call me if you need anything. Anything, Kat. You have to learn to ask for help. You can't get help if you don't ask."

"I'll be okay until you get back. I don't know what that was, Nicholas. I couldn't get my mind to stop. I couldn't shut it off," Kat wept a bit more as she spilled the truth to Nicholas.

"I know, Kat. I know exactly how you feel. And I promise, there is help for it. Call Dr. Sampson and we'll talk more later tonight," Nicholas said sternly. He stood up and flashed his charming smile as he headed for the door.

"I'll be back around seven," he promised as he walked slowly down the stairs. "Message me if you need me!" he shouted from downstairs before leaving through the front door.

Kat took a few more minutes before getting up. She looked at her clock and realized she was already late for work. She decided it was best to call in sick. Luke would have to take over for her in the client meeting. She had to get herself better or tomorrow would never come.

# CHAPTER 19

Kat watched the clock as it neared closer to seven. She was exhausted from the emotional morning, but she had called Dr. Sampson earlier in the day and made an appointment for the following Monday morning. *Another couple of hours of missed work,* she thought. But at that point, Dr. Sampson seemed like her only hope for continued sanity.

She never thought about going to therapy before. In fact, she had always mocked therapy. She believed a person was weak and fragile if they needed a paid friend to talk to. She let out a heavy sigh as she thought about her beliefs. She was always taught to seek God in situations like this. She was supposed to pray and have faith. She felt guilty for not trusting Him in this situation and trusting a psychologist over His ability to save her.

She was tired of faking her smile and hiding her pain so she didn't inflict pain on the rest of the world. As much as she wanted to tell the world about her problems and take them off her shoulders, she wasn't sure what the best approach was to doing so.

Instead, she continued to smile and laugh because that's what the world wanted anyway. *If someone asked, "How are you?" today, what would I say?* Kat wondered. *"Oh, just had a meltdown,"* or *"Just thought about offing myself."* The world that claims to care wouldn't respond very well to that type of response. Instead, other people would judge her and call her a coward. That's why Kat always smiled for them—that's what they expected. *No wonder the world is the way it is,* she thought. *Everyone wants a better world, but they have no intentions of helping to fix it.*

When 6:50 rolled around there was a familiar knock at the door. *He's early,* Kat thought to herself as she rushed to let him in. Nicholas stood outside with a pizza and a bottle of soda, just as he had promised. Kat realized she needed to trust Nicholas more. He had been good to her. He hadn't let her down yet.

"I brought soda because you and beer don't need to happen right now," Nicholas laughed. *Ah, there's that charming humor again,* Kat chuckled in her head.

"Yes, beer and me do *not* need to happen right now," Kat giggled out loud. She made her way to the kitchen as Nicholas followed with the pizza and soda.

A few minutes later, they were munching on pizza on the living room sofa. Kat was glad for the food. It did her stomach some good. After the morning chaos, she hadn't eaten anything all day. As they ate, Nicholas explained more about the horrors he had been through. Kat was captivated that his character had never been affected by the bloodshed he'd seen. He still had a good heart and still loved helping people in need.

She studied his face as he continued, noticing the dimple that appeared now and then and how it reached up to his eyes when he had a genuine smile. *God, he's beautiful,* Kat thought to herself. *I don't think he knows how beautiful he actually is.*

Their conversation flipped back and forth between laughing matters to the serious topics about their personal issues. They shared about hobbies and goals they had set. They found they shared a passion for some topics that others would likely find "nerdy". They both loved books and history. Time passed without either of them noticing.

Kat turned to look at the clock across the room and was surprised to see that it was already 9:15.

"Wow! How did two hours even pass already?" Kat asked with surprise.

"Oh, I have that ability, Kat. Didn't you know?" Nicholas tilted his head and burst into laughter. "So, movie? Do you like Denzel Washington?"

"I love Denzel! How could anyone not love him?" Kat said as her eyes widened.

"Awesome. I forgot the movie in my car. I'll go run and get it real quick," Nicholas said as he jumped up and dashed out the door.

They got comfortable on the sofa together as the opening credits came on the screen. Kat was excited. She hadn't sat down to watch a movie in months. As the first scene played, she realized Nicholas was sitting quite close to her. They hadn't been sitting so close to each other earlier. *Okay, Kat, don't make this weird,* she told herself. She could smell the cologne Nicholas wore. It smelled so good.

Kat looked up at him without making a sudden movement, eyeing him in secret. Again, she noticed how beautiful he was. She gulped hard as she began to feel her heart pound.

"Are you feeling better yet?" he turned and asked. She wasn't expecting him to turn toward her.

"I am, thank you," she replied as she turned her body to mirror Nicholas. "Thank you...for today. Thank you for not judging me. I feel silly for having a meltdown over my car."

"Don't feel silly, Kat. When you and I are in a panic, nothing we do is rational or logical. But it will get better." Nicholas smiled as he spoke in a reassuring tone to Kat.

"You saved me from myself today and I can never repay you for that," she said with a nervous smile.

"We all need saving sometimes, Kat," he returned with a warm smile.

As they smiled at each other, Kat zoned in on Nicholas' eyes. She could still feel her heart pounding as their gaze locked. This wasn't the fast-paced pounding of her heart she was used to—this was a soft and steady heartbeat that echoed through her chest pleasantly. She felt it make its way up to her throat and she gulped again. Nicholas' eyes were locked on hers waiting for an approval of some sort.

Kat continued to feel her thumping heart as Nicholas brought his hand up gently, cautious of any sudden movement, and caressed her face. He ran his fingers from her cheek down to her mouth, slowly caressing her lips. Kat gulped another big gulp as Nicholas remained silent and just stared at her. He placed his hand under her chin, caressing where her face met her neck. He was steady and thoughtful, not taking his eyes off of her.

As Kat welcomed Nicholas' touch, he pulled her slowly to him to meet her lips with his. Kat closed her eyes, the warmth of his mouth enticing her. Nicholas's hands slid up her face, touching her ear and palmed her face in his hands. She welcomed his kiss as she slowly kissed him back. He was gentle with her, cautious of every move, making sure he had Kat's approval. Kat could tell he was being careful and thanked him silently for it.

She brought her hand up to Nicholas' face, mirroring his hand placements. She turned her body, adjusting to face him better. She was lost in his touch—she had never been handled so gently before. As they continued to kiss, Kat made her way off the sofa, tugging on Nicholas' hands to direct him upstairs to her bedroom.

He retracted his lips from hers and followed her up to her room. Once there, he softly kissed Kat's neck and laid her down gently on the bed. He crawled up slowly onto her and kissed everywhere her bared skin showed.

Her heart was still pounding, not from fear or anxiety, but pounding from Nicholas' touch. She felt everything. It was her first time feeling intimacy during sex. Her mind hadn't wandered. She was there, feeling everything. She felt the world around her, she felt Nicholas inside her, and she welcomed the emotions that were present for the first time in her life.

Nicholas and Kat laid on the bed next to each other, gasping and trying to catch their breath. For once, Kat didn't have hundreds of thoughts racing through her mind. For once, her mind was actually quiet. Nicholas remained silent and Kat stared at the ceiling above them. She allowed her mind to remain blank. It was what she had desired most in her life.

Kat slept hard that night—not one nightmare, not one dream. Nicholas stayed with her through the night. He held her as she dozed into the night's peaceful slumber. All she needed was an anchor in her life to keep the storms from blowing over the lighthouse where she sought refuge and safety. Nicholas was her anchor, a friend she needed to keep in her life always.

# CHAPTER 20

Kat sat in her car outside Dr. Sampson's office afraid to go in. She was grateful that his office was in Warrenton, the small town just west of Astoria. She hated the idea of anyone she knew seeing her step out of a psychologist's office, especially being such a new part of the community.

She debated with herself whether to go in or not. She didn't know what to expect from the visit and she was scared. She was afraid that a professional would validate her fear that she was going crazy.

The nervousness only increased as her appointment time got closer, but time was ticking by quickly and she didn't want to be late for her first session. She gathered as much courage as she could muster and headed for the small building.

As she walked through the door, she was surprised by the office. She expected to see a crowded room with a line full of people waiting to see the doctor. Any doctor's appointment she'd been to before was preceded by an extensive wait time, but this was different. The front of the office was empty and she wondered if she had even gone to the right place. There wasn't even a receptionist to greet her.

She was torn between relief that the office was empty and apprehension that she wasn't where she was supposed to be. As she sat down on a comfortable brown sofa in the waiting area, she tried to focus on calming her anxiety. As she took in the soft instrumental music playing over a loudspeaker, she rubbed her temples.

"Miss Morgan?" a man's voice asked softly. *Oh God, here we go,* Kat thought as her heart rate increased.

"Yes?" she responded in a near-whisper as she stood up to follow the doctor.

"Would you like anything to drink?" Dr. Sampson offered politely.

"Just water, please," Kat said as she sat down in the chair Dr. Sampson motioned to as he fetched her a water bottle from the small refrigerator next to his desk.

The lighting in the room as soft and calming, earth-tone furniture and décor brought a sense of relaxation to the environment. It was the very opposite setting Kat had imagined earlier that morning as she drove to the appointment.

She still felt tense and uneasy, no matter how calming the room was supposed to be. It was another new situation for her to get comfortable with.

"So, what brings you here today Miss Morgan?" Dr. Sampson asked as he took the seat across from her. *Wow, that was direct*, Kat thought. She had expected more prying and small talk before getting to the big "why".

"Um…please, call me Kat," she began. She didn't like being addressed so formally, especially in such a personal situation. Dr. Sampson was difficult to read and she struggled with how to answer his first question. As she tried to think of the answer, she realized she was fidgeting with her fingers frantically. She quickly moved her hands under her legs to help control the movements.

"Um…I've been having a lot of nightmares…I've had them since I was a child. I know, it sounds crazy…an adult having nightmares," Kat revealed as she started to doubt herself. She suddenly thought it sounded ridiculous as she heard the words spoken out loud.

"Having nightmares as an adult isn't crazy, Kat," Dr. Sampson said in a reassuring tone trying to help her get more comfortable with her condition.

"Oh. Well, that's certainly refreshing to hear," Kat replied as a slight smile formed on her face.

"What do your nightmares consist of?" Dr. Sampson continued to pry gently.

"Animals chasing me or something chasing me. Sometimes it'll feel like a normal dream, but tornadoes will appear suddenly and hover in the background…the tornadoes never hit, they just hover, taunting me. It's quite terrifying actually," Kat explained, unsure whether she was making sense or not.

"I see. Have you ever had a near-death experience?" he asked.

"No," Kat said simply. She knew her answers weren't giving the doctor much to work with. She knew she needed to tell him everything, but getting her memories into spoken words was difficult. Every time she built up the courage to tell Dr. Sampson, the words got stuck in her throat.

"Have you ever experienced any kind of abuse in your life?" he asked as if he already knew the answer.

"Um, yes…my boyfriend…he would get drunk and…um, he called me names a lot. Horrible names. He…um…he got physical a couple times. Actually, it was more than just a couple times. It was many times. He was drunk and kicked me off the bed one night. Like, literally kicked me in the middle of my back to shove me off," Kat choked on almost every word as she fidgeted with her fingers again. "But mostly he screamed at me. He would get upset if the house wasn't cleaned. He slammed me against a wall one night and I left him shortly after." She continued to choke on the words as she forced them out.

"How long were you with your ex-boyfriend?" Dr. Sampson asked as he took a few notes.

"Roughly, about five years," Kat responded.

"Any other abuse other than from your ex, Kat?" Dr. Sampson continued.

Kat's heart began to pound. It was easier for her to talk about Max than it was about Daniel. Everything Daniel had done to her seemed distorted in a way. She really had to stop and try to put the pieces together. It was tough on her memory, as if little snippets would flash and she would have to gather them up and put them together like a jigsaw puzzle.

It was what made her self-esteem so low. It was what made her feel dirty, ashamed, and disgusted. It was what made her feel unworthy to the world.

"Yes," she said softly as a tear rolled down her cheek. Dr. Sampson pulled a tissue from the box on the small table between them and offered it to her. She took it gratefully and dabbed the tear from the corner of her eye.

"You're safe here, Kat. Anything you say stays between you and me," he reassured her. Kat smiled knowing he was struggling to gain her trust.

"I just feel like my memories are poisoning me. I have to get them out of my head! It's just so hard to get it out," Kat sobbed through her words. "When I was a child, a neighborhood boy would sneak into my room when he stayed the night with my brother. He…um…he would touch me…in ways he shouldn't have," Kat said, disgusted with herself that she had never screamed for help.

Kat hated reliving those nights again in her head, but as she explained what had happened to Dr. Sampson, she reassured herself that he was only doing his job. If he didn't know what haunted her, he wouldn't know how to help her. *I need his help*, Kat told herself.

Her stomach churned and she became nauseated as she revealed all of the details to the doctor. She started to rub her temples and her heart pounded as she recounted the parts she could pull from her mind. She repeatedly brushed her hair back with her fingers and fidgeted uneasily.

"Kat, breathe. Remember, you're safe. I know it's difficult for you to talk about. I'm only asking these questions so I can better understand how to help you," Dr. Sampson said calmly. *Surely, he's handled this type of thing before*, Kat reassured herself. *He's probably heard this type of story before. It's his job.*

"Can we spare the rest of the details until next time, please?" Kat pleaded. She didn't think she could get another word out about the abuse she'd experienced as a child.

"Of course we can. You can tell me more when you're ready. But one more easy question that will help, if you're able to answer it: how long did the abuse go on?" Dr. Sampson asked cautiously, his eyes showing that she didn't have to answer if she couldn't.

"Hmm…my earliest memory of it was about five years old. It stopped when I was about thirteen," Kat remembered aloud. It wasn't until that moment that she truly realized how long a period of time it had been. *No wonder I feel this way,* Kat thought to herself.

Dr. Sampson wrote down a few more notes. "So about eight years?" he confirmed with her.

"Yeah, I guess so," Kat replied, surprised with her own answer.

"Next session we'll work on some breathing techniques if you're okay with that," Dr. Sampson offered as Kat nodded in approval. "We need to bring down your anxiety level first or we won't get far in therapy."

Kat scheduled another appointment for the same time the next Monday. *I guess this is going to be my new Monday morning routine,* she thought to herself as she took the business card from Dr. Sampson showing her next appointment.

"Kat, it's going to get worse before it gets better. Eventually, we'll work on learning how to leave what's been discussed here instead of taking it with you. Call me anytime if you need me before Monday. It's going to take time, but we will get there," he promised her with a warm smile. Kat was thankful he was being so clear and honest with her.

"Can I ask one quick question before I leave?" Kat asked, needing desperately to know the answer. "Am I crazy? Because I feel like I'm crazy!" she blurted out before she could stop herself.

Dr. Sampson let out a small chuckle that revealed he'd been asked the same question many times before by other patients. "Do you see things that others can't? Do voices talk to you?" he asked with a small grin.

His response gave her relief. She already knew the answers. "No," she said as she let out a heavy sigh. "Sometimes I think irrational things or think I hear things that aren't there, but most of the time I know I'm just overreacting."

"Well, then, I think it's safe to say you're not crazy," Dr. Sampson said with another chuckle. Kat appreciated that he could find humor in her hysterical assumption of insanity.

"If I'm not crazy, then what's wrong with me?" she asked, curious to know why she felt the way she did.

"Well first, there's nothing wrong with you. But I don't give a full diagnosis until we've been through a few more sessions. However, I suspect PTSD," he explained. He noticed the confused expression on Kat's face and continued. "PTSD. Posttraumatic stress disorder. You've been through thirteen years of trauma. I suspect that's what it is. We'll go more in-depth about it next session," Dr. Sampson said.

"Thank you. I'll see you next week," Kat said softly as she picked up her bag and headed through the waiting room and out the door back to her car. Safely back in her car, she took a deep breath and realized how relieved she felt. Just getting the little bit she'd been able to share off her chest felt tremendous. She started her car and headed to work earlier than she'd expected.

*****

As she worked later that morning, she didn't feel like herself, but she tried to focus the best she could. She sent a quick message to Nicholas before diving into the pile of work sitting on her desk.

*Thanks for the referral to Dr. Sampson. Things went well. Talk later.*

# CHAPTER 21

"But I already made plans for Christmas, Mom. Can't you guys come here?" Kat pleaded with her mother. It was barely fall, but she was hell-bent in her decision that she wouldn't be going back to the city for the holidays. "I just don't want to take the chance of seeing Max."

In reality, Kat knew she was being selfish—she just didn't want to go. She missed her family, but she was also content and she didn't want to disturb the progress she'd made in Astoria.

"Katrina!" her mother spoke firmly with concern in her voice. *Oh shit,* Kat thought. *She called me by my full name.* "Your brother isn't doing well." Kat's selfishness left her mind for a moment at the mention of Jerry.

"What do you mean he's not doing well?" Kat's tone changed to one of both concern and annoyance.

"I don't know how to explain it, Kat. He's been talking about things that don't make any sense. He keeps saying people are following him and tells me not to trust anyone. I'm worried, Kat. He's just *not* himself at all. I can't leave him alone," Mrs. Morgan tried to explain so Kat would understand.

"Is he overworking himself?" Kat asked, still not clear on the severity of her mother's concern.

"I don't think so, Kat. But I have to stay with him," her mother continued.

"Well, I'll talk to Jerry and see if he wants to come here for Christmas. Would that work?" Kat asked cautiously as she could hear her mother becoming aggravated.

"Do what you want, Kat. Let me know what he says," Mrs. Morgan replied and hung up suddenly. Kat felt guilty that she had upset her mother, but not bad enough to change her holiday plans.

As she was about to call her brother, a message from Nicholas popped up on the phone's screen.

*Good morning! Lunch today?*

The message made Kat smile, but she would have to message Nicholas back after she talked to her brother.

She dialed Jerry's number and he answered quickly. "Hello," he answered, his voice sounding groggy on the other end.

"Hey bro, you feeling okay?" Kat asked in an alarmed voice.

"Not really, Kat. Not really," he responded, defeated with every word he spoke. "It's complicated. It's hard to explain. Just don't trust Rachel. She's an EMT here."

"Jerry, you're not making sense," Kat said as she started to get frustrated. He seemed to be battling issues of his own, but Kat couldn't figure out what they were.

"I can't tell you any more, Kat, or they will come for you too," he said confidently.

"Fuck, Jerry. You seem fucking crazy. What's going on? Why don't you come here for Christmas? Get out of the city and take a break. You sound over-worked," Kat said as she became upset with her brother's irrational statements.

"No, I have a lot of work here to finish. I'm not sure how much time I have left," he continued as his explanations became more vague.

"Okay, Jerry. I do love you, okay?" Kat said. She knew her brother well and she knew that when Jerry got an idea set in his mind, he wouldn't leave it alone until he finished it.

"I hope so, Kat. I hope you love me. I love you too," Jerry finished and hung up the phone as quickly as her mother had.

Kat understood better why her mother didn't want to leave Jerry alone. *It sounded like he was losing his fucking mind*, Kat thought for a moment before scolding herself. *That's not fair, Kat. You thought you sounded crazy before, too.*

The conversation was heavy on her, but she knew that as stubborn as Jerry was, she was just as stubborn if not more so. *I just don't want to go home,* Kat thought to herself. She promised herself that she would venture home for the next holiday. Then, she and Jerry could spend some time together.

Suddenly, Nicholas' message from earlier popped into her head. She'd forgotten about it while processing the strange conversations she'd had with her family throughout the morning.

*Lunch sounds good. I'll make something for us. I really don't feel like going out.*

He quickly messaged back that he'd be at her house around noon, so Kat ventured to the kitchen to plan out an impromptu date lunch.

As she prepared a spinach salad with fresh-cut strawberries and almonds, she tried to sort out the last couple of months she'd been in therapy. She'd only had one nightmare since she started going to Dr. Sampson and she welcomed the quiet slumber that visited her at night. The nightmare she did have seemed

110

mild compared to the ones she'd had before. She had dreamed she was locked in a huge room with no door. The room spun while the black and white checkered floor moved like waves in the ocean. She had still woken up in a cold sweat, but she had been able to drift back to sleep easily.

Kat wasn't as anxious lately, either. She felt less tension and didn't feel as if she needed to be on high alert all the time. The breathing exercises she did a few times a day seemed to be helping. She had also learned a lot about PTSD. The information she had found on the internet helped to reassure her that she was not, in fact, crazy, just as Dr. Sampson had told her during her first session. Different articles she'd read online said a lot of other people diagnosed with PTSD also felt like they were going crazy, so she was relieved to know she wasn't the only one who felt that way.

She had learned that PTSD was not curable, but it was manageable with therapy. She knew she had to give it time and do the work Dr. Sampson had given her. As much as she hoped he could "fix" her, in reality, she knew she had to follow through with what they discussed during the therapy sessions. *I have to allow the therapy to work*, Kat thought to herself as she began to cook bacon for the BLT sandwiches she'd planned to go with the salad.

*****

Kat had just finished setting the table when Nicholas knocked at the front door. Even as comfortable as she'd gotten with therapy, she still kept the doors double-locked most of the time, so she walked over to undo the two locks and the door chain.

"Hello handsome," she said flirtatiously as Nicholas walked in, still in his uniform.

"Hey beautiful," he replied distantly as he gave her a quick peck on the cheek. Kat was surprised. It was much different from the type of kiss he normally gave her. This time it was a quick smooch and off to the table.

He didn't pull Kat's chair out for her and he didn't even wait for her to sit down before he seated himself. He didn't seem like his usual gentlemanly self and Kat wondered if something had happened.

"I made BLTs and salad for lunch. Is that okay?" she asked softly.

"Sounds great," he said shortly. He attempted a smile, but Kat could see it wasn't genuine. It was the same type of fake smile she'd used a million times to convince people she was okay.

"Is something wrong?" Kat asked.

"Why?" Nicholas asked, a hint of frustration in his voice.

"You just seem off today—a little distant," she replied hoping for an explanation.

"Nope. Everything's fine," he said as he looked away. Kat could tell he

111

didn't want her to see his eyes. She could always tell when he wasn't being fully open and he had picked up on her ability to do so.

"Okay…" Kat replied with a tone that said she knew he was lying. She walked into the kitchen and grabbed the bowl of salad and plate of sandwiches and brought them to the table.

"I talked to my family this morning. They want me to go home for Christmas," she continued, optimistic that changing the subject would change the mood.

"Thought you were staying here?" Nicholas asked, still refusing to meet Kat's gaze.

"I am. I told them I couldn't make it. I asked them to come here, but something's going on with my brother," Kat said as she stared at Nicholas, willing him to look at her so she could see the truth.

"What do you mean?" Nicholas asked as he finally met eyes with her. Something about the mention of her brother had broken Nicholas' train of thought and he now stared directly at her. She tried to see into his eyes to see what secret he had hidden inside there today, but whatever distant place he'd been earlier was gone and his eyes looked normal again, almost excited to talk to her.

"I'm not sure. He was kind of crazy. He kept talking about people following him around and that it wasn't safe to tell me any more because they'd come after me too," she explained. "It wasn't like him at all."

"Has he ever acted like that before?" Nicholas asked.

"Not that I can ever remember," she replied. "That's why I'm kind of worried. I think he might be working too hard. I tried to get him to come here for Christmas, but he was too occupied with whatever was going on."

"It sounds sort of familiar, don't you think?" Nicholas asked before taking a bite out of his sandwich.

"What do you mean?" Kat asked, unsure what Nicholas was implying.

"The fear of being followed, the fear someone's out to get him…it sounds a little familiar doesn't it?" he continued. Kat put down her sandwich and stared at her plate. It did sound familiar. It sounded a lot like her when she first arrived in Astoria.

"I guess I see your point," she said softly. "But I've felt this for as long as I can remember. He just started acting like this out of the blue."

"Well, maybe there's more to the story," Nicholas began. "But it's probably not a good idea for him to be traveling across the country if he's got that going on."

"Probably not," Kat said as she pushed her plate away, her appetite waning. It was quiet for several minutes before Nicholas broke the silence.

"I almost forgot. I have some news for you," he said excitedly. "You know the art gallery downtown, the Riverside Gallery?" Kat nodded her head. She drove by the beautiful old building every day on her way to work. "Well, I know the owner. He's an old friend. And I told him I have a friend who does the most amazing paintings. He said he'd love to see some of your work to put up in the gallery. You could make some real money on your artwork!"

"Nicholas…" Kat began slowly with surprise and apprehension in her voice. "My art isn't that good. I don't do it to sell it, I do it because I like doing it. I'm not a professional and I don't know if I'm really comfortable with people seeing my art."

"You're wrong," he replied. "Your art is gorgeous, just like you. And I think anyone in this town would be lucky to see it on display there. Besides that, think about how many tourists go in those shops downtown. You could really get some exposure."

Kat's stomach was in knots. She had started to get comfortable with the idea of having locals see her work, but when Nicholas had mentioned tourists, it sent her into a panic. *What if someone from back home comes here and sees my art and goes back and tells Max?* she wondered silently in her head. *Worse yet, what if there's an article about the gallery and it has my name…or what if the gallery has a website…what if, what if, what if…*

She was finding it hard to control her thoughts and felt her anxiety rising once again. She started one of the breathing techniques Dr. Sampson had given her. She breathed in slowly through her nose and counted to four. She breathed out slowly through her mouth and counted to four again. She continued, adding a count each time. Nicholas watched from across the table as Kat tried to calm herself. He rushed over to her side, careful not to touch her.

"I'm sorry, Kat," he said sympathetically. "I didn't think this would upset you so much. It was just a gallery showing to get your art out there. Don't worry about it. I'll tell the guy you don't want to do it."

As she felt her heart rate slowing, Kat was able to explain what had caused her panic.

"I know it sounds ridiculous and irrational, Nicholas, but the thought of my art being up there on the wall with my name freaks me out," she tried to clarify. "What if it gets back to Max somehow?"

"I guess I see your point," Nicholas said as he sat down in the chair next to Kat and took her hand in his. It was cold and clammy from her anxiety. "Sorry, I didn't think it through."

"It's okay," Kat replied, still doing her breathing exercise. "It's stupid. I have no problem with people seeing my art. It's having my name attached to it that scares me."

"Who says you have to have your name on it?" Nicholas asked. "Lots of artists go by fake name or their initials. Why can't you?"

Kat thought about Nicholas' suggestion for a moment. *No one would know it's you, Kat,* she tried to convince herself. *Just you and Nicholas and the gallery owner. And maybe a few people you've met here in Astoria.* The idea of anonymity was starting to sound better to her and her breathing finally slowed on its own.

"You know what, Nicholas? You're right. I should do it. It would be really cool to see my work hanging somewhere other than my studio," she said as she made up her mind. "I'll go by KM."

"So I can tell him yes?" Nicholas asked with excitement in his voice. Kat nodded her head happily. "Great! I'll stop by on my way back to work and let him know. What do you have planned for the afternoon?"

"Well, I didn't have much planned, but I guess now I need to pick out some paintings to show him," Kat said as she stood up to clear the table.

"I'm so excited for you," Nicholas said as he helped her carry the dishes into the kitchen. "It's going to be great."

"I hope so," Kat said. "I guess the worst-case scenario is that no one likes my work. At least it won't have my real name on it." She laughed heartily as she began washing the dishes.

"Gotta go. I'll talk to you later," Nicholas said quickly as he turned Kat away from the sink and pulled her close for a deep, passionate kiss. He walked to the front door and turned before walking out. "See you around KM!"

Kat turned back to washing the dishes. Nicholas had acted so strangely when he'd first arrived and then he'd snapped out of it quickly when she'd mentioned her brother. He'd been distant, lost in thought. Suddenly, she recognized his quick change in emotion from her own experience. Many times she'd been lost in thought, unable to interact appropriately with the world as a flashback had filled her mind. She suddenly felt incredibly sad that she hadn't recognized it in Nicholas earlier.

*You're not the only dealing with chaos,* Kat scolded herself. *Nicholas has been through some things, too.*

# CHAPTER 22

Kat was grateful Nicholas had thought so much of her artwork, but she had never painted in an effort to get her work into a gallery. It was always just a therapeutic, relaxing hobby that gave her something to look forward to. The fact that he thought her work was good enough for a gallery showing warmed her heart.

The initial anxiety she felt when she thought about Max locating her because of her paintings had mostly subsided. Even though it still made her a little anxious, she was happy to have found a way to share her work without sharing her full name. In the week since Nicholas had shared the news about the gallery with her, she had chosen four of her favorite paintings for the gallery and prepped them for their showing.

It had been an eventful and busy week and Kat was happy to have a relaxing evening at home with Nicholas by her side. He seemed so distant lately and she was beginning to think he no longer had any interest in her. His silence and withdrawn behavior at lunch the week before had been so unlike him, even on his bad days. She respected his silence, gave him space throughout the week, and tried not to pry too much. There were plenty of days she didn't want to engage in conversation, days when she welcomed silence in her mind, days when she embraced the stillness. She had to remind herself that Nicholas needed those days too. Still, with his odd behavior lately, she was glad to have a night with him.

As she laid in bed next to him listening to his steady breathing, she allowed memories to run through her mind. She allowed them in, let them play, and let them pass through her thoughts naturally. It was a technique Dr. Sampson taught her during their therapy sessions. She was learning that trying to force the memories to stop only made things worse. As much as she wanted them to stop, she now knew that, in reality, it was impossible.

She was also learning how to cut out the stressors out of her life—at least the ones she could control. Stress heightened the symptoms of her PTSD and as she found ways to reduce major stressors, the symptoms calmed a bit. For the stressors she couldn't control, she tried her best to face them and deal with them rationally. She was finding stress relief in little things and they became a part of her daily routine. The little things helped keep her anxiety down. The little things kept her from spiraling down into the black hole she never wanted to be in again. As she rejoiced in her healing, her eyes finally grew heavy and she started to doze in and out of a light sleep.

*****

A loud thump against Kat's chest sent her into a panic. She looked around and found herself lost in a gigantic airport. *I have a flight to catch,* she told herself. The lights were dim as she struggled to find her way around. She wandered through the oversized hallways and tried to read the flickering flight menu boards that were scattered around the airport. She struggled to make out the words on the boards, but it didn't matter—she didn't know her flight information anyway.

In the distance up ahead, Kat saw a woman in an airline uniform standing behind a service counter. She hurried up to the counter where the woman stood. She wanted to get on her flight as quickly as possible and out of the strange airport.

"Ticket please," the airline employee requested. Suddenly Kat couldn't remember if she had actually bought a ticket. *I must have,* she realized. *They wouldn't let me through security without a ticket.* She dug through her coat pockets but found nothing.

"I don't think I have one," Kat said softly as she tried to gulp down her nervousness. The woman stared blankly back at Kat without saying a word. The silence and look on her face scared Kat and she slowly stepped away from the counter.

Her confusion grew as she tried to make sense of the scene unfolding before her. She was hesitant to speak to anyone else after the strange encounter with the airline employee, so she wandered around the airport with no direction and no destination. She couldn't even seem to remember why she was at the airport. *Where am I going? Why am I here?* The questions trickled into her head like water from a leaky faucet and her heart began to pound.

Looking around the airport did nothing to solve her confusion. Only a few people shuffled or sat here and there at the different gates in the dim light. *Airports are supposed to be crowded, right? Aren't they supposed to be lit up and vibrant with energy, chaos, and people rushing to make their last-minute flights?* She continued to ask herself questions hoping to make sense of everything, but the eerie feelings were hard to shake off.

*Another long hallway,* she thought as she continued to walk through the terminal. *This is a familiar walk. I've been here before. I'm certain of it.* A few hundred feet down the hall, the bright red glow of an exit sign beckoned her. It became harder to breathe in the strange environment, so she walked quickly to the exit door and flung it open to the fresh air outside.

As she took her first steps outside, the eerie feeling stuck to her. The sky was black. There were no stars shining, but it didn't look like there were clouds either. The roads surrounding the airport were empty—an oddity considering how busy most airport traffic would be. As she walked down the lonely sidewalk, something came into view in the distance. Her heart began to race, pounding hard into her throat. As much as she wanted to run, her feet suddenly felt extremely heavy and slowed her pace.

She struggled to continue a steady pace toward the road. With every step she took, it started to become clear what was standing in the distance, *who* was standing in the distance. It was Max standing next to an old Greyhound bus. Kat felt her heart pound harder and harder hitting against her chest like a sledgehammer.

"Katrina," Max said, his dark, soulless eyes staring into Kat's. She stood frozen, listening to the sound of her heart thumping. She gulped. Her mind was clouded and she choked on any words that tried to come out.

The sound of Nicholas' panicked voice woke Kat from the nightmare of Max. Her eyes popped open and she tried to focus in the dark that shadowed her bedroom.

"No! No!" Nicholas shouted. As Kat became more alert, she could see Nicholas was disturbed in his sleep. "I'm sorry! I'm sorry!" He continued to yell as his eyes fluttered under his closed eyelids. Kat had never been on the other side of a nightmare, but she was certain Nicholas was having one.

She slid herself closer to Nicholas, cautiously trying to calm him.

"Nicholas," she whispered softly as she caressed his arm. "Nicholas, it's okay. Wake up, Nicholas." She continued trying to wake him gently, nervous about his reaction if she startled him awake. He tossed and turned, slowly beginning to wake. "Nicholas," she spoke again, unsure of what else to say.

Nicholas' eyes opened suddenly and he quickly jolted out of the bed. Kat watched him in a panic as he tried to ground himself and his surroundings.

"Nicholas, it's me, Kat." She slowly followed Nicholas out of bed and turned on the lighthouse lamp on the nightstand next to her bed. Kat approached him cautiously. "Nicholas, are you okay?" She knew he was in distress and confused.

"Kat! You're here?!" Nicholas asked with confusion in his voice.

"Yes, Nicholas. You're here, too. We're in my bedroom. We're here at my house. You slept here last night," she continued in a gentle voice. His face started to relax a bit, but he still seemed tense and disturbed.

Nicholas headed back to the bed to sit down. He was careful with every word he spoke. He massaged his face as his head fell into his hands.

"I can't do this any longer. I can't do this, Kat," Nicholas spoke as he hid his eyes from her.

"I'm sorry, Nicholas," she said, unsure of how to comfort him.

"No Kat, I'm sorry. I'm so sorry. I just can't. I have to go," he said as he got up and began to get dressed.

"It was a bad dream, Nicholas. You don't have to apologize. I understand," she said softly. The confusion Nicholas had shown earlier was now contagious and Kat's mind caught it quickly. Nicholas continued lacing his boots and still refused to face her.

"No Kat, you don't understand. I'm sorry." He stood up to grab his coat off the closet doorknob and walked past Kat without giving her a second look.

Kat stood silently in her bedroom. She listened to his footsteps down the stairs. The wood floor creaked beneath every hurried step he took. Kat heard the deadbolts unlock. The door opened and then slammed shut. Nicholas had left her with little explanation and she was stunned by the situation that had just unfolded. As she wiped a tear from her cheek, she headed downstairs to relock the door.

It was five in the morning and Kat knew it would be impossible to go back to sleep. She made her way to the kitchen hoping coffee would help her process everything that had just happened. As she waited for the coffee to brew, she checked her phone hoping for a message from Nicholas, but there was nothing. With disappointment, she poured her coffee and sipped the dark liquid, this time without creamer. She let the bitter taste linger in her mouth to match the bitter feeling that brewed in her heart.

She let out a heavy sigh as she tried to sort out her nightmare and process Nicholas' behavior. The fact that he didn't even try to talk to her bothered her more than anything. They had always been able to talk to each other about everything. He was the only one, other than Dr. Sampson, who knew all her secrets, but he had been so distant lately. She wondered what she had done to upset him so much.

Her eyes shifted to the pile of unwrapped Christmas gifts that covered her dining room table. She still had plenty of time before the holidays, but she needed to wrap them and get them sent off to her family as a final sign that she would not be going back to the city for Christmas. It would consume her Saturday morning, but she was happy to have something to focus her mind and distract her from the anxiety-inducing early morning hours.

# CHAPTER 23

The rest of the weekend crept by slowly and Kat spent every minute in anticipation of contact from Nicholas. She even tried to call and message him a few times, but there was no response. By Monday morning, she finally gave up and disappointment settled in her mind.

Nicholas had been her only true friend since she'd arrived in Astoria and he had walked away without a second look. No one else knew about her secrets and understood her the way Nicholas did. *No one except Dr. Sampson,* Kat thought. *At least I still have him to talk to.* Her forehead wrinkled at the thought. *Great, my therapist is my only outlet now.*

She downed her morning coffee quickly and got ready to start her Monday morning in as positive a mood as she could muster. *I need a project,* she thought as she lined her eyes with black to match her dark mood. *A project would keep me busy, keep my mind sane. Maybe I'll start a new painting.* Her art gallery showing was scheduled for three weeks later and she was second-guessing the four paintings she'd chosen to enter. *Three weeks is plenty of time to do something new.*

Making some new friends was also on her to-do list. She giggled to herself wondering if she would actually follow through if she managed to start a new friendship. She pondered whether she would really make an effort to spend time with them unlike she had with other friends in the past. She needed to call Emily, her best friend from back home. She had really neglected her since she'd left the city nearly a year ago. Other than a few texts to let Emily know she was okay, there hadn't been much contact between the two of them. Kat also knew Emily was understandably upset with the way Kat had left so suddenly. She knew it would take more than a few texts of phone calls to make things right. Kat even wondered if a quick getaway to the city to see her friends and family would be possible with all the progress she'd been making in therapy.

The brief thought passed quickly as she rushed out the door and headed to her car. She was eager to make her way to work. The winding and wooded road would never get old to her. The trees that arched over the roadway gave her a certain peace in an uncertain time. Their hug-like stance gave her a bit of optimism to tackle the work week.

"Hey Kat, how was your weekend?" Jane asked as Kat walked into work and passed her in the hallway.

*It was stupid,* Kat thought to herself silently before answering with a lie. "Great, how 'bout yours?" She forced a smile to cover up her disappointment.

"It was busy but good," Jane replied back.

"I need some busy in my life," Kat said as she and Jane walked together down the hall to the back of the office. "I'm going to have a few pieces of my art shown in a gallery downtown." She had a sincere smile on her face as she shared her news and put her bag down on top of her desk.

"That's great, what kind of art do you do?" Jane asked as she settled at her own desk.

"I'm a painter," Kat explained. "I never thought I was that good, but apparently I'm good enough to get into an Astoria gallery."

"That's really great news, Kat," Jane said with a genuine smile. "I didn't even know you were an artist. What paintings will you be showing?"

"I'm not sure yet," Kat said. "I thought I had made up my mind, but now I think I want to do a new piece. I'll have to think on it tonight and get started this week."

"Hey Luke," Jane hollered to their boss across the room. "Did you know Kat was an artist?"

"I didn't," Mr. Stevenson answered as he looked up from the document he was reading on his desk and joked with Kat. "You any good?"

"I try," Kat joked back with a chuckle.

As she sat down at her desk, something caught Kat's eye. A bright red envelope laid on the keyboard of her computer. Only the word *Katrina* was written neatly across the front. She felt her heart begin to pound as she looked around the room wondering who had placed it there. It wasn't even close to her birthday, but the envelope looked like the type that would hold a greeting card. She wondered if it was just a card or invitation from one of her coworkers. For a fleeting moment, thoughts of Max entered her head, but she used her coping techniques to push them quickly away.

Afraid to open the envelope, she simply stared at it lurking in front of her. She wasn't sure who it was from or what it was, but she hesitated to even touch it. Still, all the hesitation in the world didn't matter. She knew herself best and she knew that curiosity would always win. If she didn't open it now, it would lurk on her desk all day taunting her.

She picked up the envelope, slowly opened it, and pulled out the single piece of paper that was tucked carefully inside. As she read the words, her heart sank into her stomach and raced faster and faster. She felt her heart shattering into millions of pieces. She suddenly felt like someone had stabbed her in the stomach with a sharp knife and kept it there twisting and turning inside her. Her confusion only grew as she read and reread the note over and over again.

*Kat, I'm sorry. I'm so sorry. Those words will never earn or deserve your forgiveness for what I've done. You truly are an amazing person, but I must go. My bus leaves this morning. This is my goodbye.*
*Nicholas*

She dropped the piece of paper onto her desk as questions raced through her mind. *Why is he leaving? Why even give me this crappy letter saying goodbye if he's just going to leave like that?* She felt herself panicking inside as she tried to appear calm on the outside. *No! He's not leaving,* she thought. *He can't leave. He's not leaving without an explanation. Why would he leave? After everything I trusted him with he's just going to leave?* She felt her pounding heart move from where it had sunk to her stomach up to her throat. She looked around and saw her office mates working away at their desks unaware of what was happening to her. *How can I just sit here and do nothing? The bus depot is just a few blocks away. I can run. I can run and stop him. I can demand answers before he gets on that bus.* She couldn't let the only person she felt a connection with slip through her fingers.

"I gotta go real quick. I'll be back," Kat said as she grabbed her phone and took off out the door. Her coworkers didn't have a chance to question her before she was halfway down the block. The shoes she'd chosen to wear slowed her down, so she kicked them off as she pushed herself to run faster. A light rain started to fall and her feet struggled to keep traction on the wet pavement.

As she jogged down the street, she tried to call Nicholas, but only got his voicemail.

"Nicholas!" she yelled, angry that he was ignoring her calls. *I have to make it. I have to get there before he leaves,* Kat encouraged herself as she felt her body tiring. As she rounded the corner onto Ninth Street, the bus station came into sight. Her breathing was heavy from the quick sprint, but the desperation to get to Nicholas before he left made it even heavier.

She pushed herself to continue as a bus pulled away from the depot. It had been the only bus parked there before and she knew Nicholas was on it.

"No! Wait!" she shouted even though she knew the bus driver couldn't hear her over the engine. She tried to increase the speed of her jog, but the bus was faster. Her run slowed to a walk as she approached the gravel area where the bus had been sitting prior to departure. She bent over and put her hands on her knees to try and catch her breath as a tear fell from her eye and joined the raindrops on the ground. She watched the bus get smaller and smaller in the distance until it disappeared on the other side of a building.

She took deep breaths as she walked back to work. She tried to put her hair and clothes back into some kind of order when she saw her reflection in the windows of the downtown buildings. Every word Nicholas had ever spoken to her ran through her mind as she bent down to pick up the shoes she'd kicked off earlier and stumbled through the last block back to her office building.

One thing stuck out from all of the things he'd ever said to her, and that was when he told her he was full of disappointment. Perhaps this was what he had meant. *He knew he would leave. He tried to warn me, I just didn't see it,* she thought. *You really know how to pick 'em don't you, Kat?* Doubt set in heavily as she questioned her judgment on men, life decisions, everything.

As she approached the office, she stopped to take one last look at her reflection. Her hair was a mess, she was sweaty, her clothes were damp from the rain and her makeup was running from her sad, tired eyes. She tried to wipe the smudges of eye makeup the best she could. Frankly, this time she didn't care if the world saw her like this. She was tired of smiling when she had every reason not to. Today she didn't feel like making the best of it. Today, she would allow herself to sulk and pout, but just for a day.

She walked into the building and quietly made her way back to her desk ignoring the questioning looks from her co-workers. If they wanted to know, they could ask, but she wasn't going to just offer up her sorrows to them. She had plenty of work to keep herself busy, so she would drown herself in work and keep to herself if they didn't care to engage with her.

# CHAPTER 24

*There's one good thing about a broken heart,* Kat thought to herself as she stared at her lifeless reflection in the bathroom mirror. *At least it reminds you that your heart is still beating.* She sighed heavily as she wondered which was worse: feeling pain or feeling nothing at all? She watched herself for another moment and the stone cold blue eyes glared back at her. A tear trickled down her face and hundreds of self-doubting thoughts ran through her mind.

*Am I not good enough? What did I do to him? We had a good thing going, didn't we?* She allowed the thoughts to run in and out of her mind. They were only questions, but she knew she would never get the answers she wanted from Nicholas and that was what frustrated her the most.

She switched off the bathroom light and lumbered down the stairs to her kitchen. As she poured her usual cup of coffee and took a sip, she headed to her favorite place on her porch. It was the same spot she'd watched dozens of sunrises and as she sat down on the Adirondack chair, she continued to ponder the same questions that had been plaguing her for weeks. With a world full of men to choose from, she'd chosen to care for the one man who was incapable of caring for her. Why did she expect someone to care for her when *she* was incapable of loving her own self? *That's the real question I want answered,* Kat thought to herself.

The silence that morning seemed different somehow. Everything looked the same, everything smelled the same, but something just felt different. Perhaps it was because Nicholas, the one friend she had entrusted with her most personal thoughts, had left. There were even some things she had shared with Nicholas that she hadn't even shared with her therapist. There were truly things only Nicholas knew about her.

He knew about the ugly side of Kat. *Maybe that's why he didn't stay.* The thought made Kat doubt herself even more than she already did. *Maybe I can just ignore my feelings for Nicholas. I can shut them out and push them away. Then I don't have to feel anything anymore.* Even as she thought the words, she knew they were impossible. You either feel everything or you feel nothing at all. There is no in between, there's no choosing which emotion to feel or not to feel. There is no local anesthetic only for heartbreak.

Kat still loved her job. She still loved the coworkers she saw every day who had welcomed her like family on that first day. She still loved the new adventure she was on and she didn't want to lose her happiness with that part of her life. She sat her coffee mug down on the wooden table and massaged her forehead. She smoothed the wrinkles that developed when she was in deep thought. She rubbed her temples and gave another heavy sigh.

The morning sun started to rise in the east as Kat finished off her coffee. She was pained as she thought about her future. She knew she would compare all other men to Nicholas. His laugh, his jokes, she would forever seek someone who was just like Nicholas. She would have to seek out someone who had the ability to have an intimate conversation or exchange different political ideas.

She daydreamed of finding someone whose smile reached up to his eyes like Nicholas' did. Would he throw his head back in laughter about something he shouldn't be laughing about? Would he be kind? Would he help humanity? Would any future man be able to look into Kat's eyes and see beyond her flaws? Would her heart long for anyone else the way it now longed for Nicholas?

The sound of her phone ringing inside disrupted her daydream and startled her from her sulking mood. "Who is calling so early?" she asked herself out loud as she rushed inside to answer the call.

"Hello?" she answered cautiously as she picked up.

"Katrina, it's Dad. I tried calling you several times," Mr. Morgan said softly on the other end. Kat glanced at the clock on the stove. It read 6:25 a.m. *Why is he calling so early,* Kat wondered.

"Is everything okay, Dad?" she asked, even though she knew it wasn't. It was never okay when someone called at the break of dawn.

"It's your brother. It's Jerry," her father answered.

"Well, is he okay?!" Kat asked impatiently. Mr. Morgan didn't reply and his silence made Kat's heart pound. "Dad! Is Jerry okay?!" She raised her voice at her father shamefully.

"No, Katrina...he's not okay," her father said, barely able to get the words out.

"What do you mean, Dad? Tell me! Just tell me!" Kat's voice began to shake as she grew more impatient with her father. "Is he hurt?" Kat made her voice quiet down.

"No, Kat," Mr. Morgan's voice said with a tremble. Kat's heart pounded harder. *If he's not okay, but he's not hurt, then...oh God.* The realization hit Kat like a truck.

"No!" she screamed into the phone. She swallowed hard and asked the most difficult question she'd ever had to ask. "Is he dead?

"Yes, Kat. He is," her father replied in a monotone voice.

"What? He's dead? Jerry is dead? He's fucking dead? How did he die?" Kat screamed in anguish. She didn't wait for her father's response. She dropped the phone and let out a cry like she'd never cried before. It was a cry that could only come from within, a cry she could feel pouring from the pit of her stomach. It was a cry from her soul. She dropped to her knees and rested her head on the cold kitchen floor. She wailed out another cry, a cry that pained her throat. "No! No! No! No!" she screamed over and over.

Tears drenched her shirt. Still kneeling on the floor, she reached for the phone and settled back on the floor with her back against the cabinet.

"Dad…are you still there?" she sobbed to her father.

"Yes, I'm still here. Do you have a friend you can call, Katrina?" Mr. Morgan's voice was suddenly filled with concern for Kat.

"Yeah, I'll call someone," Kat lied to her father. The only person she wanted to see at that moment was no longer there. *Fuck everyone*, Kat thought to herself. "How did Jerry die, Dad?" She asked the question curiously, not sure whether she wanted to know the answer.

"He committed suicide," Mr. Morgan sobbed as he spoke the words.

Everything leading up to that point in Kat's life couldn't compare to the amount of pain she felt with the news of her brother's death. This particular pain could be felt deep in the roots of her soul. It was a pain she had never experienced before, a pain that was far too difficult for her to describe to anyone—a pain that she felt so deep and so dark, that it touched every ounce of her and cut deeper than she ever knew possible.

"Okay sweetie, we have the police department here. Let us finish up and I'll give you a call back in a few minutes. I love you, Katrina," Mr. Morgan said as he ended the conversation.

Kat stood up from the floor. Her legs were weak and trembled with pain from kneeling on the hardwood floor. She looked at her kitchen table where the wrapped Christmas gifts sat waiting to be shipped to her family. The one for Jerry stood out the most to her. She looked down the hall to her dark and quiet living room. She closed her eyes and hoped that maybe this was just another bad dream.

"No. This pain is real. It's far too deep to be a dream," she said out loud to herself as she stomped to the living room. She began to yell in the isolated home she had made for herself. "This is what you wanted, Kat! Remember?! You moved away from everything and everyone you knew!" She sobbed and fell onto the sofa. She grabbed a pillow and screamed as loud as she could into it. After a few seconds, she was worn and out of breath.

She took the pillow and threw it against her bookshelf. Candles and picture frames fell to the ground, but she didn't care. She stood up as she screamed. "Jerry! Why Jerry?!" She started to throw anything she could easily grab. She ran back to her dining room and threw all the gifts to her family onto the floor. She marched back to her living room and paced back and forth. She wiped everything off her coffee table in a tantrum of anger. The TV remote flew into the wall and broke into several pieces that scattered across the floor.

Kat continued to pace the halls of her house hitting anything she walked by. "I hate this! I hate this!!" she screamed loudly. Everyone in her life had either left or been pushed away. She hated herself for it. She hated how she had allowed memories to keep her away from other people. "Nicholas, why did you leave me? I hate that I actually cared about you! I hate you, Nicholas! I hate you! I hate you, Daniel, you coward! I hate myself, I'm the one who didn't scream. I'm the one who didn't ask for help. I'm the one who didn't do shit! And Max, what did I *ever* do to you for you to stomp on me the way you did?" Kat screamed breathlessly as she started to wear thin.

Her throat hurt from screaming. She made it upstairs to her bed and laid down. Her head was throbbing from the shock and all the noise she'd just wailed out. She could feel a knot developing in her stomach. As she laid still on her bed, she knew she would have to get up eventually to make travel arrangements. The thought of having to step one foot back into the city she fled from didn't settle well with her. It was a city of destruction, a city of pain and now it had taken her brother.

\*\*\*\*\*

Kat gathered the clothes she needed to pack into her suitcase and managed to book a last-minute flight for that afternoon. Flights into the city over the next two days had been booked solid, so she had gotten a flight to the next closest airport and booked a train ticket for the last hundred miles home.

She wasn't sure how she had gotten done what needed to be done. Everything seemed like it was happening in a heavy fog. She would have given anything to replace her brother's death. The insults from Max, the pushing and shoving, his drunken nights. Kat even thought of Daniel, the neighborhood boy who had ruined her childhood. Kat would have endured those horrors all over again if it would have brought her brother back. She would indulge all the pain if she could just have Jerry back. The pain was her best friend and she knew she could hack it. She'd rather hurt than see her parents in agony.

# CHAPTER 25

Kat stood lethargically outside the train station in her hometown late in the afternoon waiting for her father to pick her up. The sun was hot and the air was dry—weather that was now unfamiliar to Kat. She had grown accustomed to the cool, damp Oregon air. She suddenly remembered the last time she had been standing in this exact place. She was hugging her parents and brother good-bye before her move to Oregon. The memory shattered her a bit more. She was standing where she'd last seen her brother alive.

He had brought her yellow flowers, daisies. They were her favorite flow-ers.

"This isn't a fairy tale, Kat. This is reality—where your heart breaks and stays broken," she spoke out loud as a tear fell down her cheek. She wiped the tear away as she kicked a few loose pebbles as hard as she could knowing that, once again, her life would be forever different.

Kat watched the pebbles bounce down the sidewalk through her tear-filled eyes. A few of them rolled off the sidewalk and into the darkness of a storm drain on the side of the street. She wished she could hide in the darkness like the pebbles. She didn't want to face the world.

As minutes ticked away and felt like hours, Kat looked into the distance to see if she could spot her father's car. She looked around impatiently when something, or rather someone, caught her eye. Her heart began to pound and confusion rushed through her blood. Nicholas was there in the distance on the other side of the train station.

"No. I'm crazy," Kat whispered to herself. She closed her eyes and rubbed them. She knew the tears must have been playing tricks on her. She opened them and tried to refocus where she swore she had seen Nicholas. As her eyes read-justed, the man she thought was Nicholas was nowhere to be found.

*I'm seeing things now. Great!* Kat thought. She dismissed the thought as she turned to see her father's car pulling up to where she stood.

# CHAPTER 26

The sun was shining brightly and the slight drift of cool air was the perfect weather for an outdoor event. Kat walked through the aisle of folding chairs that had been set up in the park and found an empty seat in the front row. It was the perfect seat, one where she would have a great view of the orchestra about to take the stage.

As she settled into her seat, the noise from the crowd around her hushed. She could still see mouths moving, but the noise was drowned out by a radiant feeling of peace that had suddenly come over her. Children were running and playing at the edge of the park, but she could no longer hear their cheerful laughter either.

She was lost in happy thoughts about the unusually calm events around her when one sound, louder than the others, caught her attention. It was a beautiful sound, a harmonic sound. The beautiful music that began to play tranquilized her. A rush of peace pulsed through her body as she listened.

Kat turned to see where the music was coming from. A smile lit up her face when she realized not only where the music was playing, but who was playing it. Jerry sat on stage dressed in a pair of black dress pants and a perfectly pressed white button-up shirt. He played the large cello confidently. *Everything is perfect*, she thought. From every stroke of the instrument's bow to the shininess of Jerry's black dress shoes, everything about his performance was flawless.

"Jerry," Kat whispered softly trying to get her brother's attention. He didn't respond, focusing instead on the angelic music coming from the cello. Kat desperately felt the need to talk to her brother. She just wanted to say hello, she just wanted one more conversation with him. As much as she wanted to run on stage and hug her brother, she couldn't. She felt glued to the chair. Even with desperation filling her mind, Kat still felt the peacefulness hanging heavy throughout her body. She made herself sit still and admire his performance.

Jerry's skin had a slight glow to it. Every hair on his head was perfectly in place. The glasses he once wore were absent from his face. Kat felt her smile grow until it touched her eyes. She was in complete awe of her surroundings. Scars she remembered on Jerry's face were gone. Though she couldn't see it, somehow she knew that the pain in his leg that had hassled him for so long was now gone.

As the heavenly music hymned from each stroke across the strings of the cello, Kat was gently awoken from the peace by her mother. It had all been a dream. But it had been a beautiful dream, probably the most beautiful and peaceful one she'd ever had.

"Katrina, honey, come on and get up," Mrs. Morgan whispered as she gave her daughter a gentle nudge.

"Okay, momma. I'm coming," Kat replied back groggily. As her mother left the room, Kat laid in bed a few minutes longer trying to wake fully from the sweet slumber that had comforted her. She wanted to replay the dream she'd just woken from. She'd never wanted to replay a dream before. She closed her eyes and the image of her brother playing the cello was still vibrant. The dream made her smile as she wished she could stay in bed and relive the dream of Jerry forever. It was certainly better than the reality of the day—it was time to begin planning her brother's funeral.

Unable to avoid the inevitable, Kat finally rolled out of bed and headed for her parents' coffee maker in the kitchen. Her body hurt from the long trip the day before and she tried to stretch her neck as the coffee brewed. She was overwhelmed. She hadn't been back to this place in nearly a year. The city she had left behind no longer felt like home and she questioned whether that was a blessing or a curse.

Kat buffered the mug full of coffee with cream and sugar like she always had. She took a sip from the mug before heading out onto her parents' porch. Though she hadn't had a drop to drink, she felt hungover. Her mouth was dry and sticky and her stomach was nauseated. She felt like she had no control over the movements she made or the words she spoke. She couldn't debate about what would happen next. *Autopilot,* she thought. *I'm on autopilot.*

Noises of the city filled her ears. Traffic, sirens, a medical helicopter in the distance, the hustle and bustle of the crowded place surrounded her and reminded her of the life she'd left behind and gave her a chill.

Though she didn't miss the city, she did miss the red brick house where so many holidays had been happily celebrated. She sat down in the same spot she'd always occupied on her parents' front porch. The chair next to her reminded her of the tragedy that had occurred. It had always been Jerry's chair and though physically empty now, it was piled full of bittersweet memories of days gone by. The thought made her forehead wrinkle as she gave a sigh full of sadness and took another sip of her coffee. The two of them had shared many conversations in this exact spot. Holidays, afternoon and weekend run-ins had been spent here. The walls that surrounded the porch knew so much.

The air was damp with a steady rain, something unusual for her hometown. Even though she now lived in a place of near-constant cloudiness and rain, this rain felt different. Every raindrop that fell was full of heartache. Every raindrop that hit the ground was a part of Jerry's pain, a pain that hadn't been fully understood until now. The rain that covered the earth was like every tear her parents would cry, every tear Kat would cry.

Still staring at the empty chair, Kat's eyes filled with tears. The sounds of the city were drowned out as everything around her turned to a blur. She could only make out the sound of the raindrops hitting the dampened ground.

Kat was still in disbelief even as the reality of the situation slowly crept up on her. Jerry would not come home. He would never again fill the empty chair beside her. He was gone—dead. Her first best friend was forever gone from the earth.

She smiled as she remembered that this was the very porch where Jerry told her about his business idea. He had been so excited starting his own journalism venture and had mapped out every detail about it including the business name and logo. The truth in journalism is what had driven her brother. His ambition had been to report only the facts, only the truth, without any biased opinions or agendas. He knew the field of journalism had become tainted by opinions and money and his goal had been to follow the traditional path of journalism.

Kat had shared in his excitement. She knew her brother well and she knew that once he had an idea, he would stick with it until the end. Good idea or not, one thing about Jerry had been his determination to follow through. *Maybe this business was one of the bad ideas,* Kat thought as she wondered whether the stress of his work is what led him to take his own life.

She knew she needed to get ready for the day. Funeral planning would not be a quick errand and time was slipping by. She had never been in a situation where she'd had to help plan a funeral before. In fact, she'd never lost anyone so close to her. Kat gave another sigh as she finished the last sip in her mug. *I should've told him I'd come home for Christmas,* Kat thought. *Maybe he would have held on that much longer.* The thoughts, the questions, and the guilt frustrated her. *Maybe Jerry just needed someone to talk to, someone to crack jokes with, someone to help laugh away the pain he had tucked deep inside him.* Kat would never forgive herself if there was something she could have done to prevent Jerry's death.

The autopilot kicked in again and Kat made her way to the shower. When she stepped out fifteen minutes later, she wasn't sure if she had actually washed herself or not. Her mind was somewhere else and she didn't really care at that point. As she wrapped herself in a towel, someone knocked at the bathroom door. Emily, her best friend, opened the door and grabbed Kat to pull her close for a hug.

The feelings of regret about her brother swelled to include the regret that she'd left her best friend behind too. Somehow, though, it seemed Emily understood why Kat had left. The hug between them seemed to imply that understanding. It was exactly what Kat needed—her best friend. They both sobbed as the steam in the bathroom dissipated. Jerry had been as much a brother to Emily as he had been to Kat. They weren't related by blood, but Emily had spent enough time at Kat's when they were growing up that she knew Jerry nearly as well as Kat and her parents did.

The two women had always been inseparable, one always there for the other to lean on. One of them was always strong enough to lift the other up. Emily's sobs subsided as she took on the role of the strong one in a difficult moment.

"I'm sorry I left without a word," Kat sobbed as Emily held her. "I wanted to tell you, but I was afraid to tell anyone."

"Shhh," Emily hushed her. "Kat, we've known each other forever and when I realized you left, I knew it was something big, something you couldn't tell anyone. You don't have to tell me now, you don't have to tell me ever. I miss you like crazy, but I know you well enough to know that if you left like that, something bigger was going on."

A wave of relief washed over Kat's body with Emily's words and her sobs grew stronger as she realized Emily had already forgiven her. She pulled away and wiped away the tears with the back of her hand.

"I've got to finish getting ready," she said as she scrambled over to the bathroom sink. "My parents are waiting on me."

"They left right after I got here," Emily explained. "They needed to go, so I told them I could drive you. Finish getting ready and we'll go together. I'm here to help however I can."

*****

"You should eat something, Kat. You're looking a little pale," Emily told Kat as they got into Emily's car an hour later.

"I'm not hungry," Kat replied with a cheesy smile.

"Too bad," Emily said as she softly smacked Kat across the arm. "You're going to eat. We'll stop and grab something on the way to meet your parents."

Traffic was heavy as they made their way to the funeral home several blocks away. As they waited for traffic to clear an intersection, a police car slowed as it passed Kat and Emily. The police officer driving the car locked his eyes on Kat and his blank stare made her heart begin to race. When he had fully passed their car, the officer sped up and continued on his way.

"That was weird," Kat said with a mix of fear and confusion in her voice.

"What?" Emily asked as she looked around to see what had frazzled Kat.

"Um, that cop. He just slowed down and he was staring at me," Kat said. As she heard the words leaving her mouth, she immediately doubted herself and knew how crazy she sounded.

"Kat, he was just driving by and then drove away, you nut," Emily replied with a chuckle.

"Emily, he slowed down and gave me a creepy stare. Who does that? Especially a cop?" Kat said as frustration grew in her voice.

"Kat, it was nothing. He was probably just looking for someone and he was trying to make sure you're not that person," Emily said, trying to rationalize things for Kat.

"Whatever. Let's just go," Kat responded with annoyance that her best friend didn't believe her. Kat knew something was off about that cop, but lately, everything felt off. *Maybe I am just a nut,* Kat thought.

\*\*\*\*\*

Kat and Emily had shopped for many things together throughout life, but neither of them ever imagined they'd spend an afternoon casket shopping. As much as she knew it wouldn't be, Kat was determined to make the funeral home an in-and-out errand. *How hard could it be?* she wondered with a small chuckle. She was grateful to Emily for taking the week off to be there with her and her family. She couldn't have done it without her best friend and she felt guilty about getting angry at Emily for not believing her in the car earlier.

# CHAPTER 27

Sleep had not been a friend to Kat since the dream of her brother playing the cello. She was desperate to go back to the peaceful moment when he filled the stage in front of her and the angelic music flowed through her ears. Desperation turned into insomnia and the lack of restful sleep was beginning to take a toll on her mental state. As much as she tried to sleep, her mind raced like a car with no brakes and a brick holding down the gas pedal.

Visitors came and went, but it was hard to remember who had actually come to share their condolences about Jerry's death. Kat's mind was still in a heavy fog and the past week had been nothing but a blur of random images.

The funeral had taken place earlier that morning and even though it had only been ten hours since then, she couldn't remember much about it. Though nearly a dozen songs had been played at the service, the only song stuck in her mind was the one her brother had played on the cello in her dream. She couldn't remember who had been at the service, nor could she remember what the pastor spoke about.

Maybe it had been the presence of her brother's cold body lying in that casket that wiped everything else away. *The funeral home did a good job*, Kat thought. *He looked like he was finally at peace.* It had been difficult for her to leave him at the end of the service. Everyone else had exited the sanctuary, but Kat stayed behind cherishing the last few moments with her brother.

Before she left her brother's side for the last time that morning, Kat found a pen and paper on the back of one of the church pews. She didn't feel like she'd had enough closure, so she wrote a quick note Jerry could take with him into eternity.

*My beloved brother,*
*I promise to always stand for you. I love you and I'll miss you forever.*
*XOXO*
*Your little sis,*
*Katrina*

135

Kat tucked the note inside Jerry's jacket pocket, kissed him on his cold forehead, and forced herself to walk away.

The scene played again in her mind as she laid in the dark bedroom at her parents' house and she let out a heavy, stuttering sigh. She had cried all the tears her body would allow her to. *I can't just lay here in bed,* she thought as she realized sleep wouldn't come any time soon. *I've got to get away for a few hours.* It was barely 9:30, still early enough to venture out on a Friday night, though she hadn't gone out in years.

She jumped off the bed and changed into a black V-neck shirt that was tight across her body, a pair of dark blue jeans that were snug around her legs, and her black combat boots. She was thankful her hair and makeup were still in good condition from earlier in the day. As she headed for the door, she grabbed her wallet, phone, and a sweater.

"Hey Dad, I'm going out for a while. Love you. Don't wait up for me," she said as she peeked into her parents' room before heading out.

"Okay, sweetie," Mr. Morgan shouted after her. "Be safe. And love you too!"

Kat got into the rental car she'd picked up a couple of days before. She was tired of relying on other people to get her around the city, so she'd splurged for her own transportation. It felt good to get away from all the commotion to spend some time alone. She hoped a night out away from reality would do her some good.

*****

"What can I get for you?" the bartender asked as Kat sat down at a pub a couple of miles from her parents' house.

"Any kind of cider on draft, please," Kat ordered with a smile. She couldn't remember the last time she'd had a drink, but it didn't matter—she was drinking tonight. She wanted to drown her reality with alcohol. *It's just one night,* she told herself to lessen her self-judgement.

"Here you go. Let me know what you think. We just got this one in," the bartender said as Kat chugged the ice cold drink.

"It's delicious," she said with a cheesy smile as she wiped a bit of the cider's foam from the corner of her mouth. "I'll take another one, please."

"Number two coming right up," the bartender replied as he fetched her another drink. The second was just as delightful as the first and she relished in the way each gulp numbed her pain more and more. "Meeting anyone tonight?" the bartender asked, though the look on his face said he knew she was the lonely girl alone at the bar tonight.

"No. More like getting away from it all tonight," Kat replied. Usually, she didn't care for small talk, especially with strangers, but tonight she needed the distraction. She would take whatever she could get if it meant not thinking about the reality that waited for her outside the bar.

"Don't make it a habit," the bartender told her with a genuine smile. "I've seen too many lives wasted here on a weekly basis to get away from whatever they're avoiding."

"Thanks," Kat replied, half annoyed and half thankful for his honest advice.

"Hey! Can I get another round over here!" a man hollered from the other side of the bar.

"Duty calls," the bartender said as he walked away giving Kat the space she was hoping for.

*****

An hour later, she sipped on her fourth glass of cider and finished the wings her stomach ached for. The numbness from the cider allowed Nicholas to come into her thoughts. *A quick message wouldn't hurt,* she pondered doubtfully. *Maybe he'll answer me.* The anger started to boil in her as she remembered the way he'd just left without any sort of explanation. He had simply walked away without a care. She still wanted an explanation. In fact, she demanded it as she typed out a quick message.

*Where are you? Why did you leave?! How could you do this to me?!*

Minutes passed with no reply. Disappointment hit her again and she let out a heavy sigh as she realized she'd set herself up to be disappointed yet again.

"Hey, you know drunk texting is never a good thing. It'll drive you mad," an unfamiliar voice said behind her. She jumped in her seat, unaware anyone had been watching her. Kat turned quickly to see the handsome man who'd given her the unsolicited advice. His eyes were a familiar brown that matched his dark skin. He smirked at Kat and a dimple appeared on the side of his mouth. *Nicholas,* Kat thought. *His features look so much like Nicholas.* She was suddenly drawn to the mysterious stranger.

"Yeah, I'm slowly learning that the hard way," she replied as she finished off the glass in front of her.

"Can I buy you another one?" the man asked.

"Yes, please," Kat replied without hesitation, not caring about the amount of alcohol she was consuming. *I'll regret this in the morning,* she thought, though the idea didn't stop her from continuing her careless night. Through blurry vision, she watched the man walk over to order their drinks.

"I'm Alex," the man said as he sat down and handed her one of the glasses.

"Cheers," Kat said as she clinked her glass against his. "I'm Kat. Nice to meet you."

"What brings a gorgeous lady like yourself to a bar alone?" Alex asked curiously as he sipped his drink.

"Just needing a distraction from life at the moment," Kat slurred as she gave Alex an inviting smile.

"Can I help with that distraction?" the man asked, prying at Kat.

"Depends on what you have to offer," Kat said as she tried to focus and stare into the stranger's eyes.

"Wanna get out of here?" Alex asked confidently. An intoxicated Kat didn't debate with herself, she didn't assess the danger the way she normally would have. She wasn't hesitant in her reply at all.

"Yes. Let's go," she said as she tried to stand up.

"I like your answer," Alex said as he put his hand gently on her arm. "You can finish up your drink and we'll go." He didn't take his eyes off Kat as she chugged the rest of her fifth glass of cider. When the glass was empty, she stumbled off the barstool, took his hand, and followed him out to his car.

*I know I shouldn't be doing this,* Kat thought briefly as they neared his car. *But I want to do this.* Her urge to replace Nicholas overpowered any doubt she had as Alex swung her around and pressed her gently up against his car for an eager kiss. Kat welcomed the attention from the man she'd just met and allowed him to do whatever he pleased.

"I want you so bad," Alex whispered as his hand crept up her shirt.

"Take me to your place," Kat whispered back knowing she wanted him as well.

*****

Once inside Alex's townhouse, clothing items dropped to the floor one by one making a trail to the bedroom. The thrill of a stranger's seduction excited Kat. She welcomed everything as Alex laid her in his bed. Her mind was far from the week's events, far away from Max and Daniel and Nicholas, far from the nightmares that haunted her. She was far away from any reality that awaited her. The night was successful at distracting her, just as she had planned.

*****

The next morning, Kat awoke and looked around. She was lying naked next to Alex. *Crap,* she thought as regret finally kicked in. Her head was throbbing and she felt dehydrated. She sat up in bed looking for her clothes, only able to spot the undergarments. *Crap,* she thought again.

"Good morning," Alex said as he rolled over and caressed Kat's bare back.

"Hi. Do you have any pain reliever?" Kat asked as the naked stranger sat up.

"Yeah. I have some Gatorade too. I'll go get some," Alex replied. The man got up and walked over to grab a pair of sweatpants from his dresser. As much as the view of his naked body made her feel awkward, it was also a pleasant view.

When he returned from the kitchen, Kat sipped on the Gatorade and downed the pills so she could gather her clothes and leave. She stood up and walked through the house collecting each item of her clothing. Alex walked up behind her and gently kissed her on the back of her neck.

"Again?" he whispered into her ear as he caressed her body. As tempting as it was, she knew she needed to get back to her parents' house. *Ugh, I feel horrible,* she thought as she pulled away.

"No, I have to go," she said as she got dressed.

"Well, if you insist. Maybe we can meet up for dinner sometime?" the man asked with a grin.

"Not likely. I'm only in town for a few more days," Kat responded bluntly.

"Oh, I see," Alex responded with a strange sound in his voice.

"Can I use your bathroom to freshen up?" Kat asked. She was eager to leave but didn't want to go anywhere if she looked the way she felt.

"Yeah. Just down the hall and to the left," Alex explained as he gestured the directions and looked her up and down before she headed down the hall.

As she came out of the bathroom and neared the kitchen, Alex was waiting for her.

"Would you like some breakfast?" he asked politely.

"No thanks. Umm…can you take me back to my car please?" Kat asked, ready to get out of the hall of shame. The man's face displayed a hint of disapproval, but he smiled and agreed to take her.

"No problem. Let me go make a quick phone call and we'll go," Alex replied as he headed back to the bedroom.

"Sounds good," Kat smiled, though the smile was one of nervousness more than politeness. She used the few minutes Alex was gone to send her parents a message that she'd stayed the night at a friend's house.

She felt like a teenager again lying to her parents about where she'd spent the night. She always hated lying to them, but there was no way she could tell them what she'd really been doing the night before. As she hit send, Alex finally came out dressed and ready to go.

"Ready?" he asked.

"Yep," Kat responded simply. Alex drove silently back to the parking lot outside the bar where they'd met.

"Thanks for the fun night," Kat said as she got out of the car. "I needed it."

"No problem. Here's my number in case you change your mind about dinner," Alex said as he handed a small piece of paper to her. *Again, not likely,* Kat thought as she grew more annoyed.

"Thanks. Have a good day," she replied, carefully holding back the sarcastic comments she wanted to make. She shut the car door and headed toward the rental car sitting alone in the parking lot.

She crumpled the paper and tossed it into the floorboard of the car and erased all thoughts about the stranger she'd slept with the night before. She pulled out of the parking lot and ventured her way back to her parents' house. For the first time in a week, her mind wasn't racing with thoughts. Her mind was quiet from the reality that surrounded her and that thought alone was enough to make her smile in her solitude.

As she turned onto the street where her parents lived, Kat glanced in the rearview mirror to see red and blue lights flashing. "Ah, crap," she said aloud. *I'm only a few blocks away from home. Why now?* She slowed the car and pulled over to the side of the road.

"License and registration, please," the officer said as Kat rolled down her window. As she started to gather the documents, the officer spoke again. "Do you know why I pulled you over, ma'am?" He spoke sternly, more sternly than a simple traffic violation warranted.

*Hmm,* Kat thought. She wracked her mind trying to remember whether she'd been speeding or missed a turn signal. Her mind had been elsewhere just like it had been all week. *Maybe I did forget to use my blinker,* she thought. As she looked up to hand over her information to the officer, her heart began to race and she swallowed a hard gulp. It was the same officer who had slowed down as he passed her and Emily days before—the same officer who'd given her that blank, creepy stare.

"Someone called in a theft from their residence. Your car matches the vehicle description," the officer continued as he took Kat's paperwork. Her heart pounded even harder with anxiety and confusion.

"Oh, well you can search me and the car. I can assure you it wasn't me," Kat said nervously. *What is going on?* she wondered. *Theft? I didn't steal anything.* Her thoughts raced along to the quickening speed of her heart.

"Okay, Miss Morgan. Can you please step out of the car?" the officer requested, again in a stern voice.

"Yes, sir," Kat said as she stepped out the rental car. "But I assure you this is some kind of a mistake."

"Turn around and place your hands on the car," the officer spoke as Kat followed his instructions. *Is this really happening?* Kat questioned in a panic.

The officer conducted his pat down on Kat and stopped mid-search.

"What is this?" The officer's tone changed from stern to downright angry. *What is what?* Kat thought as she turned around to see what the officer had found. Her heart pounded into her throat with nervousness.

"This is the wallet and badge reported stolen this morning. It was in *your* coat pocket, Miss Morgan," the officer continued. Kat examined the open wallet and saw a driver's license on one side and a police badge on the other.

*Alex? Alex is a fucking cop?* she thought to herself. As her confusion grew, she began to get angry.

"I didn't take that! I've never seen it before!" Kat said with a raised voice. *This doesn't make any sense. I didn't take it,* Kat thought as the confusion and anger dug deeper.

"You're under arrest for theft, Miss Morgan. Turn back around and place your hands behind your back," the officer directed. *This can't be happening,* Kat panicked. *What the fuck is going on?* The questions raced through her mind as she felt the metal cuffs latch around her wrists.

As she was placed in the back of the police car, a tear rolled down her cheek. She was overwhelmed with emotions once again. *How did I miss that Alex was a cop? How did his wallet end up in my coat?* Nothing made sense. She had come home for a funeral and now she was headed to jail for something she knew she didn't do. A reckless night out was going to end up costing her more than she'd ever imagined.

# CHAPTER 28

It was an unusual ninety degrees in the city in late fall, and Kat couldn't help but think her own chaos was the cause of the wild weather around her. She'd only been in the jail for two hours waiting for Emily to bail her out, but it felt much longer. *I'm not jail material,* Kat thought. *This is too much.* There was no way she could tell her parents what happened. They had already been through so much and they didn't need any added stress.

"Dude, what's up with you? What the hell happened? Do I even want to know, Kat?" Emily scolded Kat as they walked out of the building.

"Emily, chill! You know me!" Kat snapped back.

"Apparently not so much anymore, Kat. You move away without a word, then I get random short text messages from you throughout the year, and now you're getting arrested," Emily continued to scold.

"That's not fair, Emily, and you know it! I'm sorry for hurting you, but I had to leave. I had to!" Kat shouted as she felt the tension taking hold throughout her body.

"I just want you to talk to me, Kat. Ever since you left, you don't talk to me. We've been best friends forever. I've *always* been there for you. But lately, you don't even talk to me. It's like you don't care anymore," Emily said as the two girls got into Emily's car.

"Again, I'm sorry, Emily. I'm sorry!" Kat yelled at her friend. Her heart was racing as frustration grew. She finally broke down and gave Emily a summary of the events that had taken place in her life. "Look, Max was toxic for me. He was always drinking and yelling at me…he got physical. He was fucking crazy! I was scared, so I left. I couldn't tell anyone, Emily. I was scared he'd find me. Then I thought everything would be fine when I got settled, but I was paranoid that Max was following me and I was having nightmares all the time!

"But then I met someone—a friend. He helped me and then I started going to therapy. Things were getting better. *I* was getting better. Then Jerry died! I just went out for drinks, Emily. I went home with this guy, Alex, and left this morning and bam—here I am! He said I stole his wallet and badge. I didn't even know he was a cop, Emily!"

Kat felt the slightest relief as she spilled her pent-up secrets to her friend. Emily sat in the driver's seat with a concerned and shocked look on her face. Silence filled the space thousands of words had just filled for a few seconds.

"Emily, I didn't take his wallet. I didn't. He must have placed it in my coat pocket," Kat continued, desperate for her friend's help.

"Kat, honey," Emily began softly as concern rose in her voice. "I love you, but why do you think a cop would plant a stolen wallet in your coat?" Kat started to doubt her irrational thoughts as she heard Emily say them back to her. It did sound absurd, but it was the only thing Kat could think of.

"I know it sounds crazy, Emily. But the cop who arrested me was the same cop who passed by us that day—the one who gave me that creepy stare. He was the one who arrested me and he acted like it was all planned out," Kat pleaded desperately.

Emily let out a heavy sigh and continued. "Kat, you're under a lot of stress right now. Can you give your therapist a call?"

"Seriously?! My fucking therapist, Emily? I just want you to believe me. That's it. You're talking to me like I've lost my mind, not like a friend in need," Kat said with defeat in her voice. She tried to calm herself. She hated talking to her best friend so angrily, but she couldn't seem to get through to her. She knew she wasn't crazy.

"I'm sorry, Kat. Okay, let's say this Alex cop guy did plant his badge and wallet in your coat. What would he have to gain from it? Why would he do this?" Emily asked as she tried to reason with Kat.

Kat sat quietly for a few moments allowing the questions to reel through her mind. *True, what would he gain?* Kat thought, realizing that once again she had jumped the gun to the worst-case scenario and made a scene. As Emily's words sunk in, Kat began to relax, though doubt still weighed heavily in her mind.

"Yeah, you're right. I'm sorry. It's probably just a misunderstanding. Just take me to get my car, please," Kat said. She knew she sounded crazy, but the situation still bothered her. Kat knew that from now on she would have to keep her assumptions about the current situation to herself.

"You don't need to apologize. A lot has happened. I'm the one who's sorry," Emily said genuinely. "Go eat and rest…give your therapist a call, okay?" *Great, she thinks I'm fucking nuts,* Kat thought.

"Yeah, thanks," Kat said shortly as she stared out the window without another word as they crossed the city to the impound yard.

"Thanks for the ride. I'll wire you cash after my phone charges," Kat said as she was closing the door.

"Get some rest," Emily shouted out the window as she pulled away and left Kat to herself. *Rest. Yes, I need rest,* Kat thought. *And a shower. And food.* It was three in the afternoon and Kat was hungover, emotional, and wandering around like a zombie in a movie. She paid the impound lot and headed back to her parents' home. *What a mess,* she thought as she drove back through the city.

*****

After a hot shower and a leftover plate of the food others had brought her family, Kat finally made it to her bed. The funeral was over, the house was quiet again, and guests had stopped coming by to check in. Kat's anxiety began to grow as she thought about her summons for court the next morning. She just wanted to go home—her real home in Astoria. *Home,* she thought. *I miss it so much. Maybe I can just skip town? What's the worst that will happen if I don't go to court?*

The thought quickly passed as she remembered the charge wasn't a simple parking ticket. This was theft, and not just any theft—it was theft of a police officer's badge. There was no way she could just scoot off to Astoria and avoid the consequences. Justice would follow her back to Oregon. Besides, even if she could hide away in Astoria, she could never go back to the city to visit her family without the constant fear of the allegations catching up with her. Though it was morning, her eyes became heavy as she realized the only option was to face her fate, whatever it would be, in court the next day.

*****

"Hey Katrina…sweetie…are you doing okay? You've been out for quite some time now," Mr. Morgan said as he gently roused Kat from her much-needed slumber.

"Yeah, Dad. I'm just tired," a groggy Kat replied.

"Your mother and I want to get out of the house for a bit. Wanna meet us for a late-night dinner in a little while?" Mr. Morgan asked.

"Yeah, that sounds good," Kat said with a yawn as she rolled out of bed. "What time is it, anyway?"

"It's almost eight," Mr. Morgan replied. *Crap,* thought Kat. *I slept away the whole afternoon.*

*****

Later that night Kat joined her parents at their favorite restaurant as promised. They sat in a booth near the back of the restaurant and munched on the chips and salsa they had all grown to love over the years. The three of them were excited to spend time together that didn't involve planning a funeral. Between all the crises, they hadn't had a chance to catch up at all. Kat informed her parents of the details her new life in Astoria—most of the details, that is.

"I entered a few paintings into a local gallery right before everything happened," she said with mild excitement.

145

"That's great, Katrina! I'm so proud of you. I've always loved your art-work," Mrs. Morgan exclaimed, her voice full of pride.

As the family enjoyed their dinner, it warmed Kat to see her parents laugh again. It was something she hadn't seen in the time she'd been back in the city and she had been worried there was no getting over the loss of a child. Now, however, it seemed like they might actually be able to move on from the tragedy that had taken place. In the midst of their laughter, Kat saw a glimpse of hope that, in time, healing was possible.

Even in a moment of happiness with her family, Kat could only look down and pick at the food on her plate. When she finally looked up, she saw a group coming in to eat that made her heart sink into her stomach. The hostess guided the group directly to the table right next to where Kat and her family were seated. She gulped hard as she tried to move her focus back to her parents and ignore the group next to them.

"Good evening, officers. What can I get you guys to drink?" Kat over-heard the server ask the group.

Mrs. Morgan continued her story, but Kat was too distracted by her rac-ing thoughts. *Alex! Why is Alex here? And he's with the cop who arrested me! The one who gave me the creepy stare that day with Emily. Why are they together?!* The thoughts raced around the track of her mind as she tried to piece together the puzzle before her.

"I'm gonna run to the restroom real quick," Kat tried to whisper to her parents so the table next to them wouldn't hear. She rushed through the restroom door and began to splash cold water on her face in an unsuccessful effort to calm herself down. *I'm fucking crazy! I really am,* Kat thought. *No! This doesn't make sense. How can this possibly be a coincidence? Breathe, Kat! Four in, four out. Four in, four out.* She continued the breathing techniques Dr. Sampson taught her. She was aware her thoughts were paranoid and irrational, but she still struggled to calm herself down.

"Get yourself together, Kat," she said out loud to herself while staring into the mirror. Her own frigid eyes stared back at her in the reflection. "It's just stress. That's it." She took one last deep breath, adjusted her shirt, and headed out the door.

"Alex!" Kat said as she bumped into the stranger she'd spent the previ-ous night with.

"You never called," Alex said with a dirty grin on his face.

"You're fucking kidding, right?" Kat responded as anger boiled inside. The officer chuckled in response, amused at Kat's dismay. "You're a fucking joke. You put your wallet in my coat pocket!" Her voice began to rise before she re-membered her parents were in the restaurant as well.

"Shhh, no need to make a scene, Kat. You're pretty good at that, right?" Alex's grin grew larger as he taunted Kat.

"What are you talking about?" Kat asked as her forehead wrinkled with concern.

"Oh, nothing. But you did steal from me. Why would I put my own wallet in your coat? That sounds a bit…um…crazy, don't you think?" He lingered over the word *crazy* for a moment allowing Kat to soak it in. *It does sound crazy*, Kat thought. *But I'm not crazy.*

"No. It's not crazy. I'll get a lawyer and prove it," she snapped back.

The officer leaned in closer to Kat, invading her personal space, to whisper, "Oh yeah? Who's going to believe you? You're just a grieving sister whose brother just died. And, you go to a therapist for your history of paranoia, right?" Kat gulped hard as she processed what Alex had just whispered in her ear and she was at a loss for words. "Seems like you're getting a little paranoid again, Kat," the officer added with an evil chuckle before turning to walk away without a second look.

Kat could feel her heart pounding again. Confusion and fear were both loud within her. No part of the situation made any sense to her. *I'm not crazy. I know he put it in my pocket, right? Why would he say those things?* The questions continued with no answers. Fear grew larger with every thought, especially as she struggled to understand how he knew about her therapy. *How did he know? Did I tell him a drunken story? No! Emily! Why would she tell him? Why would she tell such personal things to a total stranger?* Kat had to get out of the suddenly sweltering restaurant. Her thoughts were suffocating her.

As she rushed by the group of officers, Kat quickly told her parents something had come up, but that she would see them at home. Her father and mother looked at each other with confused looks on their faces. Kat didn't want to see their disappointment if Alex or the other officer decided to let them in on her secret. She couldn't be near the group of officers who would surely continue to taunt her, so she hurried out of the restaurant without further explanation.

With tears in her eyes, Kat peeled out of the restaurant's parking lot without a destination in mind. Instead, she drove around the city as she contemplated her next move. After cruising for several city blocks, she pulled into an empty parking lot and grabbed her phone from her purse. She dialed Emily's number and demanded to know why she had broken their trust.

"Hey Kat, feeling better?" Emily said as she picked up.

"No! I'm not! Why did you tell Alex that I go to therapy? That's personal! And you told him I thought Max was following me, didn't you? Emily, why?!" Kat shouted into the phone.

"Who the hell is Alex?" Emily asked calmly.

"The cop who accused me of stealing from him!" Kat continued to shout into her friend's ear at the other end of the call.

"Kat, chill the fuck out. I promise I didn't tell anyone. I promise, Kat," Emily said, sounding defeated that her friend would accuse her of such a thing. "Kat, you're really worrying me. Go home and rest. You need sleep." Emily's voice was full of concern for her friend and it was clear she was being honest.

"I did sleep, Emily. I slept the whole fucking afternoon away," Kat said as her eyes teared up.

"Kat, you're just not making a whole lot of sense lately," Emily continued. Kat stayed silent as she processed Emily's words and sincerity. Emily had never lied to her before and she knew she had to trust her even if she didn't want to.

"I'm sorry, Emily. Fuck," Kat replied as she massaged her forehead.

"Dude, it's okay. Why would you think that anyway?" Emily's voice perked with curiosity.

"It doesn't even matter. I'll talk to you later. Love you," Kat said as she hung up to avoid further conversation and accusations that she was crazy.

*I don't get it,* Kat thought. *If Emily didn't tell Alex, then who did? How did he know something so personal and something that happened so far away from here? Did he go through my phone?* The realization that her personal business had been invaded made her feel even more uneasy and on edge.

# CHAPTER 29

It was close to midnight by the time Kat made it back to her parents' house. She walked slowly up the sidewalk to the front porch. She stared at Jerry's empty chair under the glaring brightness of the porch light.

"Jerry," she whispered to herself. "What a crazy day, Jerry." She spoke out loud to the empty chair as if Jerry were right in front of her. She let out a heavy sigh as her forehead wrinkled in thought. "Jerry!" she said again, this time louder and more confident as if a light bulb had just turned on in her head. She gulped hard as she remembered the last conversation she'd had with her brother.

"Don't trust anyone, Kat." The words rushed through her mind like a freight train and her heart pounded fast to meet the speed of the racing thought. *Is this what Jerry was talking about?* When she'd spoken to him that last time, he sounded crazy, just like she did now. Why had he said what he said about trusting people?

A soft crackling sound came from the shadowy yard behind her. It sounded like dry leaves crunching under someone's feet just beyond where the porch light's illumination reached. Kat jumped at the noise but didn't turn around. Her heart pounded again, but she didn't want to see what lurked in the dark. She rushed up to the door and into house locking the door behind her quickly. *It was nothing, Kat. Nothing is outside. It's just the wind,* she reassured herself silently.

She hid away in the guest room that had once been her bedroom and hoped whatever was outside wouldn't be able to find her. She laid on the bed alone with her racing thoughts. She had to find out what was going on. She had to find out what her brother had been talking about. She needed to find answers— her sanity depended upon knowing the truth.

How would she ever find the answers she needed? Why would a cop do what Alex and the other officer did to her? Who would even believe her if she did find out what happened? Her best friend didn't believe her.

As she laid in the quiet with her racing thoughts, she heard her parents' car pull into the driveway outside. She knew it would be another night of restless sleep, so she let out another heavy sigh trying to let the thoughts exhaust her. *Rest, I just need rest.* Sleep would either be her best friend or her worst enemy, but either way, her body longed for a good night's slumber.

A knock came at her door.

"Hey, hun. Just checking on you," Mrs. Morgan said as she opened the door. "Katrina are you okay? You rushed out of the restaurant so quickly." Kat jumped out of bed and rushed over to her mother.

"Mama, I need Jerry's house key. Please," Kat begged, ignoring the question her mother asked. Mrs. Morgan's face grew with deep concern, the same concern she'd had for Jerry before his death.

"What's wrong, Katrina?" her mother demanded sternly.

"Nothing, Mama. I just need to…um…look for something…something I gave Jerry a long time ago. Please," Kat continued pleading, hoping her mother would buy her story.

"Katrina, it's after midnight. Can't it wait until daylight?" Mrs. Morgan asked.

"No. I can't sleep. This will help and it will give me something to do, something to keep my mind busy," Kat pushed.

"Okay, Katrina. Just don't be gone too long. Please?" Mrs. Morgan said with concern.

Questions and thoughts raced through Kat's mind on the drive over to Jerry's house. *What the hell am I doing? Maybe Alex was just kidding. Maybe it was all a joke and I'm just blowing this out of proportion. Maybe I'm just being paranoid.* Doubt set in as Kat tried to analyze the situation and her thoughts. *But how did he know such a personal thing?* That question alone brought reason back to Kat's late-night excursion.

Kat pulled into the driveway of her brother's lonesome house. She took a deep breath and debated whether she should go snooping around his house at one in the morning. *I should wait until morning,* she told herself as her heartbeat picked up again. Curiosity erased the last trace of doubt in her mind and she opened the car door to creep up the steps to her brother's front porch.

Jerry lived at the far edge of the city, far enough out that the stars shone brightly. The air was cool and dry and only noises from the nearby freeway broke the stillness of the night. The door creaked as she slowly pushed it open, afraid of what she might find inside. She closed it quietly behind her, not wanting to disturb the silence.

She flipped the light switch and stood still for a few moments to observe the lifeless room that stood before her. Kat's forehead wrinkled with disbelief and her heart thumped hard against her chest as she made her way around the room. She carefully stepped around the papers scattered all over the floor. Things seemed to be out of place.

In the bedroom, the dresser drawers were pulled out. Clothes had been thrown around and every closet door was flung open. Items that seemed to once have a place on a shelf now laid unusually on the floor.

Kat's heart pounded harder and faster. *Something isn't right,* she realized silently. *Someone has been here. But who?* She knew her parents hadn't been to the house since Jerry's death. She rationalized that Jerry must have gotten upset before he took his own life. She tried to resist the hysteria and irrational thoughts, but she *knew* someone had been there. She could feel it deep in her conscience. Someone had been there to look for the same thing Kat was.

As she entered Jerry's office, she ran her fingers over the surface of his desk.

"Jerry," she whispered as she picked up a business card that laid on the desk.

*Jeremiah Morgan*
*Breaking News Reporter*
*Metropolitan Online News*

She took the card and slipped it into the pocket of her jeans as a memento of her brother's hard work to build his career. "What happened, Jerry?" she whispered, knowing there would be no response. Just then the sound of a clink came from the other side of the house and she jumped in fright.

"Fuck! What was that?!" she exclaimed in a soft voice to herself. She gulped hard and froze, debating whether she should investigate the unknown sound. *Oh Kat, just calm down,* she told herself as she stood frozen in place. *It was just the house settling. It's nothing.* She tried to reassure herself that she was still alone.

Her breathing was heavy and her heart pounded up into her throat making it difficult to swallow. *Clink, clink,* sounded again, this time louder. Kat armed herself with a baseball bat sitting in the corner, the closest thing to a weapon she could find in the disorganized room. She crept slowly out of her brother's office toward the noise that left her trembling with fear. With every step she took, her heart pounded louder with the unknown.

"Hello?" her quivering voice said with fearful curiosity. *Clink, clink,* was the only response and it terrified her.

The rhythm of her breathing was the only thing grounding her at the moment. She allowed herself to listen to the fast breaths she took, hoping it would calm her. Just as she turned the corner back into the living room, she saw the window opened and let out a loud shriek.

"Who's in here?!" she shouted as she looked behind her in fear. She quickly scanned the room and held the bat above her head, ready to fight.

The pounding of her heart grew and the drift of air through the open window caught the blinds and flung them back against the window sill. *Clink, clink,* sounded from the window as the blinds tapped against the glass. Kat hurried to the window, closing and locking it quickly. Afraid that someone was looking in, Kat rushed around the house and closed the other blinds as she double-checked each room for any possible threat.

*Was the window open when I got here?* she asked herself, struggling to remember. *Surely I would have noticed, right?* She continued to ponder and question everything around her. She could no longer tell what was real and what wasn't. She let out a sigh hoping it would relieve the tension overwhelming her.

Back in the living room, Kat allowed herself to plop down on her brother's sofa and rested her head against the back. *God Kat, what are you doing?* she asked herself silently. She took a deep breath and moved herself to the edge of the sofa letting her head fall into her hands. She had been running on adrenaline for too long and her body was starting to fight back. She massaged her temples as she tried to regain some energy.

As she opened her eyes and lifted her head, something caught her attention across the room. The rug that laid under the small TV stand was out of place. The corner of it was folded upward exposing a seam in the hardwood floor beneath. *That's unusual,* she thought.

Curiosity rose again and helped her regain her energy. She jumped up to examine the area. She lifted the part of the rug that was free and saw a board placed in the floor where a piece of the hardwood flooring had once been. Kat's heart pounded again, a familiar feeling that seemed to be her norm.

Needing to satisfy her curiosity, Kat stood up and pushed the TV stand away from the wall and slid the rug along with it. The board was a lot heavier than she thought, but she managed to get it up from the floor. Beneath the board, a black trunk was hidden and covered in a thin layer of dust. *What is this,* Kat wondered. *What the hell did Jerry have to hide under his floor?*

She grabbed the large trunk and struggled to pull it out onto the floor next to its hiding place. She took a deep breath and swallowed a hard gulp, not knowing whether she wanted to see what her brother had to hide from the world. She tucked her hair behind her ears and slowly opened the trunk. The inside was filled with different folders of paperwork, newspaper clippings, and several flash drives. As Kat picked up one of the folders, dozens of photographs spilled out.

"Oh God," she whispered as she bent down to pick up the fallen photographs. "What is this?" She held in her hands the photos of two seemingly dead bodies. Other photographs showed Alex, the man from the night before, disposing of the bodies into a makeshift grave. Kat's stomach turned in knots.

Overwhelmed, she could feel vomit starting to rise in her throat. She swallowed hard again, forcing her nausea to settle. Two other men Kat didn't recognize were also in some of the photographs and a fourth man stood out from the rest—it was the officer who arrested her.

"Fuck, fuck, fuck!" Kat said as her anxiety shot through the roof. She wasn't sure what she was looking at, but she knew whoever had been to her brother's house had been looking for the same thing. Whatever secrets this trunk hid weren't good.

Kat picked up the rest of the photos and placed them carefully back into the trunk. As she gathered everything, she read one of the headlines from a newspaper clipping: *Local missing couple still not found.* The headline made her shiver—the photo of the missing couple in the newspaper looked just like the two dead bodies in the photographs. Another headline caught her attention: *Officer found dead in home, death ruled suicide.* As fear began to overtake Kat, she knew she had to get out of Jerry's house. She shoved everything back into the trunk and secured the latches.

The trunk wasn't easy to carry, so she slid it across the room and out onto the porch. She hurried to lock the door behind her as she noticed the quiet of the night. The quiet scared her, the darkness panicked her, but she forced herself to leave the porch defenselessly into the open yard and dragged the trunk to her car.

She secured the trunk in the backseat of the rental car, feeling the whole time as if someone was watching her. She hurried into the driver's seat and backed out of her brother's driveway. *Just hurry, Kat. Get back to the freeway,* she encouraged herself silently.

As she pulled away, she saw a car's headlights turn on in her rearview mirror and follow behind her.

"Oh fuck. Fuck!" Kat said as she drove faster. The faster she went, the faster the car behind her followed. *Get back to a more populated area. Get back to the city. Get away from whoever is following you.*

Kat's heart slowed as she approached the freeway. Familiar and busy territory comforted her and she hoped she could lose the car behind her in the heavier traffic. In a few minutes, the car that was once behind her was no longer visible in her mirror. She hoped it was gone, but she knew it could be lurking a few cars behind in the freeway traffic out of her view.

"Oh God, Jerry. What were you into?" Kat frantically asked out loud. "What is going on? So I'm not crazy, right? I'm not paranoid, right?" The new information she found overwhelmed her. It was four in the morning and she had to be in court by eight going on no sleep and plenty of adrenaline.

"Crap! Court!" Kat exclaimed. *The trunk—where will I hide the trunk?* She couldn't risk anyone finding it or taking it. All the answers she sought could be in that trunk. There were probably more answers than she wanted to know, but if she expected to sort out Jerry's death she would have to go through everything. She had to understand what drove her brother to kill himself. *Just get back home,* Kat told herself. *I'll figure it all out then.*

# CHAPTER 30

Kat pulled into her parents' driveway at nearly five in the morning. The death of her brother and his funeral had been draining enough, but the events that unfolded since then had sucked the last bit of energy from her tired soul.

Her heart finally gave her a break from the rapid speed it had been racing at all night. She had court in three hours and she was in possession of a large trunk of disturbing information her brother had hidden from the world. Despite this, Kat was calm. She was too exhausted to care or process any more of the situation. She only cared enough to focus on hiding the trunk full of secrets.

As quietly as she could, Kat slid the trunk to her parents' front door and down the hall to the guest room. She closed and locked the door gently behind her as she searched the room for a hiding place. She cleared a spot in the back of the room's closet and buried the trunk under a pile of clothing where it was once again hidden from the world. She pushed the closet door closed gently and sat a chair in front of it hoping no one would find it in the little time she'd be away for her court appointment.

*I need sleep. Just a little,* Kat thought. *Just an hour. That would be enough.* Although she was afraid of oversleeping before her court hearing, her body demanded sleep. She set an alarm for one hour and fifteen minutes hoping it would give her enough rest to get through court. Her heavy eyes closed and she drifted into a pleasant slumber.

\*\*\*\*\*

"Jerry, can you get the veggies from inside, please," a pretty, red-haired woman called out to Kat's brother. Kat had never seen the woman before, but she obviously adored Jerry.

"Sure thing, honey," Jerry called back as he left the grill to fulfill the woman's request. Kat sipped her cold lemonade under an umbrella in the middle of Jerry's back yard. The trees had just bloomed and the soft green grass was vibrant in color.

"Here you go, hun," Jerry said as he walked back outside and gave the woman a kiss on her cheek as he handed off the plate. As Kat watched, she thought to herself that there was something different about her brother. It was the way he walked—he walked without a limp. His skin had a slight glow again and he was perfect. His hair was neatly combed and the clothes he wore fit his frame perfectly.

Birds were chirping loudly and a rush of peace and happiness came over Kat. As she continued to sip from her glass, she wondered why Jerry never came over to talk to her. That's all she wanted—one more conversation with him. As much as she wanted that one last conversation, she was still joyful watching Jerry and the woman interact. She looked at them laughing together and their happiness made Kat's smile stretch from ear to ear.

"I love you, Charmeine, my beautiful wife," Jerry told the red-haired woman.

"I love you too," the woman said gently while blowing him a kiss.

*Ah, his wife. His beautiful wife who adored him. That's who she is,* Kat realized. It made her smile even more. Jerry was happy and at peace and it comforted Kat. She was filled with joy knowing that he now had a peaceful and happy life, finally married to a happy and caring woman.

Kat was woken by the alarm on her phone. Her body felt heavy and it was difficult to make herself get out of bed. When she did finally manage to stand up, she took a quick shower and got dressed up the best she could with the few clothes she'd brought with her in her rush from Astoria. Because of the lack of time, she skipped her usual morning coffee and stumbled around to try and prepare for the rough day ahead of her.

*How am I going to get out of this?* she wondered. It was Alex and the other officer's word against hers and now she knew there was more to the story than she originally thought. The consequences of a conviction this serious could be harsh and she knew the outcome had the potential to change her life forever. The thought made her anxiety even worse.

At five minutes before eight o'clock, Kat pulled into the court parking lot and rushed inside the courthouse. She was quickly passed through the security checkpoint and took a seat in the back of the courtroom. As she waited for her name to be called, the arresting officer and Alex walked in and found a seat across from her. Her heart pounded the familiar fast-paced beat as the two men gave her a glare from across the main aisle making her more uneasy. After seeing the pictures of the two men with the dead bodies, she knew the men who accused her were full of deception.

*Crap! Why didn't I bring the pictures I found,* Kat thought quickly to herself. *Surely I could have used them somehow today. But how?* She had no idea who she could trust in the city with the new information she'd just uncovered. It was completely plausible that the judge might even be in on whatever scandal the officers were wrapped up in.

156

*I just want to go home,* Kat thought. She hadn't been able to book any sort of return trip to Astoria yet, but she had already decided that after her hearing she would go straight to the travel agent who had booked her secret move to Oregon in hopes that she could help her get home as quickly and safely as she had done before.

"Next on the docket, the State versus Katrina Morgan, arraignment hearing twenty-five dash one zero six," the court clerk announced. Kat's heart beat faster and nervousness grew inside as she stumbled to the front of the room and waited in front of a microphone. The district attorney stood at another microphone awaiting the judge's instructions.

"Please state your full name, Miss Morgan," the judge asked as everyone settled into their new seats closer to the front of the courtroom. Kat swallowed hard and, with a shaking voice, she did as directed.

"Katrina Marie Morgan," she said as she looked the judge in the eye trying to determine whose side he was on.

"Miss Morgan, you are being arraigned today on charges of theft, specifically the theft of a police officer's wallet, a misdemeanor under state law, and his badge, a third-degree felony under state law. The theft of the officer's badge has resulted in an additional charge of attempted impersonation of a police officer, a state-level misdemeanor. Before we present any evidence, how would you like to plea, Miss Morgan?"

"Um…not…" Kat began presenting her not guilty plea, but she was quickly interrupted by the man who had been taunting her.

"Your honor," Alex said as he stood up from the courtroom bench where he'd been seated quietly. "May I approach the bench, your honor?" His voice was suddenly sweet with false sincerity and he gave Kat the crooked smile he'd given her the night before at the restaurant. The judge signaled for Alex to proceed to the front of the room with an annoyed look on his face. As he began speaking to the judge, Kat strained to hear the words he was quietly speaking to the judge.

"Your honor, I would actually like to request that the charges against Miss Morgan be dismissed. This was all a misunderstanding. It turned out to be an honest mistake on my part and I apologize to the court," Alex said as he looked back toward Kat with another sleazy grin. "I forgot that I asked Miss Morgan to hold my belongings as I used the restroom at the pub the night before. I forgot to ask for my wallet back and didn't remember giving it to her, so I assumed she stole it from me. I haven't had a chance to clear this up prior to now and I'm very sorry for wasting the court's time."

"Okay, then," the judge said with impatience in his voice as he wrote something down. He looked Kat's direction sympathetically as he continued. "Let the victim's statement be entered into the record. Miss Morgan, this case is dismissed with prejudice. I am truly sorry you were falsely accused. You are free to go." He gathered the papers in front of him and handed them to the court clerk before striking his gavel.

*What?! That did not happen!* Kat thought as anger boiled inside her. *I don't remember any of this happening. He's lying!* As she walked out of the courtroom, she was torn between relief that the case had been dismissed and anger that it had been dismissed under such circumstances. She massaged her forehead as she tried to make sense of what happened in the courtroom. *Saturday night was a blur, but surely I would have remembered Alex handing me his things, right? Maybe I am a nut,* she thought as she remembered Emily's words. *So it was just a misunderstanding, then?* Confusion mounted and Kat doubted everything that had happened the past two days, including the trunk she'd found in her brother's house.

As she walked quickly to her car, Alex ran up behind her.

"Kat!" he shouted. She cringed at the voice that called her name.

"What?!" Kat snapped as she turned around.

"I just wanted to apologize for accusing you of stealing from me. I'm truly sorry," Alex said in the same charming voice he had the night she met him. Kat stared blankly back at him and squinted, allowing rage to fill her emotions.

"You're kidding, right?!" she said as she attempted to process Alex's apology and whether it was sincere.

"No, I'm serious. I'm sorry," Alex apologized again.

"You planted that wallet in my coat, falsely accused me of stealing, called me paranoid, and then fabricated some bullshit story. I don't get it, Alex! Just stay away from me!" Kat said as she raised her voice in the parking lot, not caring who heard.

"There you go with that, Kat. No one planted anything! I made an honest mistake and I'm sorry," Alex said with the sneaky grin creeping up on his face once again. "Sleep deprivation will do that to you, Kat. Maybe you should spend more time sleeping and less time wandering the city at night." He turned and walked away, not giving Kat a chance at rebuttal.

Her heart pounded as her mind raced back to the hundreds of thoughts she'd been processing the past few days. *I've got to get home,* she thought again. *Things around here are too fucked up.* She tried to understand all the crazy things happening around her, but nothing made sense. *Why would Alex admit what he did last night in the restaurant? Why did he tell the judge those lies? What is the whole point of all this?* The questions kept piling up in Kat's mind, but she was too tired to process it all.

*Fuck! Maybe I was too drunk to remember? Maybe he was telling the truth?* Kat's doubt grew larger and larger with every passing moment. She started to doubt whether she could even trust herself anymore.

She took a deep breath and tried her best to push the thoughts out of her head. *Home…let's just focus on getting home to Astoria,* she thought as she made her way back to her parents' house.

# CHAPTER 31

Kat stopped on the way back to her parents' house to buy the biggest duffel bag she could find. Dragging the heavy trunk all the way back to Oregon was out of the question. The bulky box would slow her down and draw unwanted attention she didn't need. The duffel bag was large, but she could easily use it to carry both her clothes and the contents of the trunk.

She rushed into the house as soon as she pulled into her parents' driveway. She carried the empty duffel bag to the guest room and began to transfer everything from the trunk to the bottom of the duffel bag. Kat quickly cleared out her suitcase and placed all her clothes into the duffel bag to hide the contents at the bottom. If anyone decided to snoop through her bag, they would have to sift through her clothes to find what lay at the bottom.

*I should really try to sleep more before I leave*, Kat thought as she zipped the duffel bag closed and shoved the empty trunk and suitcase into the closet. *I hate to leave my parents on short notice again.* It was becoming an ugly trend in her life, but she had to leave today before some other unknown chaos from the city invaded her life.

"Hey, mom, dad, there's a big project waiting for me at work, so I need to head out today," Kat said as cheerfully as possible, hoping they would buy her lie.

"Oh. Well, okay, Kat. We understand, honey," Mrs. Morgan replied, trying to hide the disappointment in her voice. "We knew you'd have to go back eventually. Do you want us to take you to the airport or train station?"

"No thanks. I'm okay. I need to a make a quick stop somewhere before I head out," Kat said, hoping her parents wouldn't pry.

Kat hated herself for leaving what was left of her family after Jerry's death. But she also knew she had a life waiting for her in Astoria and she missed it dearly.

"We will be okay, Katrina. So will you," Mrs. Morgan said, noticing the concern on Kat's face.

"I just hate leaving you guys after everything," Kat said as a tear rolled down her cheek and she choked back a sob.

"Life must go on, Katrina. It *will* go on. It *must* go on," Mrs. Morgan replied with a smile. Kat hugged her mother tightly, wishing she could take her parents home to Astoria with her.

"I love you, Momma," Kat whispered as she gave her mother another tight squeeze.

"Dad, I love you too," Kat said softly as she wiped another tear away and gave her father the same tight hug.

"We'll come visit soon," Mr. Morgan said as Kat finally let go.

"That sounds wonderful. Love you guys. I'll check in with you when I get home," she said as she grabbed the heavy duffel bag and headed to the door.

"We love you too. Be safe," Mr. Morgan said as Kat walked out the door.

*****

The sun was bright and the weather was breezy and dry. *I can't wait for that coastal air,* Kat thought to herself as she drove to the travel agency to arrange her last-minute trip back home. Nothing Alex said had made any sense to Kat. His newfound charm in court had put her even more on edge. *Stop thinking about it, Kat,* she told herself. *Just focus on getting home and you can deal with everything else later.*

When she parked outside the agency where she'd arranged her first journey to Oregon, she grabbed the duffel bag out of the backseat of the car and held it close. She couldn't risk leaving it anywhere out of her sight. It was a hassle carrying it up to the office building with her, but it was a necessary hassle.

"Hi, I'm looking for a woman who helped me arrange my travel about a year ago," Kat said to the young man at the reception desk.

"Well, good afternoon ma'am. I would love to help you. Do you know her name?" the man asked politely.

"Oh...actually, I don't. But she had light brown curly hair and...um... her office was right over there, to the left of the filing cabinet," Kat said as she pointed to the office where the woman had helped her find a way to leave the city in secret nearly a year earlier. Though she was nervous about her trip back home, she was excited to let the woman know about all the good things that happened when she'd arrived in Astoria and that she had succeeded in removing Max from her life.

"Oh...Mrs. Roberts..." the man replied as his smile faded and he looked down to the floor.

"Oh yes! That's it. Is she available?" Kat asked as her voice perked.

"I'm sorry. Mrs. Roberts isn't with us any longer," the man said quietly, avoiding eye contact.

"Oh, okay. Do you know where I could find her? She's...um, kind of a friend," Kat replied as her concern grew.

"Ma'am, I'm sorry to tell you this, but Mrs. Roberts passed away almost a year ago. It was all over the news. I'm surprised you didn't hear about it."

"Oh…I've been out of town since the last time I saw her," Kat clarified as her voice shook.

"Her cause of death was ruled unknown, but the rumor is that it was a possible homicide, probably a poisoning," the man explained.

"What?!" Kat asked quickly. *Oh God! Homicide!* she thought as she tried to process the news. "Oh, that's just horrible!" Kat said as her forehead wrinkled with concern. She wasn't sure what to do next.

"Is there something *I* could help you with instead?" the man asked cautiously.

"No, thank you," Kat replied as she shifted the weight of the duffel bag on her arm. "I'll just buy the tickets at the train station. I was hoping to see Mrs. Roberts, but this is just terrible news." Kat turned and walked to the door as her brain fogged with confusion.

"Safe travels, then," the man replied as he focused back on his computer.

Kat stuffed the bag into the back seat again and climbed in the driver's seat to drop the car off at the rental office. There were two blocks between the car rental office and the train station and she knew she would have to walk quickly between the two. The thought of walking in the open with a bag of incriminating evidence made her anxious. She was going on little sleep, no caffeine, and an empty stomach, and her adrenaline was fading quickly. If someone did try something, she wasn't sure what she could do to stop them.

*I'll sleep on the train,* she told herself. *I just have to make it to the train and I'll be okay.* She parked the car in the rental lot, grabbed the bag out of the back seat and rushed inside to drop off the keys. Outside, she quickly scanned the area before proceeding. In the city, she once again felt like she was constantly being watched.

*Only two blocks away, Kat. Just two blocks.* The noisy and busy streets gave her a headache and heightened her anxiety. Every honk made her jump and every loud engine startled her. *Just breathe, Kat. Just breathe.*

"Food. I need food," she spoke out loud to herself trying to drown out the noises around her as she entered the train station and walked up to the counter.

"When is your next train leaving? I need a ticket to Portland, Oregon," Kat said groggily to the clerk on the other side of the window.

"It leaves at 1:05 this afternoon, ma'am," the clerk replied. "You have about an hour before boarding begins."

"Perfect," Kat said with relief. "I'll take one, please. Is there room in a sleeping car available?"

Kat finished her ticket purchase with a sigh of relief. She was almost out of the city once again. Her stomach growled with hunger when she saw a man selling hot dogs at the edge of the station. *That will have to do,* Kat thought as she adjusted the heavy bag on her shoulder and made her way over to satisfy her hunger.

Kat was careful to keep the duffel bag close to her as she waited for the train. Finally, it was time to board and she hugged the bag against her body as she climbed onto the train and found her assigned cabin. She happily forked out the extra money for the sleeping room to have the rest and privacy she desperately needed. Her next forty-eight hours would be spent on the train and she figured she might as well use the time to catch up on her lost sleep.

She felt like she could breathe easier the moment the train departed. It was once again a relief to be going as far away as possible from the tragedy of her brother's death, far away from Alex and the men who were taunting her, far away from the sadness that lingered in the city.

With the cabin door securely locked, Kat stretched out on the bed and entwined her arms in the straps of the duffel bag as it laid next to her on the narrow mattress.

"Finally," she spoke out loud to herself. Quiet finally surrounded her once again. The rattle and clack of the train over the rails reminded her of the ticking of a clock and helped ease her into the isolation she had grown to love.

*Things don't add up,* Kat thought to herself. Again, she struggled to make sense of Alex's superficial sincerity. *Why did Jerry have that trunk full of dark secrets? Was he a part of it? Surely not, right? And the travel agent—dead!* As much as she wanted to rest, her mind kept racing. The unknown answers troubled her. Confusion clouded her thoughts and her judgment. Every passing thought or question she pondered made her doubt everything around her.

Kat had been so irrational in the past that she couldn't tell whether there was a valid reason to be fearful in this case. She didn't know whether to trust her surroundings, no matter where she was. Her forehead wrinkled at the thought. The only person she could truly trust was herself, and now even that seemed questionable.

*Just wait until you get home. Just wait,* she told herself silently. *You can go through everything and, hopefully, get answers then.* As much as she wanted clarity in the situation, her body overpowered her mind and finally fell into a long, deep slumber she had longed for.

*****

Gasping for air, Kat woke up in a panic. "Crap! Where am I?!" she wondered as she tried to untangle herself from the duffel bag's straps to jump out of bed. Her body finally felt rested, but she was disoriented and her mind was groggy.

She peeked out the closed curtain and saw the familiar Northwest coastal trees she had fallen in love with.

"What day is it?" she whispered to herself. The unknown made her heart pound. *Calm down, Kat. Calm down,* she told herself. It took a moment for her to wake fully and check her phone for the date and time. Just then, she felt the slowing of the train and an announcement broke in over the speaker on the wall.

"Arriving in Portland, Oregon," the message declared in a soft computerized voice.

"Crap! I slept two days away!" Kat whispered again with surprise that she had slept such a long time.

Before exiting, she pulled her keyring out of the duffel bag and held it in her hand with the keys poking through the spaces between her fingers like claws. *Just in case,* she thought. She threw the bag over her shoulder and headed for the train's exit door.

# CHAPTER 32

As Kat stepped out onto the platform from the train, her senses welcomed the smell of fresh rain and the sight of the vibrant greenery all around. The sky was overcast—no more bright, glaring sun. It was just the weather she liked. *Almost home*, she thought.

It was nine in the morning when she spotted Mr. Stevenson waiting to pick her up at the curb, just as he promised. As Kat had munched her hot dog back in the city two days ago, she had called Mr. Stevenson asking him for the favor. *What a great boss*, she thought to herself as she approached him standing next to his car.

"Oh, Kat, I'm so sorry about your brother," Mr. Stevenson said as he gave Kat a hug. "We've all missed you at the office."

"Thank you. I've missed you guys too," Kat said warmly. The truth was, she really *did* miss them. Her coworkers were now part of her new home. *Home*, she thought. *I've missed home dearly.* "You're a sight for sore eyes, Luke," Kat said as Mr. Stevenson opened the door for her and she climbed into the car.

"Here, I'll put your bag in the trunk," Luke said, trying to be helpful.

"Oh, no thanks…um…I'll keep it with me in the front seat. No biggie," Kat said, taken off guard by the thought of being separated from the bag when she was almost home.

"You truly are strange, Katrina Morgan, but that's why we love you," Luke joked with a chuckle as he closed the door and walked around to the driver's side. Kat smiled, remembering that her brother's sense of humor was so much like Luke's.

Kat stuffed the large bag between her feet on the floor board.

"Two hours will seem a lot longer sitting like that," Luke continued with a chuckle as he climbed in and started the car. "You act like you're carrying hidden treasure." He grinned as Kat gulped hard.

"Yeah, something like that," she said with a nervous laugh. "It's just some of my brother's stuff and I want to make sure it arrives safely." She quickly changed the subject before Luke pushed any further. "Can we get some food for the road?"

165

"Yeah, no problem. What sounds good?" Mr. Stevenson asked with a smile.

"A huge, juicy cheeseburger would be nice," Kat said as she rubbed her stomach.

"Good choice, but I'm not sure where we will find a cheeseburger at 9:30 in the morning," Mr. Stevenson replied with a laugh.

"Valid point. Breakfast burritos could do? And coffee, please?" Kat replied with a grin. *Coffee, my dear friend,* Kat thought to herself with a quiet laugh.

As the two headed out of Portland, Kat's stomach knotted every time they drive over or under a bridge. She thought of Jerry. All she could see was her brother hanging lifeless from each bridge. Her imagination overwhelmed her. *Oh Jerry, why?* she questioned silently, knowing she would get no response from her brother. She took a deep breath and swallowed a hard gulp, trying to push out the disturbing thoughts entering her mind. Every time she closed her eyes, all she could see was her brother's limp body, hanging with a noose around his neck.

A tear trickled down her cheek and she wiped it away quickly before Mr. Stevenson noticed. She didn't want to open any discussions about what was racing through her mind at the moment. *I wonder who found him?* Kat pondered. *I pray whoever did is able to find comfort.*

Kat smiled at a sign up ahead on the side of the road:

*East Mooring Basin Boat Ramp, Next Right*

"Yes, finally home!" she exclaimed with excitement.

"Home, sweet home?" Mr. Stevenson asked.

"Yes, home. Very sweet," Kat replied anxiously. She couldn't wait to be in her house again.

A few minutes later, the two pulled into Kat's long driveway from the winding road.

"Thank you so much, Luke," Kat said gratefully as she climbed out of the car and heaved the duffel bag over her shoulder.

"Anytime. I'll see you Monday," Mr. Stevenson said as Kat closed the door and he backed out of the driveway. Kat was thankful for a few more days off before she had to go back to work. It would give her the time and peace to try and find the answers she sought.

Kat was pleased to be home. She carefully walked up the steps to her front door. The thought that there could be someone inside waiting for her crossed her mind. With the turn of events, she couldn't take any chances. After unlocking the door, she grabbed the keys between her fingers as she had done at the train station and prepared to defend herself.

She stepped inside and quickly locked the door behind her. The house was quiet. Only the creaks from the hardwood floor sounded as she stepped forward. She examined the house carefully, only noticing the objects she'd thrown to the floor, still laying haphazardly about. The items she'd wiped clean off the dining room table were still scattered on the floor where she had left them.

A heavy sigh escaped her lips as she headed upstairs dragging the large duffel bag. *I'll clean up later,* she thought. Once in her room, she closed and locked the door behind her. She felt she needed the extra privacy even there in her own empty house.

She sat down next to the bag in the middle of the floor and opened it quickly. She took all the clothes out and threw them next to the hamper by the closet.

"Okay, Jerry. Let's see what you were doing," Kat said quietly to the silence around her. She took everything out of the bottom of the bag and looked over the pile of documents and photographs.

Her heart began to race as she indulged herself in the pile of disturbing items scattered around her on the floor. As she looked through the newspaper clippings and photos, confusion and questions grew. *Nothing links Jerry to any of it, so why did he have all of this?* she wondered to herself.

A hard knock sounded on the front door downstairs and Kat jumped at the loud banging. "Shit!" she said out loud. Her heart's speed raced as she quickly shoved everything under the bed and ran downstairs. She slowed her speed as she neared the door.

"Who is it?" Kat shouted nervously.

"Mrs. McKay, darling," the voice on the other side responded.

Kat let out a sigh of relief and opened the door.

"Hi, Mrs. McKay. How can I help you?" Kat asked, hoping the conversation with her neighbor would be quick so she could get back to her investigation.

"I have a piece of mail for you, dear. It was delivered to my house by mistake. I've had it for a while now, but you haven't been home since then. I'm so glad you're back. Mr. McKay was on the porch and saw you pull up," the elderly woman said as she handed Kat a bright yellow envelope.

"Thank you," Kat replied simply as she reached for the envelope. Her heart sank into her stomach as she read the name on the return address: *Jeremiah Morgan.* She remained frozen for a moment as she stared at the envelope in her hands.

"Are you alright, dear?" the woman asked her with concern. "You look like you've just seen a ghost."

"Um…yes. I'm fine, thank you," Kat replied as she snapped back to the present. Questions and curiosity had filled her mind after seeing her brother's name and she was momentarily lost in thought.

As soon as Mrs. McKay walked down her steps, Kat shut and locked the door and hurried back upstairs. The envelope was postmarked a week before Jerry's death. Kat swallowed hard and opened the envelope.

*Dear Katrina,*

*I have an unwavering feeling that something bad is going to happen to me. You're the only one I trust to help me. About a year ago, a black trunk was placed on my front porch with a note from a police officer named Duke Conway that read, "Help me". Two days later, he was found dead in his home. I started to investigate the disturbing information I found inside. I'm so close to breaking this story, Kat, but I feel like I'm losing my mind. I really think people are after me. I think they're following me, Kat. I can feel them watch me. I can hear their whispers. Kat, if anything happens to me, get the trunk to a media source outside the city. I don't trust anyone here. And Kat, be careful who you trust. I love you.*

*Jerry*

Kat read the letter twice, and both times her heart pounded faster and faster with each word. Questions flooded her mind.

"Is he saying he thought someone was going to hurt him? So he *was* involved, but it was a story he was working on?" Kat asked out loud over and over.

The thought that came next made her boil with rage. *If there is a possibility he didn't kill himself, then who did?* she wondered.

"No! No! This is crazy, too crazy! Just calm down, Kat!" she yelled out loud to herself as she paced around the room.

The chaos was too much, too strong. She doubted everything around her and every thought she had. It was overwhelming and Kat couldn't tell if the information she was drowning in was real or not.

She continued to pace in her bedroom and with every step she took, her anger rose. "Did they...did they murder my brother?!" Kat screamed as she picked up the lighthouse lamp and threw it against the wall as hard as she could.

"No! No, Jerry! No!" Kat screamed again. Pieces of the ceramic lamp shattered across her floor. She grabbed a pillow and screamed the loudest scream she could into the fluff of the pillow.

Kat's body grew heavy and she laid down on the floor in a quiet sob. Tears found her again as she imagined what could have happened to her brother. *This can't be real,* she thought. *Nothing makes sense and these things don't happen in real life.*

"I've gotta get out of here," Kat said as she quickly rose and loaded all the papers back into the bag under her bed.

*****

Kat drove fiercely down the winding road into town and passed by the diner.

*Kyle! I can talk to Kyle,* Kat thought, remembering the time he told her if she ever needed a friend to come and find him. *It's all I have at the moment,* she thought.

She parked her car and ran up to the diner, quickly observing her surroundings. Even though she was out of the city, the feeling of paranoia and the sensation of being watched were still very much present.

"Is Kyle in?" Kat said as she rushed through the door clanging the bell loudly. Her hasty and noisy entrance startled a waitress near the front of the diner.

"Yeah, he's back in his office," the waitress answered as she gave Kat a disapproving glare.

"Thanks," Kat said as she hurried back through the kitchen doors and back to Kyle's office.

"Kyle?" Kat inquired cautiously as she crept into his office breathing heavily.

"Kat!" Kyle said, shocked to see her.

"I need you, Kyle...I need your help! I don't know who else to turn to," Kat said, winded and struggling to catch her breath.

Kyle stood up quickly with his eyes widened. "What is it, Kat? Are you okay?" he asked with nervousness in his voice.

"Things are happening, Kyle, things I don't understand. I feel crazy, Kyle. I think I'm losing it," Kat revealed as tears rolled down her cheeks.

"Kat, Kat. Breathe. Slow down," Kyle said trying to calm her down.

"Kyle, I think my brother was murdered. I think people were following me. I think they're watching me. And not just anyone, Kyle—the cops. I think some cops murdered my brother...and...made it look like a suicide. I know it sounds crazy, but there's so much going on," Kat said, speaking quickly between labored breaths.

"Oh God, Kat. Oh shit. No!" Kyle said as he stared into Kat's fragile blue eyes. He started to pace back and forth in his office and quickly combed his hair back with his hands. "Oh, Kat, I'm so sorry."

"I know I sound crazy, Kyle, but—" Kat continued, but was interrupted quickly by Kyle.

"No Kat, you don't sound crazy. You don't," Kyle said nervously. "Fuck, Kat! Fuck!" He walked over and slammed the office door closed. "Kat, I should've told you something a long time ago," he continued, taking a step back from her.

Kat's heart pounded hard at the sound of Kyle's words. "Should have told me *what* a long time ago? What is it, Kyle?!" Kat shouted angrily.

"Kat, I'm sorry. I'm so sorry. I didn't know they were serious. I didn't know they would do something so cruel. Fuck!" he responded in a shaky voice.

"Kyle, if you don't explain to me what's going on, I swear I'll cut your throat right here and watch you bleed out," Kat said as her voice quieted and her teeth clenched together. Kyle took another step back and gulped a hard gulp.

"A week before I met you in the diner I got a phone call. It was a man's voice. He told me to befriend you—to get close to you, to listen if you said any-thing unusual or incriminating and report back to him. He sent me your picture and everything," Kyle said with his eyes locked on Kat's waiting for her reaction.

Kat stood silently as more fear, more rage, and more confusion grew deep within her bones.

"*That's* why you were so friendly to me, Kyle? Really?! So I'm guessing you didn't just overthrow your dog's ball by accident that day at the beach, right? You told me if I ever needed anything, to let you know! *That's* why, Kyle?! *That's* why?!" Her voice was loud and demanding as she commanded answers from Kyle. "Why Kyle?! Why?! Why didn't you just tell me?!" she continued to yell.

"Kat, I'm sorry. They threatened me. They knew my address, they knew my family's address. He knew everything about me and my family. He said he would kill them. I'm sorry, Kat. I'm so sorry," Kyle said, struggling to explain his actions. "After I saw your face banged up that day I just assumed it was them. The reality of the situation hit me then and I backed out...I backed out, Kat. It scared the shit out of me seeing you like that. I didn't want any more to do with it. I'm sorry!" he continued.

Kat could feel her body start to tremble with anger and she suddenly spoke softly. "And you never thought once to tell me? I'll *never* forgive you, Kyle." Kat didn't give him another look. She flung open the office door and rushed out of the kitchen and the diner without so much as a glance back in his direction.

She walked quietly and calmly outside to process the information Kyle had just given her. *Be careful who you trust, Kat.* The words in Jerry's letter ran through her mind again. This whole time she had been paranoid about Max but something else, something much bigger and more sinister had been lurking in the shadows the whole time and she was too naïve to see it. The line between fantasy and reality was slowly fading away as she realized things she had imagined over the past several months may have been real.

As she stood outside, a slow rain began to fall. She stood still in the wet air, allowing the droplets of water to cool down the rage she had steaming inside her. She closed her eyes for a moment to soak in the cold rain and took a deep breath. When she opened them, she spoke only one word.

"Nicholas." Her heart raced from hearing his name out loud and she hoped her irrational thoughts about him were wrong.

170

Even after sleeping two days away on the train, Kat's mind and body once again felt exhausted. It seemed as if every new day brought a different kind of disturbance and she was quickly wearing thin. The chaotic events overwhelmed her and she felt lonely with no one to turn to. Even Emily, her best friend from childhood, thought she was just sleep deprived and overstressed.

As she laid in bed, all of the recent events left questions and doubts in her mind. *If they contacted Kyle, who else did they contact? Surely no one at work, right?* The questions swam through her mind, grabbing hold of her and pulling her down to drown underwater. *How did they even know I'd be in Astoria? I tried so hard to keep it from everyone. How long have they been watching me? And why? What is their motive?*

Kat let out a heavy sigh. She felt stuck, she felt alone. *Nicholas,* Kat thought. *There's no way he's in on this, right? He was so gentle, so understanding. He helped me through so much. Why would he want to hurt me? He was so sincere.* The questions continued to rattle her mind and she knew that, again, it would be a night of restless sleep. *I'm getting out of here,* she told herself as she jumped out of bed.

"I can't just stay here," she said aloud to herself. *I'll go mad before dawn,* she added silently.

Kat dressed quickly and tucked the duffel bag in the bottom of her laundry hamper. She piled the dirty clothes on top. Before she hurried downstairs and out the door, Kat grabbed a pocket knife she kept in her nightstand drawer. *Just in case,* she thought.

She stepped outside and down the steps to the damp ground as she took a deep breath. The smell of rain invigorated her and the cool air felt good in her lungs. She hopped in her car and drove into town desperate to get out of her own head.

Without a destination in mind, Kat ended up at the only place in town open at this hour—the local tavern. *Just one drink tonight, Kat. Just one.* As much as she wanted to be responsible and clear-headed, she also wanted to drown out the chaos surrounding her. *Alcohol got me in trouble the last time,* Kat thought as she pulled the brass handle on the oversize door and walked into the tavern.

There were quite a few people at the bar for a Wednesday night, which she appreciated. *Socialize, Kat. Be normal for a night,* she encouraged herself. She quickly downed her first mug of cider and found herself pacing around the pool table.

"May I join you?" an unfamiliar voice spoke behind her. Kat turned around to see a handsome man with vibrant green eyes that matched the Oregon trees.

"You'll probably win fairly quickly," Kat said with a chuckle. "I'm horrible at pool."

"I see. Maybe I can teach you something so you have a chance at least?" the green-eyed man said with a friendly laugh. "I'm going to get another drink. Would you like one?" *Crap. No Kat, you said one drink. But what's two drinks?* She hesitated for a moment but found some reason within herself to justify it.

"Yes, please. Cider on draft," Kat said with a smile. *Don't trust him. Even if he is beautiful, trust no one. Those eyes are inviting, but be good Kat,* she thought as the stranger fetched their drinks.

Every sip Kat took washed away another piece of the chaotic puzzle her life was now a part of. She was laughing and enjoying life for the moment. The two had been laughing and talking for over an hour and time seemed like it had stopped briefly. Not one thought of Jerry, not one thought about the hidden secrets she found in that trunk, not one thought about Kyle. Kat had found a glimpse of peace.

"I think the way you're holding the cue stick is your mistake. Let me show you a better way to hold it," the stranger said.

"Is it because you feel sorry for me because of my horrible losing streak?" Kat said as she laughed.

"It is. I've seen ten-year-olds play better than you," the handsome stranger replied with a chuckle of his own.

The green-eyed man walked around the table and stepped close behind Kat. "Okay, place your hand like this," the man said as he placed Kat's hand on the cue stick. "Now, give me your other hand and place it like this. Much easier, right?"

"Oh yeah, what a difference," Kat exclaimed.

"Okay, bend your body like me," the man said as he placed his hands on Kat's waist to guide her into position. "Everything comfortable?" He was whispering in Kat's ear as he mimicked her body position against her back.

"Yes," Kat responded simply.

"Great. Now line up your shot and go for it," the man said softly. As Kat focused on her shot, she also focused on the man's steady breathing on her neck, trying to ignore the enticing feelings that came with it. *Okay, Kat. Focus on the ball,* she thought to herself.

Kat found her perfect stance and right when she took it, something across the room distracted her, making her miss the carefully placed shot.

172

Nicholas, with his eyes attached firmly to Kat, was across the room and quickly walking her way.

"Damn it!" she said as she stood up straight.

"Hey, no worries. You almost had it," the friendly man said, trying to encourage her.

"No, it's not that. I got distracted," Kat said quickly as her frustration grew.

"Kat," the familiar, sweet sound of Nicholas' voice spoke. Kat's heart began to pound with anger and anxiety, but it also pounded because she had missed him. Nicholas, the one who had enraged her and disappointed her, the one she had a thousand questions for, stood right in front of her and she was speechless.

*I hate you…I've missed you…How could you?…I can't trust you.* The thoughts raced through her mind in circles. Stuck in her throat, she couldn't get one word out. She had been waiting for this very moment to demand answers and instead, she stood frozen and speechless.

Kat stared into the dark eyes she had been missing. She took a deep breath and remembered her brother. *Jerry,* she thought. Saudade changed to an anger that dug deep into her bones once again. She swallowed a hard gulp and clenched her teeth, allowing herself to fume even more.

"Kat, I'm sorry. I'm so sorry," Nicholas said genuinely with sadness in his tone. He pleaded for Kat's forgiveness. *Sorry? He's not sorry! For what? Leaving without a word? Ignoring me after everything? Or sorry for only pretending to be my friend?* The thoughts raced and rage grew larger.

Silent, and without hesitation, Kat glued her eyes on Nicholas as she pulled back her hand as far as she could and swung it around to smack Nicholas as hard as she could across his face. He quickly grabbed his cheek trying to rub out the sting.

"Your apology is nothing to me, Nicholas," Kat said, finally getting the cemented words out.

"I deserved that," Nicholas said wincing in pain from Kat's slap.

"You deserve much more, Nicholas," Kat said as she put the pool cue down and headed for the exit.

*Damn it, what did I just do? I left a huge handprint across his face,* Kat thought as she walked quickly down the sidewalk to her car.

"Kat! Please, Kat. Come back. Let me just explain," Nicholas shouted as he ran after her down the damp sidewalk. It had started to rain while they were inside and Kat wasn't dressed for the wet weather.

"Just stay away from me, Nicholas. Just go!" Kat yelled with her back still facing him. Her mind seemed like it was running at five hundred miles an hour. As much as she wanted answers from Nicholas, she also wanted him to stay far away from her. She couldn't trust him, not after what Kyle disclosed to her at the

173

diner.

Nicholas picked up speed and quickly ran in front of Kat, obstructing her from her destination.

"Kat, stop. Please," Nicholas said as he left her no other choice but to stop.

"What, Nicholas? What is it that you want?" Kat demanded with her voice rising louder and louder. "I just want to go home, Nicholas. Move out of my way!"

"You've been drinking, Kat. Don't drive home," Nicholas said, trying to reason with Kat.

"Now you care, Nicholas? Now you fucking care? So much shit has happened since you left and now you fucking care? Forget you, Nicholas!" Kat screamed as she took a step to the side and continued to her car.

"Kat, I know. I know. I'll explain everything to you, Kat. I will!" Nicholas said as he hurried to catch up to her again. Kat turned around to face him as she continued to shout.

"You left, Nicholas! Remember, you left and gave me some crap good-bye in a note with no explanation. But of course, you didn't give a fuck, Nicholas, since you only had to pretend to be my friend. Isn't that right?" Kat shouted as Nicholas' eyes widened at her words.

"Pretend to be your friend, Kat? What the hell is that?" Nicholas asked with concern.

"Seriously, Nicholas. You know exactly what I'm talking about! Those corrupt cops from my hometown called you, didn't they? They told you to be-friend me, to watch me. Right?!" Kat continued shouting her demands and ac-cusations. "How could you, Nicholas, after everything? You know some of my deepest secrets and used them against me! Then you left! You're sick, Nicholas. There's something seriously wrong with you. Just stay away from me!"

"Kat, listen to yourself. You're being irrational. What cops? And I *never* pretended to be your friend. Kat, breathe! No one is watching you! Do you hear yourself? It's me, Nicholas…Kat, just breathe," Nicholas said as his voice calmed and took on a gentle tone. "Kat…it's me. I know I messed up. I'm sorry for leav-ing like I did. I'll explain everything. Let's just get out of the rain. It's freezing."

Kat's breathing was still heavy as she stood still, confused, and untrust-ing. *Don't trust him, Kat. Don't trust him,* she thought. Her heart beat quickly and question after question raced frantically through her mind.

As she debated silently with herself, Nicholas cautiously took a step clos-er mirroring her stance. Kat swallowed a hard gulp as Nicholas placed his hands on her arms and squeezed gently.

"Kat, you're soaked. You're freezing," he said softly. "Kat, let me take you home. I don't want you to get pulled over." He gently wiped a drop of rain from Kat's eye with his soft hand. "You're freezing."

Kat's heart pounded a soft hum. She missed his touch. She hadn't realized how much until that very moment. *No! Kat, he's lying. Don't trust anyone, Kat. Be careful who you trust.* Jerry's words raced over again in her mind. Her confusion grew and she had no idea what to do.

"No, Nicholas. It's all too much. I can't think straight. Anything out of your mouth or anyone else's—I don't know if it's true or not. I can't tell the fucking difference," Kat said as she began to sob. "Just let me be," she added as she wiped the tears falling from her eyes.

"I can't say sorry enough, Kat. Please, I don't want you to get pulled over," Nicholas said once again in hopes of getting through to her. "Kat, I'm here now. Let me help you."

"Okay then. Take me home," Kat said with defeat as she handed over her keys.

"Come on, let's get you out of the rain," Nicholas said as he opened the car door for her.

*What am I doing?* Kat thought to herself as Nicholas drove her through town and up to the winding road to her house. *What if this is all part of his plan to keep me close?* Kat wondered as she stared out the window and watched the rain falling on the glass. Silence filled the space between them.

Nicholas parked in Kat's driveway and kept still for a moment longer before Kat broke the silence.

"Thank you," Kat said shortly. *Don't do it, Kat. Don't invite him in,* she told herself silently. "You can come in while you wait for a cab," she said softly, still gazing out the window. *You caved, Kat. You fucking caved,* she thought.

"Thanks," Nicholas whispered as the two got out and headed up the steps to the porch. *Maybe he is telling the truth. Maybe I am being irrational. Maybe it was only Kyle,* Kat thought as she opened the door to the house.

Inside, the creaking floor sounded beneath their steps. Both of them were drenched from their confrontation in the rain. They headed upstairs silently for towels to dry off.

"My handprint is fading," Kat said as she stood close to Nicholas in the middle of her bedroom. She reached her hand up to his face and gently massaged the spot where she'd smacked him. She whispered softly as she rubbed his cheek. "I'm sorry, Nicholas."

"No, Kat. Don't apologize. I'm the one who's sorry," Nicholas whispered back. Kat's hand slowly moved over to his lips, caressing them where her lips had once been. *He tasted good,* she thought to herself. Her judgment was clouded with the memories of her and Nicholas—the way he handled her, the way he kissed her, the warmth of his body on hers.

As pleasant memories filled her mind, Kat leaned in and kissed the soft lips before her. She kissed him hard and aggressively. Nicholas welcomed it and quickly took off his shirt.

*He still tastes good*, Kat thought as Nicholas undressed her. His body heat felt good on her cold, damp skin. Nicholas held her face in his hands and continued to kiss her. He moved his kiss down to her neck and down to her toes. Nicholas led her by the hand to the bed and laid her down gently.

"I've missed you so much, Nicholas," Kat whispered as he continued to kiss her bare body.

"Oh, Kat, I've missed you too. So much," Nicholas replied as he gazed deep into her eyes.

# CHAPTER 34

Kat's heart beat at a slow and steady pace while she laid in Nicholas' arms.

"Where were you?" she asked him softly, still needing answers to the questions that frustrated her. "Why did you leave me that night?"

Nicholas took a deep breath and kissed her softly on the forehead.

"I'm not sure how you'll react, Kat, but when you're not around, I think of you constantly," he replied. "I'm always wondering if you're okay or not. I love how I feel when I'm with you...and that scares the hell out of me."

"I don't understand. Then why leave?" Kat asked with more confusion.

"I don't know what to do with these feelings, Kat," Nicholas attempted to explain. "I don't deserve you, not even a bit of you."

"So you thought ignoring me would work? Did you ever consider *my* feelings, Nicholas? Did you ever think how *I* felt?" Kat pressed back.

"I didn't ignore you, Kat," Nicholas continued. "That morning after I got home, I found out my mother was in the hospital. She lives in Peru and when I got the call, they told me they weren't sure if she would make it through the night. I went there as fast as I could and I haven't had cell service until I got back in town two days ago. I know it looks bad and I'm sorry for hurting you. When I left, I thought it was best to cut ties, but I didn't have time to explain. You deserve better, Kat. You deserve so much better." As he spoke, he caressed Kat's arm.

"Oh man, now I feel like such a jerk," she replied. "I'm sorry about your mother." She was embarrassed about yet again jumping to conclusions that weren't real. *Great Kat, he was with his sick mother and you were thinking the worst about him*, she thought silently to herself.

"Kat, stop apologizing. You had no idea. It's okay," Nicholas said as he kissed her once more on the forehead. *I should make him leave*, Kat thought. *I'm sleepy and I need to get some rest. But I like him by my side.* She continued to debate with herself as Nicholas held her close. Without another word or thought, Kat gripped him tightly and hoped to fall into a deep slumber.

The nightmares that had plagued her at night no longer visited her unconscious mind, perhaps because the world around her had turned into a living nightmare. Soon, in the comfort of Nicholas' arms, Kat drifted into a good night's sleep.

*****

Dawn hit and Kat crept out of bed as quietly as possible to avoid waking Nicholas. Carefully, she pulled the duffel bag out of her hamper and went downstairs to her computer. She opened an internet window, navigated to a search engine, and typed what she was looking for:

*Newspapers near Portland, Oregon*

Kat's heart progressively beat faster as she scrolled through the results. She knew she needed to get the information she'd found to a newspaper, but it had to be a big newspaper, the type a bigger city like Portland would have.

"Which one, Jerry? Which one?" Kat whispered aloud. She couldn't make up her mind, so she settled on the third one in the list and found a contact email for an investigative reporter at the *Portland Times-Republic*. She carefully wrote out the message she'd been mulling over in her head.

*To whom it may concern,*

*I need your help. My brother was a breaking news journalist in my hometown and was working on a disturbing story before he died under unusual circumstances. I have a duffel bag full of evidence, including photos of uniformed police officers disposing of two dead bodies.*

*Before my brother died, he sent me a letter telling me to help him if anything happened to him. He directed me to contact a media agency.*

*Please see the attachments to this email. I have taken a few pictures of the contents inside the bag. I need to get this to you as soon as possible before someone comes looking for it. My contact info is below.*

*Thanks,*

*Katrina Morgan*

Kat let out a heavy sigh and hit the send button, hoping they would be able to help her. *I just want this bag out of my hands already*, Kat thought. The responsibility of keeping its contents safely hidden had worn her out.

"Kat?" Nicholas called out as he entered the dining area. Kat jumped with surprise.

"Nicholas!" Kat exclaimed as she hurried to put the items spread out on the table back into the bag.

"What is all this?" Nicholas asked with concern glaring from his face.

"Nothing, Nicholas. Just some stuff from my brother's house...it's personal," Kat answered quickly, too quickly, as she struggled to gather the contents into the bag. Nicholas approached the table with curiosity in his eyes. "Nicholas, please, just leave this alone." Panic was rising in her voice.

Nicholas picked up one of the photographs showing one of the police officers disposing of the bodies. Nicholas gasped frantically. "Kat! What the hell is this?! Where did you get these?" he asked as his voice trembled with fear.

"Nicholas, I told you to leave it alone!" Kat snapped back quickly as her heart pounded with anxiety. She tried to grab the picture from Nicholas' hands.

"Kat, this is serious stuff. Where did you get this?" Nicholas asked hastily as he pulled away, not allowing her to grab the picture.

"Fuck, Nicholas! I got it from my brother's house. I told you that I thought he was murdered! This is why I feel like somebody's watching me, Nicholas!" Kat shouted with the same tremble in her voice.

"Kat, think hard. Do they know if you have this stuff?!" Nicholas pried more.

"Damn it! The night I went to get it, it was late. It was dark. I don't know!" Kat snapped. Suddenly, her heart sank into her stomach as she remembered that night. *Oh God, I didn't cover the hole in the floor. I left it wide open,* she thought to herself in a panic.

"Oh, Nicholas! Oh crap! I forgot to cover the hole in the floor where I found the trunk. The trunk had all this inside!" Kat said as she started to pace back and forth from the dining room to the kitchen. "I slid the trunk to my car and...I think someone followed me back to my parents' house. I don't know, though. Everything back home seemed off. I just don't know!" Kat continued in a panic. "Damn it, Nicholas! I'm not sure about anything anymore! Anyone could have been watching me! Kat shouted.

"Shit, Kat," Nicholas said as he slowly started to pace across the floor along with her. "This is bad, Kat. This is very bad! I gotta take this to my lieutenant. We gotta get you out of here."

"No! I have to get this to the media. The police can get involved then!" Kat said frantically, grasping for hope that she could grant Jerry's last wish. *I have to get this to the media like Jerry said,* Kat thought to herself.

"The media! Kat, we have to get this to the police! Let me just take all of this and I'll get it to the station. You shouldn't have this in your possession!" Nicholas shouted.

"No! These are cops, Nicholas! No! I can't risk it! I'm sorry, but I can't even trust a cop with it. Not even you!" Kat snapped back again.

Their debate was suddenly interrupted by the ringing of Kat's phone. She took a deep breath before answering.

"Hello?" she answered with the hint of a tremble in her voice.

"Yes, Katrina Morgan?" a stranger's voice asked on the other end.

"Yes, that's me," Kat responded cautiously while Nicholas stood frozen with his eyes glued to her.

"This is Todd Jennings with the *Portland Times-Republic*. I just read your email and I would like to discuss this further," the man said with a stern voice.

"Oh, yes sir. Are you able to help me?" Kat asked with desperation.

"I can meet today. I'm in Portland. Would you be willing to give me all the evidence you have?" the reporter asked.

"Um...yes," Kat responded nervously. *It's okay, Kat. It's okay. He's gonna help,* she reassured herself. "Can we meet halfway? I'm in Astoria." She didn't want to deal with another big city so soon after returning to her small-town life.

"For sure, um...let me think," the man replied. "There's a restaurant near Elsie. We can meet there. How about this evening around five? Do you know where Elsie is?"

"I'll figure it out. That sounds good. I'll see you then," Kat said as she hung up the phone.

"What was that?" Nicholas asked with a stern and demanding look on his face.

"Um, I emailed the *Portland Times-Republic* earlier while you were sleeping...about all of this...I, um, sent them a few pictures so they would believe me," Kat explained nervously, concerned about Nicholas' reaction.

"You used your computer to email about this?" Nicholas asked with the concern growing in his voice as he raced over and shut down Kat's computer as quickly as he could.

"Yes, I used my computer. You know, that's what people normally use for email," Kat replied sarcastically.

"Fuck! Go get ready, Kat. We've got to go. I'll take you to the reporter tonight. Let's just get out of here, now," Nicholas said as he gathered the rest of the contents and placed them in the bag for Kat.

"Nicholas, why?! I don't have to meet him until tonight. I don't want to leave yet!" Kat snapped back. "Why are you in such a hurry to leave?"

"I just think it's safer, Kat. If you're not willing to take all this down to the station right now, there's no way for the police to protect you. If they don't know about it, how can they help? So that means you need to get out of here. Whoever is in those pictures is probably gonna want them, Kat! They're pretty fucking incriminating!" Nicholas shouted with a tone she had never heard him use before. "Now stop being so damn stubborn. Please, just get ready. Please!" he pleaded.

"Just give me the bag, Nicholas. I'll go get ready," Kat said as she grabbed the bag from his hand and headed for a shower. *Why didn't you just wait until he left, Kat? Stupid fucking move,* she thought to herself as she took the bag upstairs and carried it into the bathroom with her where she could keep a close eye on it. She locked the door behind her before stepping into the shower. *Certainly they wouldn't come all the way here, right?* Her new home was the shield from all the chaos back home. Surely they wouldn't hunt her down here.

180

"I want to show you something," Kat said as she and Nicholas took the winding road into town. "Let's stop at the art gallery for a minute. I want to show you one of the pieces I entered."

"I'm glad you were finally able to make a choice for the show," Nicholas responded with a friendly, but nervous smile. The two of them had finally calmed down enough to make it out the door. Kat drove with the duffel bag close to her and always within sight. Even if Nicholas truly had nothing to do with all of it, she still didn't feel like she could fully trust him again. *Not after the way he walked away without a proper goodbye, sick mother or not,* Kat thought.

"Me too," Kat responded shortly. Her mind was going in so many different directions that she didn't want to engage with the world any more than she had to.

Kat pulled up in front of the local gallery where she'd submitted her painting and directed Nicholas to follow her inside. She carried the duffel bag with her, not daring to risk leaving it in her car.

There were several paintings from other local artists on display. The two of them walked in silence as they strolled slowly observing the beautiful artwork around them.

"Here, this one is mine," Kat said softly as she approached a large painting showing a lighthouse signaling to a ship in a dark storm. "I had originally made this as a gift for your birthday next week." Kat spoke flatly, with no emotion in her voice as she remembered her disappointment when Nicholas had disappeared.

"You made this for me? It's amazing, Kat!" Nicholas said with excitement.

"I made it for you when I trusted you—before you let me down. It was a 'thank you' for helping me seek refuge in the storms that constantly surround me," Kat explained as she stared directly into Nicholas' eyes.

"Kat, I'm—" Nicholas began to say before Kat interrupted him.

"No, don't apologize again. Just don't," Kat said quickly. "Let's go. I'm hungry. When I get it back from the gallery, I'll give it to you." She turned and started to walk back to the front of the gallery, bumping into Nicholas as she walked past, but not stopping or looking back to apologize.

Her mood matched the weather outside—gray and dreary with no sign of sunshine any time soon. She had a goal in mind—to get the evidence from the trunk to the media—and she wouldn't let herself lose focus until that happened. She walked a few doors down with Nicholas quickening his pace behind her to try and catch up.

"This is my favorite pizza place," Kat said as she stopped outside the small pizzeria. She opened the door and held it as Nicholas finally caught up to her.

"Oh yeah, I've eaten here a few times before," Nicholas said as they took a seat in an empty booth. "It's pretty good."

"Yeah, we could have enjoyed delicious pizza together before, but while you were avoiding me that time, this is where I ate…alone," Kat added with a smirk on her face.

"Okay, Kat. I get it. You're still pissed. You should be, but can you stop already?" Nicholas said with defeat.

"If you don't like it, Nicholas, then why are you still here? I can handle this on my own like I always do and like I have been doing," Kat said as she clenched the duffel bag closer to her body.

"I know you can, Kat. I just gotta make sure you stay safe. I don't like this at all," Nicholas replied.

"I'm sorry, Nicholas. I know I shouldn't still be upset with you," Kat said only half apologetically. "These last few weeks have been overwhelming. I don't know about anything anymore. I don't know if Jerry just couldn't take it anymore, or if something else really did happen. I just don't know." She tried to hold back the sobs as she continued. "But what I do know, Nicholas, is that I miss my brother so much. I just want one more hug, one more laugh. I just wish I could've told him goodbye. There's nothing I or anyone else can do to bring him back. I hate this! I hate it so much, Nicholas," she exclaimed as she wiped a tear and a few other patrons in the restaurant looked over.

Her heart began to race at the speed of her quickening words. She massaged the wrinkles starting to develop on her forehead and let out a heavy sigh.

"I'm losing my fucking mind," she added.

"You're not losing your mind, Kat. You're not. I promise," Nicholas said, trying to comfort her.

"Nicholas, I don't even know what I'm doing. I don't even know if I should be meddling in all this, but I feel like I have no other choice. It's like it's meddling with me! Maybe I *should* just take it all to the local police, but I feel like I need to do what Jerry said to do," Kat continued, trying to quiet her voice as much as possible. "I just want my brother back. It's all I want. But if I can't have him back, I have to do this for him. I have to finish what he started or…or, it was all in vain. I'll stand for him, always, like I should have done all along."

"Kat, you did what you were able to do for him," Nicholas said, concern deep in his voice and empathy on his face.

"No, I didn't. That's just it, Nicholas! I was too worried about taking care of myself to realize what the hell he was going through! Family shouldn't desert each other and that's exactly what I did when I hopped on that train to come here! I even told him and my parents I wouldn't go home for Christmas all because I couldn't want to face what I had left behind," Kat continued.

Her breathing began to get heavy as her anxiety and anger rose. "It's sad when people start caring more for a person when they're no longer here as if their death meant more than their life. I'll never forgive myself, Nicholas," Kat said with guilt she couldn't swallow.

Nicholas was silent, unsure of what to say or how to help. He handed Kat a few napkins to wipe away her tears. He comforted her the best he could from across the table.

"We better order something," he said as Kat dried her eyes. "We gotta get on the road in a few. It's almost three."

# CHAPTER 35

A light fog started to roll in as Kat and Nicholas left the pizzeria.

"Can you drive? The visibility sucks and you know these roads better," Kat asked as she tossed the keys to Nicholas.

"Sure thing," he said with a warm smile.

They began the cloudy drive slowly going in and out of thick fog.

"The restaurant near Elsie is about an hour away," Nicholas said as he turned onto Highway 202. "The drive is beautiful and hopefully we'll get to see some elk if this fog clears up."

*I just want this to go away,* Kat thought as she enjoyed the tall spruce trees peeking through the fog along the highway. *I want everything to go back to normal. Normal…what is normal?* Her life of nightmares had become a sense of reality that made her question everything around her. *Maybe this is just a nightmare I can't wake from,* Kat added to herself silently.

"Hey, we're here," Nicholas suddenly said, startling Kat from her deep thoughts. "Right over there is where we're meeting," Nicholas added as he pointed toward the restaurant.

"Where did the time go?" Kat asked with confusion. She was certain they had just left Astoria, but somehow an hour had passed and they had reached their destination.

"Oh, it went. You were just off somewhere else," Nicholas said with a chuckle, attempting to change Kat's gloomy mood.

They walked into the small restaurant and looked around at nothing but empty tables and booths. Kat clutched the duffel bag tightly as they walked to the back of the restaurant and sat down in a dark corner booth.

"May I have a water?" Kat asked the server as she walked by.

"Of course, I'll bring you a couple waters right away," the server replied as she walked into the kitchen in the back.

Kat massaged her forehead again, trying to relieve some of the stress that had built up within her.

"Where is this guy at?" she wondered as she checked the time. "It's already twenty after." Her anxiety rose as she looked around the empty restaurant.

"He'll be here, Kat. If that's what he said, he'll be here," Nicholas replied, hoping to calm her down.

"What if it really wasn't a reporter that I talked to? What if…what if it's them?" Kat said as she frantically scanned the restaurant.

"Kat! Calm down. I'm sure it was a reporter, okay?!" Nicholas said as he reached to cup her hands in his. "Kat, look at me." He studied Kat's frail and tired eyes as he spoke. "He'll be here, the reporter. He *will* be here. Take a deep breath."

Kat took a deep breath as directed. "I'm losing my mind, Nicholas…I can feel it," Kat said, sounding defeated.

"You're not losing your mind, Kat. I wish I could take all this away," Nicholas replied with anguish in his eyes.

"Katrina Morgan?" a voice asked. A tall, dark-haired man stood at the table with a briefcase and a lanyard around his neck. *Todd Jennings, Investigative Reporter* was written on his nametag.

"Yes!" Kat said with relief as she jumped up to shake the reporter's hand.

"I'm so sorry I'm late. Traffic getting out of Portland was heavier than I expected today and the fog slowed everything down. My apologies for keeping you waiting," the man said genuinely.

"Please, have a seat," Nicholas chimed in. "Are you hungry?"

"Very," the reporter replied. "Have you two eaten?"

"Earlier, but I could eat again," Kat said, realizing she had only picked at her pizza back in Astoria.

"Great! Let's order some food," the reporter exclaimed excitedly.

The man wasted no time in getting down to business. "Katrina, please tell me more about the evidence you have. I'm going to be up all night working on this. I would like to investigate everything you have and hopefully break the story in the next day or two," he said.

Kat unzipped the duffel bag next to her and started handing the contents to the man. "Look at this headline, 'Officer found dead, apparent suicide'," Kat said as she handed one of the articles to the reporter. "This is the same officer my brother mentioned in a letter he sent a week before his death. Officer Duke Conway—he's the one who dropped all this on my brother's porch with a note asking for help." She spoke quickly, trying to get all the details in.

"Here's the letter my brother wrote me as well," Kat said as she handed the folded paper over.

The reporter examined the newspaper clipping carefully, then moved on to the letter and the photograph of Alex disposing of the dead bodies. He flipped quickly through the journals Jerry had left behind.

"I wonder if this Officer Conway was the one who took the photographs?" the reporter wondered aloud as his expression showed he was in deep thought.

"I didn't even think of that, but, yeah, I think he would have to be the one, especially since he was asking for my brother's help," Kat said softly.

"Why haven't you gone to the local police department with this? I'm not criticizing, I'm just curious," the reporter questioned as concern grew on his face.

Kat swallowed a hard gulp and ignored the gaze Nicholas was giving her, seemingly in agreement with the reporter. "I…I don't know if I can trust them…I don't know if I can trust anyone. I'm taking a huge risk talking to *you* about this," Kat said.

Over dinner, Kat filled in all the gaps for the reporter: her brother's paranoid talked prior to his death, Alex's seduction and Kat's subsequent arrest, the rumors of the murder of the travel agent who'd helped Kat escape to Astoria, Kyle being contacted and asked to keep an eye on Kat. Nicholas visibly cringed during the parts of the story where Kat slept with Alex and looked away several times when she mentioned being followed. Kat couldn't help but notice Nicholas' nervousness as she told the reporter more and more about the happenings of the past several weeks.

"I know it all sounds crazy, but I think it's connected somehow," Kat said. "Kyle said someone contacted him a week before he met me at the diner. Maybe…maybe it was all staged to cover their tracks?" Kat's heart pounded into her throat, making it difficult to get her words out. "There are also some flash drives in the bag. I'm not sure what's on them, but they are there for you."

"I don't think it sounds crazy at all. I think something huge is here and I'll get to the bottom of it," the reporter said confidently, reassuring Kat.

"Thank you so much. And please, be safe. This bag is full of despair," Kat said as she handed the duffel bag over to the reporter.

"I certainly will. Watch for the newspapers in the morning. I'm going to have something by then, but I have to go. I have lots of work to do before midnight," the reporter said as he threw the bag over his shoulder and stood up to leave. "One more thing," he said as he turned back around and faced Nicholas. "No one ever tried to contact you about any of this, correct?"

"Of course not," Nicholas replied, though he seemed unsure of his answer. "I knew nothing about this until today."

"Okay, no problem," the reporter said. "I didn't mean to sound accusatory. I just thought if they contacted her other friend, maybe they tried to contact you too. So long." With that, the man turned and rushed out of the restaurant.

"Let's go," Kat said with relief, finally rid of the secret materials that had caused so much destruction. She couldn't help but wonder about the reporter's question. It was a valid question—if they'd contacted Kyle, why hadn't they tried to contact Nicholas? *Maybe they knew he was too close to me,* Kat reasoned with herself as they headed for the car.

Night had fallen and the fog was much thicker by the time they left Elsie. "You're definitely driving back," Kat said with a small chuckle.

"She laughs!" Nicholas said playfully as he bumped into Kat.

"She does, indeed. What a rare delicacy you get to experience," Kat replied with a smile as she got into the passenger side of the car.

As the two drove the curvy highway home, Kat continued to massage her forehead with her fingertips. Even though she no longer had the bag, she found it hard to relax. Something still felt off about the events that had unfolded over the past weeks and months.

*Maybe I'll give Dr. Sampson a call this week,* Kat thought as she tried not to focus on the thick fog creeping across the dark highway. *Dr. Sampson,* she thought again as her heart started to pound with a combination of curiosity and anxiety. She swallowed a hard gulp as she stared out at the eerie fog in front of them. *Only Emily and…Nicholas knew about Dr. Sampson,* Kat frantically thought to herself. *If Emily wasn't the one who told Alex about my therapy…oh God, was it Nicholas?*

Kat continued to ponder the unanswered questions. Her breathing sped up, becoming more rapid with every breath she took.

*In fact, Nicholas was the one who conveniently referred me to Dr. Sampson, business card and all, right in his pocket.* Kat's mind was racing with the memory of that day when she no longer wanted to be here on Earth. *He just seemed to know the right things to say, the right things to do.* Her heart thudded against her chest and the thoughts piled up in her mind. Her train of thought was broken by the sound of Nicholas' phone beeping. He looked at the phone briefly with a worried look on his face. Kat hated when people looked at their phones while driving. It was bad enough in fair weather, but in fog, it was downright deadly. She huffed a bit on her side of the car.

"I've got to pull over," Nicholas said suddenly, his voice shaky and distraught.

"What?" she responded, startled by the tremble in Nicholas' voice.

"I have to pull the car over, now!" he repeated loudly.

"You're not pulling over on the side of the road in this visibility. It's dangerous!" she replied nervously to his sudden, irrational need to get off the road.

"I don't care. I have to pull over! I have to throw up!" he shouted louder.

"It's dark and foggy! Where are you going to go, anyway?!" Kat said, her voice rising to meet Nicholas' shouts.

"I've gotta get out, Kat! It's either that or I puke all over your car!" Nicholas shouted even louder.

"Fuck! Okay, pull over!" Kat said with frustration and worry as Nicholas pulled the car to the side of the road. He flipped on the hazard lights to alert any other vehicles of their presence. The car barely came to a stop before Nicholas slammed it into park and jumped out.

"What's wrong, Nicholas?" Kat hollered after him as he ran through the fog toward the woods next to the road. She watched him disappear into the mist as she stepped out onto the wet pavement. It was quiet on the deserted highway and it reminded her of her dream—the one where something or someone lurked in the woods waiting to attack. She heard a crack in the woods, just like the one in her dream, and she began to wonder whether she was, in fact, dreaming once again. Another cracking sound came, this time closer, as she heard Nicholas retching nearby.

Kat began to panic as she rationalized whether the sound was real, whether the woods were real, whether her entire trip to meet the reporter was real. She tried desperately to determine whether she was in reality or dreamland. The line had been blurred so much recently she couldn't trust her own judgment. *Quick, try to think about something you wouldn't know in a dream,* she told herself. As she reviewed the last several weeks, she tried to hone in on little details that were tucked away in her mind.

She relived her trip back to the big city—her flight and the short train ride at the end of the trip. She remembered the platform at the train station when she'd thought about Jerry and the yellow daisies he'd brought her before her move. Then, like a neon sign lighting for the first time in her mind, she remembered the man she had seen across the crowd on the platform. She thought she had seen Nicholas—she would have sworn it that day and now as she stood next to her car in the still fogginess, hazard lights flashing in the mist, she realized it *was* Nicholas. In the stress and hopelessness of the moment that day, she had convinced herself she was seeing things. But as she remembered that day with a clearer mind, she suddenly knew, without a doubt, Nicholas had been the man there that day. He had been in the city with her.

"Nicholas!" she screamed, suddenly filled with rage as the pieces clicked together like the last missing corner of a jigsaw puzzle—the feeling of being watched, the way Alex had known intimate details of her life in Astoria, the way Nicholas had just *accidentally* walked in on her going through the documents and trying to convince her to give them to her. "Nicholas, get back here now!" She heard him rustling through the brush toward her, and he finally emerged through the thick fog with a terrified and nervous look on his face.

"Kat, what are you screaming about?" he asked as he wiped vomit from his face with the back of his shirt sleeve. "What's wrong?"

"*You,* Nicholas! *You* are what's wrong. I can't believe you used my deepest secrets against me!" Kat yelled and started to pace back and forth on the side of the highway.

"Kat! What in the hell are you talking about?!" Nicholas demanded.

"Enough, Nicholas. Enough playing dumb already! You're the one who told Alex I see Dr. Sampson, aren't you?! Is that why you told me to go to him? So you guys could hold it against me later?! So they could screw with me and call me crazy?!" Kat shouted quickly and loudly. "I suppose Dr. Sampson is probably in on it, too, isn't he? That's why you referred me to him, isn't it?"

Nicholas stood frozen at Kat's accusations, sorrow filling his eyes.

"Kat, let me explain," Nicholas said cautiously.

"Explain?! You keep saying that, Nicholas, but you never fully explain, do you?!" Kat shouted. "Tell me, Nicholas. Did you tell Alex about Dr. Sampson? Are you a part of all this?! And don't lie to me! Don't you fucking lie to me one more time!" Kat added with a heavy breath.

Nicholas swallowed loudly and took a couple steps toward Kat. The thick fog crept across the dark road, the only thing filling the space between the two of them.

"Get away from me, Nicholas! Get away!" Kat shouted as she stepped backward putting more space between them.

"Kat…at first, I didn't know the extent of it all. They told me you were involved in some drug activity. I thought I was just helping out another department. I thought I was just doing my job, Kat," Nicholas said as his voice trembled. "When I told them I thought you had PTSD, they were so excited and that's when I knew something was horribly wrong with what they were doing. They wanted to use the PTSD against you, make you feel even more paranoid until you snapped."

Kat's heart sank into her stomach, vomit ready to come up at the sound of Nicholas' finally honest words. Anxiety hit hard and racing thoughts fluttered through her mind.

"So…so you did tell Alex? And was Dr. Sampson in on this, too?" Kat asked as she clenched her teeth. "Tell me!" she screamed.

"Yes! Yes, I did, Kat and yes, Dr. Sampson was part of it. I'm so fucking sorry! They told me to. They told me that maybe you'd confess some illegal activities to a therapist they could use against you later. That's why I did it. I'm so sorry, Kat," Nicholas said as he stepped closer. "It got out of hand, Kat. I realized you weren't involved in drugs the way they talked about…but, I wanted to stay close to you, to them. I had to stay in the loop. It was the only way to keep you safe from them! That's why I followed you back to the city. I care about you, Kat! I really do," Nicholas said, continuing to explain himself to Kat as quickly as he could.

"Liar! You're a fucking liar! So everything, *everything* has been a lie! Running in the rain, huh? Your favorite thing to do, huh? No! I just caught you spying on me that day, didn't I? So you just pulled that charm right out of your ass, right?!" Kat screamed as panic rose. "I felt crazy. I have felt crazy this whole time! And you did nothing!"

"Kat, I know it's bad. I know! I should have told you. I didn't know how. I was trying to protect you and your brother. I was too late. I'm sorry," Nicholas said quickly with exhaustion in his voice.

Kat's fast pace came to a complete stop at the words he spoke. Feeling as if her heart had just skipped a beat, Kat turned and looked into the eyes of the man she once trusted.

"Me…and my brother? You were too late? What the fuck are you saying, Nicholas?"

"After I realized they were lying, I had to do my own investigation on them. I found out they were going to get rid of your brother. So I went and I tried to stop them, Kat. I did! That's why I left town so suddenly. But I was too late," Nicholas said as his voice still trembled.

"Get rid of him? So they did kill him? They killed my brother? And you were there? Peru was just another lie?" Kat said, this time in a quiet voice. The words she spoke were slow. "So that *was* you at the train station that day. I thought I was losing my fucking mind, Nicholas! I fucking hate you!" Kat said as she pushed him as hard as she could, making him stumble back.

"Kat, I'm sorry. I couldn't do it anymore. That's another reason I had to leave for a while. It was eating at me! When they told me they would handle it, I knew what they meant. I had to go for myself and see, to stop them. Kat, I fled to the airport that morning. I tried to stop them! I tried to save him!" Nicholas pleaded.

"You never thought to tell me? I could have warned him, Nicholas. He could still be alive, Nicholas! He didn't have to die!" Kat screamed and pushed Nicholas again, this time making him fall to the pavement.

Nicholas quickly got back up on his feet and rushed over to Kat, grabbing her by the biceps to shield himself from her blows. "Kat, I know, I fucked up. I could've done things differently. I thought I was doing the best I could. It eats at me every day!" he said, still pleading with Kat. "I saw you getting off the train when you went back for your brother's funeral. I knew you would be there and I had to see you before I came back to Oregon. I even thought about staying back there in the city to follow you and make sure you were okay, but I couldn't. They wouldn't let me."

"I thought you were my friend! I told you so much and after everything, you were still okay sleeping with me?! Your conscience is pretty fucked up! Either that or you're still lying to me right now and this is all part of your act. You're sick, Nicholas! You're fucking sick!" Kat screamed into his face.

"I told you, Kat. I still had to make sure you were safe. The only way was to keep going along with them. But my feelings for you never changed. They still haven't," Nicholas replied, hoping to get through to her. "I don't expect your forgiveness, but please, try to understand that my intentions were good, Kat. They were! They still are! I promise!"

"You're lying! Your promises don't mean anything, Nicholas!" Kat shouted again into his face.

"Kat, they're waiting for you right now. They're fucking waiting for you at your house! That's why I needed to get you out! That's why I pulled over. I couldn't take you back home with them waiting there for you," Nicholas continued, failing at all attempts to gain back Kat's trust. Kat's breathing was rapid and rain suddenly started falling on them.

"You could've saved Jerry. You could have fucking saved him, Nicholas. I

191

hate you. I hate you so much!" Kat sobbed and screamed before reaching into her back pocket and pulling her pocket knife out. She walked slowly toward Nicholas with a crazed look in her eyes. She stood in front of him as the knife shimmered in the blinking of the car's hazard lights. She screamed once again, pulled back her hand, and stabbed the knife into Nicholas' lower abdomen.

Nicholas let out a loud moan. "Kat, no…" he said as he tried to pull away from the knife and away from Kat. Every time he tried, Kat twisted the knife around and plunged it deeper into his body, blood pouring from the wound onto her hand and down to the pavement below. Kat felt its warmth as she stared into Nicholas' eyes, watching his suffering.

She pulled the bloody knife out and pushed Nicholas again, making him fall onto the wet pavement. Nicholas winced as he covered the wound.

"I hate you, Nicholas. I hate you for everything!" Kat screamed as she kneeled down beside him and quickly dug the knife in once again.

"Kat, stop. Please," Nicholas said as he choked on the words he spoke. "I'm sorry," he added softly. Kat pulled the knife out of Nicholas and dropped it next to him on the road. She stayed there, frozen, for a few moments as Nicholas gasped before lying down and closing his eyes for the last time.

Minutes passed and the puddle of blood Nicholas laid in grew bigger. Kat was suddenly in shock of what she had done, trembling at the sight of Nicholas' lifeless body. She raised her hands in front of her face and stared at them, drenched in blood. Her heart pounded quickly. As she stared at her hands, the rain droplets slowly began to wash them clean. But no amount of rain could wash away the reality she had just created. She had killed a man.

The heavy fog dissipated and only the heavy rain hummed throughout the dark wooded area. A vibration coming from Nicholas' pocket interrupted Kat's shock. Curious, she dug into his pocket and answered the ringing phone.

As she placed the phone up to her ear, she listened in silence. "Hello? Where are you, man? She's not here yet. Where the hell are you, Nicholas? Hello? Hello? Can you hear me?" the familiar voice said on the other end. Kat hung up immediately and whispered one word, "Alex."

She jumped up quickly and started pacing. "Oh God, he was telling the truth," Kat screamed as she threw Nicholas' phone across the wet pavement.

*What have I done?* Kat wondered as her pace stopped and she stood still over Nicholas' body. *No Kat, he deserved it*, she countered.

Kat's energy was quickly draining and she sat down on the wet pavement next to Nicholas' dead body. She sat there for a long time, allowing the rain to drench her. She still hoped she might suddenly wake from the nightmare around her. She sat calmly as the bitter taste of vengeance filled her mouth. The sound of another car approaching sounded nearby and as the vehicle's lights came into view Kat could see it was a police car. She didn't know whether it was a good cop or a bad cop, but either way, she knew there would be consequences. If they were connected to the cops in her hometown, she would be dead. If they were not, she had just killed a man. Either way, she was ready for the outcome.

As the officer turned on his red and blue lights and pulled up behind her car, Kat raised her hands in the air to surrender to whatever her fate would be.

With the steady uproar in her life, Kat had determined that pain itself was the only constant thing she could count on. Pain, terror, and agony would never leave her side. Pain—the only thing in life that wouldn't leave her alone would forever leave her lonely.

# SPECIAL THANKS

*Jennifer Coats - Cover and Marketing Photography*

*Will Hughes - Cellist and Model (Jerry)*

*Ariana Hernandez-Caballero - Model (Kat)*

*Edina Olvera - Model Hair and Makeup*

# ABOUT THE AUTHORS

## JENNIFER TUCKER

Jennifer Tucker is a design draftsman in the Dallas-Fort Worth area where she lives with her two sons, Julian and Adrian.

Tucker spent most of her youth in Denver, Colorado, and Roswell, New Mexico. Aside from her career in the architecture and design field, she has also worked in public service with the US Department of Labor's Job Corps program.

Writing has been a hobby of Tucker's for more than three years. *Irreparable* is her first book, but she promises it is not her last.

## RUTHERFORD RANKIN

Rutherford Rankin is the author of *Fighting Against Gravity* and co-author of *Irreparable*. He has also worked as a journalist, copywriter, and ghost writer under his own and other names.

Rankin was born in southwest Kansas and grew up in Satanta, Kansas. He holds a bachelor of arts degree in Spanish literature and journalism from Emporia State University and a master of arts degree in educational administration from New Mexico State University.

Rankin is also the co-founder of Michelkin Publishing and serves as president of the company as well as acquisitions editor. He lives in Roswell, New Mexico, and works at the local community college as a student services director.

Made in the USA
San Bernardino, CA
07 August 2017